Live Free or Die b

MW00398302

"Well-written and expertly crafted, *Live Free or Die* explores the lives of ordinary people who become key characters impacting all of the reader's senses—you can see them, hear them, and either love or mistrust them. A hero you can root for, surrounded by characters who inhabit his town in Connecticut, balancing the line of detached and respected professional and loving husband. Settings and dialogue support and enhance this second book of the Parker Havenot series. It is a journey down the rabbit hole of suspense into the lives of teachers, police, and the mind of a self-appointed avenger. Once you begin reading, be prepared to either stay up late or steal time the next day to get back to *Live Free or Die*."

—Ethel Lee-Miller,
author of *Thinking of Miller Place* and *Seedlings*

"'Sometimes we can still see over or through the cracks of the walls we've built to shield us from the past,' says one of the character in Duke Southard's excellent *Live Free or Die*. What happens when those walls are being shattered from the other side by a psychopathic killer? Where is the thin line between vengeance and warped vengeance? How do citizens protect themselves when technology moves faster than the law? These are a few of the important elements explored in Southard's follow-up to his equally excellent *Agent for Justice*. His story line is complex, but easy to follow; he has a powerful way of intertwining plot lines while keeping the pace of the overall story moving. The characters are well-drawn. The dialogue is crisp and believable. He has a knack for making the landscape a vital part of the story rather than descriptions tacked on as filler. *Live Free or Die* is a terrific book and highly recommended."

—Dan Baldwin, author of *Sparky and the King*,
the Caldera westerns, and the Ashley Hayes mysteries

Praise for *Agent for Justice,* the first Parker Havenot novel

" . . .Creatively combined a teacher's world with mystery and a psychological tailspin. Great characterizations, foreshadowing, and building to a surprise but realistic conclusion."

—Ethel Lee-Miller
author of *Thinking of Miller Place* and *Seedlings*

". . .Entertains us as characters deal with their own inner turmoils. A great read!"

—Shauna Smith, Amazon review

"Life isn't fair. This book demonstrates that lesson from its riveting first chapter to its shocking surprise ending."

—*Green Valley News,* July 2014

"This novel will appeal to readers who enjoy suspense as well as those who are looking for realism and drama with just the right touch of romance. Southard, a former educator, takes us into the world of high school teachers but adds a psychological twist that leads to an unexpected powerhouse ending."

—Kathleen Sammartino, instructor, creative writing and English

"*Agent for Justice* truly portrays the heroic work that great teachers do while effectively demonstrating how an unmitigated idealism leads one man into a spiraling descent of mental deterioration and madness. The story plays like a classic tragedy, with a well-drawn, sympathetic character fighting his obsession toward righting injustices on his own terms."

—Christie Sarles, author and library director

" . . .The subtle description of Brad Wallace's mental decline creates a fascinating account of human psychology."

—Kathleen Noone, *Villanova Magazine*

Praise for other works of Duke Southard

A Favor Returned

"Integral backstories and smooth time transitions allow us to form a personal relationship, both positive and negative, with each unique character."

—Bonita Papenfuss, poet and book reviewer

"A masterful work that kept me reading, with plot twists that were exciting and unexpected, yet completely believable in context. The characters were well-drawn and complex."

—Dan Baldwin,
author of *Trapp Canyon* and the Caldera series

"Your characters are fantastic. You manage to make the supernatural seem natural."

—Christopher Allan Poe,
award-winning author of *The Portal*

"Intellectual stimuli, adventure, and romance jostle one another for your attention."

—Dr. Gerald Gares, Burlington, New Jersey

The Week from Heaven and Hell

"Only once in a great while does a book evoke the emotions that yours did."

—Nguyen Lam, Phoenix, Arizona

"Read this book. Duke Southard tells the tragic yet insightful story in a way that grips the reader from the first page and never stops."

—James Castelli, Amazon review

Live Free or Die

Duke Southard

Duke Southard

Live Free or Die

*To Karen —
With my appreciation
for your support and
gratitude for the
Country Bookseller!
Sincerely,
Duke Southard*

Live Free or Die

Published by Wheatmark®
1760 East River Road, Suite 145, Tucson, Arizona 85718 USA
www.wheatmark.com

ISBN: 978-1-62787-224-9 (paperback)
ISBN: 978-1-62787-225-6 (ebook)
LCCN: 2014956888

Special Author's Note

Univac Redux is a fictitious company. However, there were technology companies working on miniature computer chip research similar to that used in the location and time period of this novel. I take full responsibility for any liberties taken with that research for the purposes of this story and for any attendant errors based on that research.

To Barbara, who is truly the BEST

Acknowledgments

MY THANKS TO HILLARY and Gary Metzger, innkeepers, for their earlier permission to use the name of the *Winnipesaukee Belle* in *Agent for Justice.*

My heartfelt gratitude to family and friends whose constant support is always an inspiration and a revelation.

To those who wanted more, especially Betty and Carlos, here it is...

My thanks to the Green Valley Writers Group—you will see the many results of your insightful, thoughtful, and helpful remarks in the book.

Finally, my thanks to Lori, Grael, Atilla, and Sam, the true professionals at Wheatmark.

A Failed Mission

August 8, 1992

"GET THE HELL OFF this boat, NOW!"

Gordon's shout carried that edge of desperation that borders on hopelessness. Parker reacted to his friend's cry with the instinct of a veteran policeman, sensing the impending danger instantly. His frantic glance around encompassed almost three hundred and sixty degrees.

"Josie," he whispered.

Relief swept over him when he saw both Josie and Becky well clear of the patrol boat. The next millisecond, just as he started to jump, the first blast struck him in the back, the intense shock wave flipping him into the water. The sky overhead turned a bright white then faded into darkness.

Several minutes later, his world gradually came back into focus. He looked up into Josie's face from his position on the deck of the second lake patrol boat. She cradled his head in her lap as he struggled to make sense of his situation.

His questions began in staccato fashion. "Is everyone all right? Where's Becky? Is Gordon OK? What the hell happened?" Josie finally interrupted.

"Everyone's fine, Parker. Relax. We really are all OK." The soothing sound of his wife's voice brought him back to the present and he sat up. He stared over the edge of the boat at the still burning

1

debris floating between the patrol boat and the *Winnipesaukee Belle* anchored to the west.

"Oh, my God," he whispered as the memories formed. "Brad?" He asked the single word question while his eyes remained fixed on the flames licking at the oil slick rising and falling with the soft swells of the lake.

"Gone, Parker. He's gone," Josie said simply, her eyes filling. "He brought that preserver over to me then just let himself go."

BRAD WALLACE HAD PRACTICED the maneuver so many times that it was second nature to him. The weight belt did its job nicely, dragging him beneath the surface as water began spilling into the top section of his wet suit. Josie had already slipped Parker's limp arms through the ring and found room for one of her hands. As Brad sank into what she was seeing as his personal oblivion, he saw her stunned expression forming the crazed image of a rippling fun house mirror as she clung to the life preserver.

When he reached a depth of about eight feet, the light faded. It was time. The single snap he had used to secure the belt around his waist came loose as easily as it had in his practice sessions. The weights brushed past his legs, just nipping at his toes as they tumbled to the bottom of the lake. He shrugged his shoulders and pulled the sleeves of his suit off his arms. The water was well over one hundred and fifty feet deep in this area of the lake. The belt would sink into the sandy bottom and never be found but the suit needed to stay with him. He immediately went into the second part of his well-practiced routine and began a scissor kick down and away from the confusion on the surface, the drag of the wet suit barely noticeable. The chop on the lake this late in the day would have quieted considerably since the heavy boat traffic earlier and his approach to the surface would have to be cautious at best. Based on his best performances, he estimated he could be at least a hundred yards from the patrol boat when he came up for air. With the chaos that still would be churning above, he would draw at least two or three deep breaths before diving again. The second dive would take him far enough away that he'd be able to float to shore without being seen. He envisioned himself collapsing on the shore, dead to those still out on the lake, but Brad Wallace would be very much alive and ready to carry on.

After all, he had so much more to accomplish, especially with his former wife and his favorite detective, Parker Havenot, apparently ready to live happily ever after.

The Return of Brad Wallace

As Brad dragged his exhausted body onto the shore, he glanced over his shoulder in the direction of the *Winnipesaukee Belle*. Wisps of smoke floated above the partially submerged patrol boat but showed signs of dissipating altogether. Despite the distance, Brad could see the ornamental paddle wheel on the *Belle* churning while the real motor driving the craft created a string of bubbles on the surface. The boat was slowly getting underway. He observed nothing in the appearance of the scene that indicated any degree of panic, a fact that somehow annoyed him.

"The great Parker has it all under control," he muttered as he made his way toward the stand of pines bordering the sandy beach. When he reached his temporary headquarters under cover of the towering trees, he grabbed his backpack and rummaged through it until he found his binoculars. A quick scan of the lake convinced him that all attention was focused on tending to those in the second patrol boat. Determining his fate did not appear to be on anyone's agenda. His elation at his successful escape progressed until it reached acute euphoria.

To those left out on the lake, any search and rescue mission for Brad Wallace needn't be rushed. That mission was sure to be announced as a recovery operation, and with dusk settling over the lake like a gray mist, the search would be placed on a priority list for another day. Josie would have passed along her description of his mental state just before he slipped beneath the surface. In her mind, there would be no question about it. Brad was gone. Any momentary regrets she might have experienced would be dispelled by the happiness of knowing that Parker was all right.

All that remained now for him was to execute the next part of his contingency plan. He would soon be back in Connecticut, probably before they held a memorial service for him.

"As if they'd even be planning one," he mumbled to himself.

THE DETAILS OF THE weekend on Lake Winnipesaukee assumed a surreal quality as Detective Parker Havenot tried to relate them to his colleagues at the Covington County Sheriff's Department. Halfway through the description, he finally gave up.

"Just unbelievable; totally beyond belief. That's all I can say. I mean, the guy is about fifty years old and still . . ." His voice trailed off and his colleagues knew that they would hear no more about the weekend, at least for now.

Parker disappeared behind the door to his office and began sifting through the pile of notes and phone calls that always accumulated over long weekends. It appeared that Covington County, that bucolic escape from the big city problems of Hartford to the east and Danbury to the west, had not been very quiet over the weekend. The reports of robberies, domestic disputes, check frauds, DUI arrests, and the myriad of other minor infractions presented the usual daunting task of lining up the evidence and witnesses needed for prosecution. The sheer volume of the reports was unusual but without any dramatic, high-profile cases like murder or rape. As the senior and by far most competent investigator on the staff, Havenot had first choice of the cases he would handle. His standing with the department precluded the possibility that anyone would ever disagree with him. His challenge for this day leaned toward finding something to help him forget his incredible weekend.

Back to Connecticut

"LIVE FREE OR DIE" is the state motto of New Hampshire, a maxim some consider macabre. Brad Wallace had chosen to die so that he could live free. His stealthy return to Connecticut could not be called triumphant in any sense, but his backup plan for leaving the sunny shores of Lake Winnipesaukee worked to perfection. Anyone who even pretended to care about what happened to him would be convinced that he had committed one of the most bizarre suicides in Granite State history. While he wished that his efforts had gone better on the big lake, the unfolding story of his planned assault on the *Belle* would have everyone who was on the boat that night thankful that his scheme had been interrupted.

After he read the Wednesday edition of the *Granite State News*, informing the general public that his body had not yet been recovered, he knew it was time to put the second part of his plan into action. He threw a few pieces of clothing that would not be noticed as missing into an old briefcase from his educator days and began the four-mile trek to the Concord Trailways bus station in Moultonborough. As he expected, within a quarter of a mile, a pickup truck pulled over and the driver asked if he needed a ride. Also as expected, the driver, being a New Hampshire native, had little to say and the conversation didn't go any further than "where ya headed?" and Brad's answer.

The bus ride from Moultonborough to Boston provided a

6

time to savor the chaos he had created. The most dramatic event, the explosion of the *Winnipesaukee Belle,* had been foiled, but his imagination allowed him to picture the pieces of the vessel floating in slow motion against the crystalline blue New Hampshire sky. As agent for justice for those aboard, especially George Metcalf and Rich Lane, he would have to wait for another opportunity.

It would be a long time before he could be declared legally dead without his body being recovered from the bottom of the lake. Much like his subtle inquiries into the technical and mechanical aspects of the *Winnipesaukee Belle* that were crucial for his failed mission to sink it, Brad had conducted another quiet research project. His lengthy chats with a few knowledgeable divers with a wealth of experience on the big lake led him to several grizzled old-timers, the type who believes that anyone not from a family living in New Hampshire for five generations really can't call themselves natives.

The shared information he gained from his sources convinced him that it was uncommon but still possible that a body lost to the lake might never reappear. In the winter, skimming snow-mobiles, ice racing, and just plain stupidity on the part of drivers chancing the thrill of racing their cars across the ice led to many bodies sinking to the bottom. A fair number of these were never recovered. With the addition of open lake boating accidents in the spring through the fall, the number of bodies or parts of them that remained in the lake might even double. The shifting currents and the plethora of rocks and shifting sands on the bottom had disappointed many families in their frantic search for the elusive closure that comes with discovering the remains of a lost loved one.

Brad could not imagine that much effort would be placed on finding his body if all the other pieces of his disappearance fit together. Watching him disappear beneath the surface would be all the closure that his ex-wife Josie would need. He doubted that the others needed any degree of closure.

Establishing a new identity for his life in what he laughingly called his Post-BW period would require some clever planning but people did it all the time. In the meantime, he would remain wary and live his life under the noses of his past comrades, who would not exactly be watching for him. If he were careful, he would be free to roam for a long time.

After leaving the bus station, he hailed the first cab he saw and asked the driver if he knew of any used car lots with cheap transportation.

"Yeah, but it'll cost you. Quite a ways out but it'll be worth the trip."

A year and half of living the life of a hermit while on significant pension and early retirement payments allowed Brad to accumulate a substantial amount of cash.

"Not a problem, as long as you forget you ever saw me afterwards." The driver looked him straight in the eye.

"Not a problem for me, either," he said.

A half hour later, Brad found himself standing in the lot of Paul's Used Cars. Another hour later, he was heading toward Hartford in a drab and innocuous gray 1982 Ford Escort.

"You'll be fine as long as you keep it under the radar, so to speak," Paul said, grinning at his own joke. "The plates are current and nobody'll bother you unless you rob a bank." Paul let loose with a salesman's guffaw. Brad couldn't get out of there fast enough.

The two-hour ride to Hartford, normally a deadly bore in his past life, allowed sufficient time to plan his reunion with Brad, Jr. and a return to the exhilarating Connecticut black periods. The imitation of his infant son's gravesite in New Hampshire never came close to equaling the real thing that he had missed so much. The forthcoming visit to the true grave fully occupied his mind and, in what seemed a few minutes, he approached the exit from Interstate 84 in West Hartford that would eventually lead him to his temporary living quarters. Estimating that the execution of the next part of his plan would take only a few months, he could deal with the tiny rental house and with a landlord who asked no questions as long as the rent came in on time and in cash.

Back in Connecticut and deceased, he could continue to be an agent for justice in his home territory.

Gordon's Paranoia

"COME ON, GORDON. LISTEN to yourself. I mean, the whole idea is ludicrous!" Parker smiled as he imagined Gordon Tibideau flinching at his taunting. After sharing the whole incredible Brad Wallace saga, he and Gordon decided that nothing would ever again surprise either of them. Gordon even bought into Parker's mantra that nothing ever surprises him anymore. From everyday simple events like a trusted police officer calling in sick and spending the day on the golf course to the life-changing like infidelity or terminal illness or loss of a child, there were no surprises in the life of Parker Havenot, only varying degrees of disappointment. Human beings were capable of just about anything and seemed determined to prove that capability on a regular basis.

This phone call from his New Hampshire friend puzzled Parker. Gordon's suspicions were usually well founded and his law enforcement instincts matched that of the most astute of Parker's detective colleagues. Parker's teasing was half-hearted and his good friend sensed it in spite of the limitations that telephone conversations have on the participants.

"What exactly is it that has you so riled up?" Parker asked, his voice softening, well aware that his young friend worshipped his talents as a detective.

"It's just a little weird, that's all. I mean, I know that all that stuff with Wallace was strange but this adds a whole other dimen-

9

sion to it. He should have come up by now, for sure. I just don't get it." Gordon paused long enough for Parker to jump in.

"It's only been a couple of days and he had a weight belt on, or at least we assume he did, then a wet suit to boot. Besides, it's a huge lake with all sorts of strange currents. You've told me that many times yourself, Gordon. He could pop up nearly anywhere."

"That's the thing that has me stumped. One of our divers found the belt in about a hundred feet of water. The buckle had been replaced with a snap. Much easier to get rid of if a diver needed to."

Parker remained silent, waiting for Gordon to come out and say what he was thinking. His friend cleared his throat several times before going on.

"I'm wondering if maybe Wallace had another plan in case things didn't go his way. I'm thinking he could be alive, Parker. I hate to even mention that but just maybe we should consider it. This is really awful to say but every time the phone rings I'm hoping that it will be someone telling me he had surfaced. All I'm saying is that without that belt on, his body should have shown up by now, no doubt about it."

"From what I'm hearing, it seems to me that my influence on you has been pretty negative. When I met you, you were the ultimate idealist, trusting everybody and figuring that if someone said something, it must be true. Don't let Brad Wallace get in your head. But if it will make you feel better, we can talk about it when Josie and I come up next weekend. I'm guessing that by then, we'll have nothing to talk about as far as Wallace is concerned."

"Do you really think so or are you just patronizing me?" Gordon asked, a friendly sarcasm evident in his voice.

"Come on now, you know that's not me. I'm only trying to process everything just like you are. I would never do that to you, you know that."

"Yeah, I do. It's just that…" His voice faded and it appeared that Gordon wanted to end the conversation. He needed the benefit of face-to-face contact so he could see Parker's reaction.

"Hey," he said, false enthusiasm gushing through the phone

line, "thanks for listening. I'll look forward to seeing you and maybe my paranoia will sound better in person." His hearty laugh offset the negative vibrations of the whole conversation. "By the way, you're the cause of all this, you know. I used to be a pretty normal guy until you got me involved with Brad Wallace."

Parker smiled. "Yeah, right. You loved that and you know it. See you this weekend."

"Former Teacher Still Missing"

WHEN JOSIE AND PARKER arrived at the lake cottage late Friday night, Gordon was waiting. He had, as usual, opened the windows to let some of the knotty pine scented air escape from the closed-up cabin.

"It's pretty late, Gordo! What are you doing still up?" Parker hollered from the car window when he saw Gordon climbing the steep path toward them.

"Just thought I'd give you a welcome back," he said. "Plus, I wanted to make sure you came after our conversation the other day. You probably thought I was crazy."

Parker laughed and reached out to give Gordon a warm hand-shake. "Of course I think you're crazy," he said. "But I wanted to see your delusion in person."

Gordon followed him to the trunk of the car and grabbed one of the suitcases. "Hi, Josie. You're looking better than ever!" he called out to her as he stumbled down the path toward the house.

"I'll just drop this off then leave you two alone. You didn't come all this way to have me intrude on your first night here." He set the suitcase just inside the door and started back up the hill toward his car. "I'll see you tomorrow sometime, Parker.

Give me a call whenever you feel like it. I'll be at home. Big day off, you know!"

"LET'S JUST TAKE A look at his house, Gordon."

After a romantic and memorable night on the lake with Josie, Parker called his good friend unexpectedly early the next morning and closed the conversation with the suggestion.

"I know we did that drive-by the day after but maybe we should just take a closer look. After all, no one really will care much one way or another. Unless, of course, we bump into Wallace's ghost." Parker chuckled but Gordon wasn't biting.

"I've got an uneasy feeling about that, I must admit. I mean, I don't even think the police have been over there yet. We might be assuming too much, even though the Chief likes you." Gordon hesitated, giving Parker an opening.

"So, there you go. There's nothing to worry about. Chief Grover probably won't get to it for a while and he couldn't care less if we just look around. Besides, maybe Brad'll invite us in for coffee." Parker laughed again. His years of experience in law enforcement with its often sanity-saving, gruesome humor once again shocked his younger compatriot.

"OK, OK, you win. I'll pick you up at your house in about fifteen minutes but you can stop giving me the willies any time now. Wallace is somewhere at the bottom of the lake; that much we can be sure of. If he's serving coffee, it sure as hell won't be in his old house. I'll see you in a bit." Gordon hung up the phone with a nervous giggle.

THE LAST TIME THAT Parker had seen Brad Wallace's house, he had been confused by what he saw. Only after Gordon, with his "gee whiz" enthusiasm, confirmed what he suspected did Parker begin to believe that Brad might indeed be a true psychopath. According to Gordon, the damage to the boats had to be purposeful. Brad Wallace was deliberating sabotaging boats on the big lake. This visit, he was prepared.

The pieces of the hulls of the boats still littered the backyard. It seemed that nothing at all had changed, at least as far as the outside of the house was concerned.

"OK, Gordon, let's see if we can find any answers in there," Parker said.

They approached the back door like nervous young children creeping toward an abandoned and surely haunted house.

"It'll be open, I'm sure of that," Parker said as they climbed the porch steps, one at a time. The knowledge that Brad Wallace was somewhere at the bottom of the big lake did little to assuage their cautious approach. As expected, the door was unlocked. Parker inched it open while Gordon hung back as if anticipating an apparition to appear at any moment.

Both finally cleared the door and stood inside.

"This is really weird," Gordon said. "It's like Brad left with every intention of coming back but never made it."

"Speaking from experience, that's exactly how it is. I've been to a lot of places where people left in the morning then had some catastrophe wipe 'em out, just like that. Pretty unsettling but also more common than you'd like to think."

"Yeah, I guess everybody expects to come home from work in one piece."

They walked through the house almost on tiptoes, treading as though walking among graves in a cemetery. After the cursory trip through the small cottage, Parker was the first to speak as they stopped in the middle of the kitchen.

"Looks pretty much like I recall when I peeked through these windows. I'm not seeing any hint yet that would indicate that he's anywhere but where we think he is, under a hundred and fifty feet of water, as you said. I think we'd be able to tell if he'd returned here. There would certainly be some sign and I'm not seein' it. What about you?"

After the uneasy beginning as they entered the house, Gordon had regained most of his composure during the inspection and now stood a little taller and answered Parker's question.

"I guess I agree with you. This house sure doesn't seem to have any secrets to give up." He smiled as he looked at the veteran policeman whom he had come to respect so much. "Guess we'll have to hit the diner for coffee; doesn't look like there's much chance of getting any here."

"Maybe we should take a look around the outside before we go," Parker said.

"I really don't think we have to this time around. Let's leave that to the Chief. It'll give him something to do." Gordon was the first one out of the door and he paused to look around the mudroom serving as an entryway to the house. In one corner, a large cardboard box held a stack of newspapers that Brad either was saving or getting ready to take to the landfill.

"What the hell is this?" he whispered. Parker was close enough behind him that he heard the quiet exclamation.

"What's up, Gordon?" As he asked the question, he followed Gordon's gaze and saw the pile of papers just about overflowing the box. The front page of the paper on top of the pile explained Gordon's reaction. It was the edition of the *Granite State News* that came out on Wednesday after the incident on the lake.

The headline fairly jumped off the page at them.

"FORMER TEACHER STILL MISSING," it shouted.

"How in the hell did this get here?" they said, literally in unison.

"There's no way, no possible way that this paper should be here. I mean, unless it is Wallace's ghost that brought it back here." Gordon's hands shook as he picked up the paper, not wanting to probe all of the implications.

"Let me just see that for a second, will ya?" Parker said. "There's got to be a logical explanation." Parker's voice didn't hide the skepticism about what he had just said. After glancing at the headline again and checking the publication date, he just looked at Gordon.

"Let's go see the Chief. Maybe he'll take this a little more seriously this time." With the newspaper held firmly in his sweating palm, Parker led the way back to the car, glancing over his shoulder at the graveyard of boat hulls. Both men grumbled to themselves as though ashamed to announce out loud what now was a realistic possibility.

Brad Wallace may not be gone after all.

A Wallace Sighting

LIKE MOST HUMAN BEINGS, Dr. John A. Simms remained a creature of habit. Tuesday was what he called his day in the park. After a trip to the deli to pick up his triple decker turkey club, he crossed Highland Avenue and entered Memorial Park, an oasis spreading more than twenty acres in the center of the new complex of buildings between West Hartford and Hampton Village. The huge commercial development sprouted within a year of a major change in Covington County's zoning regulations, allowing business and industrial use of land on the eastern border with West Hartford. Local residents viewed it as just an expansion of the city, the beginning of the end of the rural character of the county. Politicians salivated over the burgeoning tax base, and developers who controlled the politicians celebrated the infinite financial possibilities. The Covington County Sheriff's Department saw it as nothing but an albatross, bringing city-like problems under their jurisdiction.

Simms found his favorite bench, always empty when he arrived at ten minutes before twelve. A few minutes later, the bench would be occupied for the duration and he would have to settle for a far less desirable spot. He chose the locale for its position on a short cut between a large insurance company building and the favorite lunch spots of many of the beautiful young women who worked there. His bench rested just off the path so he could

17

spend his time, as the old song said, "watching all the girls go by." On this Tuesday, an exceptionally warm one for the Connecticut Berkshires with the approaching fall, the solution to his dilemma about Alison came to him.

He had no reason to be jealous. Although Alison was a beautiful young woman, she had demonstrated no propensity toward other men.

"If ever there was a one-man woman, you're looking at her," she often remarked when he pursued the subject. During their two-year relationship, he observed not a single sign that she might have other interests. Yet, by all measures, she was so damned attractive that he couldn't let it go. The casual attitudes toward sex among the young in the world of the late twentieth century infuriated him, an unwelcome intrusion on his generally balanced sense of well-being. He couldn't shake the suspicions that his beloved Alison, almost fifteen years his junior, would have to succumb to the temptations so prevalent all around her.

"It wouldn't really even be her fault," he told himself. "It's just the way things are these days."

Submerging that worry required an almost physical effort, leaving him drained after each wave of trepidation passed by, crashing on the not-too-distant shore of reality. As strong as she was, she still existed in a world of professional young men and the sensation gnawed on the pit of his stomach like an incipient ulcer. The feeling, he decided, must be similar to the sensation a few of his millionaire clients complained about shortly after receiving their implants. They described it in a variety of ways but the common thread was plain. The knowledge that a minuscule foreign body rested somewhere just beneath the surface of their skin produced an ill-defined discomfort that resisted all attempts at relief. The sensation was not unlike the back itch between the shoulder blades, tantalizingly out of reach.

The answer suddenly became so clear that it might have been a headline screaming at him from the newspaper that lay folded open to the front page on his lap. He paused in his rapid munching on the huge sandwich, allowing time for his swallowing to catch up. Once his mouth was clear, he made a quiet pronouncement, barely audible and certainly not understandable to the man hurrying by at the moment.

"I'll just make her one of my clients." There would be no need to tell anyone. Alison herself wouldn't even have to know. His furtive glance around his environment found nothing noteworthy until he noticed that the man in a hurry had stopped. He peeked over his shoulder at Simms then turned away, walking even faster.

The fifteen-minute walk back to his office allowed ample opportunity for the doctor to outline a simple plan. He found himself whistling and feeling a little more bounce in his step than usual. His four o'clock appointment would provide a sound, practical experiment and would focus the still vague details of his scheme. His pace quickened in equal measure with his excitement. He would have to concentrate hard on the intervening appointments, likely boring cases of the flu or indigestion or imagined maladies that brought so many hypochondriacs to his office. Four o'clock and the appointment with Ralph Brookins couldn't come soon enough.

As he unlocked the door to his office, the image of the man who had hurried past him flitted through his mind.

"I'll be damned. I know that guy," he said to his receptionist, who had no idea what he talking about.

"What do you mean, Doctor?" she asked.

Simms shook his head.

"Never mind, Clarisse. It's really nothing. I thought I'd seen an old patient of mine. Think his name was Wally or Walter or something like that. No, no, wait a second. It was Wallace. Anyway, it couldn't have been him. He's dead, or at least I think so."

"You're pretty good with faces and names, Doctor. I'd be surprised if you made a mistake."

"You know what? You're absolutely right. I'm curious now. Why don't you look up a Wallace in the old records and see if you can find a phone number then when you get a chance, call them up. Just tell him what happened and apologize profusely for being intrusive but you can make me the bad guy if you want. You probably don't want to ask him if he's dead but you'll think of something. Let me know what you find out."

Several days later, she found the note she had left for herself on her desk and made the call.

The Four O'Clock Appointment

"Now, what's on the docket for this afternoon, Clarisse? I mean, before the four o'clock?"

"Just a physical at two then a couple of kids with stomach problems. Everything should be over with well before Mr. Brookins gets here at four."

"Look, Doctor, if you think this is a mistake, just come right out and tell me."

Thus far in the project, John Simms had dealt with twelve obscenely wealthy men. Ralph G. Brookins typified their arrogance. He clearly was a man used to having things his way.

"Mr. Brookins," he said, his voice soft yet firm. "I believe in this project. Its ramifications reach far beyond the present use. I respectfully suggest that if you're having any doubts, you need to make the decision, not I." His formality betrayed the agitation behind his pronouncement.

"I didn't mean anything by the question, Doctor. Certainly no offense was intended," Brookins said.

"None taken," Simms said with an affected wave of his hand. "Have you any last-minute questions before we perform the procedure?"

"Actually, I did have just a couple that occurred to me during the night." Then, with just a hint of sarcasm, he added, "Of course, that's if you don't mind."

"Let's hear them. We believe it's important that everyone stay well-informed in case of any glitches."

Brookins flinched. "Glitches is not a word I like to hear. It carries an implicit indication of possible failure."

Simms did not respond.

RALPH G. BROOKINS WAS a self-made man, as they say. His original small neighborhood food store blossomed into a true empire of supermarkets throughout the country and he constantly fought an internal paranoia, a war where most of the battles centered on his ability to control his empire. His eighth grade education was a personal and profound secret, one that he determined had to be kept at all costs. Blessed with natural intelligence and possessed of a voracious reading habit, he could easily discourage most acquaintances from challenging him on any issue of substance and his employees remained in awe of his commanding presence. Yet, the danger that he would be discovered, his weaknesses exposed, often consumed his arrogant confidence. The imagined threats to his position and even his personal well-being occupied an increasing amount of his time.

"Powerful people have powerful enemies," he explained to his reflection in the mirror every morning. His inordinate fear that the cutthroat food business would lead a competitor or, worse yet, a conspiracy of his own employees, to plot some evil against him inspired his first call to Henry Bouchard at Univac Redux and Project TRAC. From there, his path led to Dr. Simms.

"IS THERE EVER A time when the trackers would be out of touch with me?" he asked.

Simms heard this one literally every time he performed an implant but discretion forced him to respond as though Ralph Brookins were the first to ask it.

"That's entirely your call, Mr. Brookins. Obviously, there may be times when you'd rather not have anyone know what you are up to." He grinned and winked but Brookins didn't appear to be amused.

"This is a rather difficult decision for me, Doctor, as I'm sure you realize. To most people, what I'm worried about is nothing but a product of a vivid imagination, but to me the danger is very real. I'd appreciate it if you wouldn't try to inject any humor into this."

Simms recovered quickly. All his clients had their little idio-syncrasies and clearly Brookins was no different.

"I apologize. I didn't mean to be flip but I've used that line when I get similar questions. I'll try to be more direct. There will never be a time when you are out of touch with your tracker unless you choose to be. It is very important to us that you are satisfied with the product. We haven't lost anyone yet; at least not unless they wanted to be lost."

"OK," Brookins said. "That's question one. Next thing—what's the point of the anesthesia being so strong? Why not just use a local? It's not like you're doing a major surgery here."

"Purely for your own protection, Mr. Brookins. You really don't want to know where it is just in case the bad guys think you have one. They could have ways of forcing you to let them know about it before we could respond to your location."

"I didn't really want that answer but I guess I understand. Why don't we just get on with it?"

LESS THAN AN HOUR later, Ralph Brookins sat staring at the monitor. The screen reminded him of the one in his new Lexus.

"Your tracker had the signal within seconds of the implant, Mr. Brookins. From that moment forward, someone will know exactly where you are every minute of every day."

"And you won't let me know where the implant is, right?" The inflection in Brookins's voice as he asked the question indicated a deep ambivalence. Without the doctor's "bad guy" remark just before the procedure, he would have demanded to know. It was, after all, his body that now contained an intrusive foreign object. He listened as Simms added to his previously sketchy explanation.

"You seem like a man who would accept any challenge but I'll pass this along anyway. If you can go one day without giving a lot of thought to this, you'll probably never find the scar. I'd almost say that if you went home right now and searched for it, you probably wouldn't find it. The point, Mr. Brookins, is very simply this. You had this procedure done for a very specific reason. I doubt that you'd want to jeopardize the effect of it just because you're curious about the location of the implant."

"Of course not, Doctor. It's just that I'm used to being in charge or at least feeling like I've got some control."

"I'm sure you are and I can't blame you for that. And you do have some control. Even though your body supplies the power to run the thing without you even being aware of it, you can have the receiver end turned off. The generator for your signal is your own body heat, which you can't control, but this isn't a spy network, Mr. Brookins. We are just performing a service for you, a service you can decline at any time."

Brookins, a pragmatist used to controlling everything that affected his life, smiled.

"OK, Doctor Simms. You've kind of got me by the short hairs. Apologies for the crudeness but I'm not declining. I just want to know that someone will know where I am when I disappear." Realizing what he had just said, he tried to recover. "I mean IF something should happen."

"No need to worry about that, sir." Simms's sarcasm matched that of Brookins earlier and would have overwhelmed even the most naïve. Brookins suddenly felt like a pawn, a lowly one at that, whose destiny was now entwined with many people that he didn't even know, and the few he did know he didn't like.

"You really can't tell me where it is? I mean, God, you've just put something into my body and you think I won't be able to find it? That is absolutely absurd!"

"Our instructions are very simple; if you want to stand in the shower and search for the opening, that is certainly your prerogative. Our experience has been very consistent. Our clients don't want to know where it is. Sometimes, when you involve yourself in a project, it truly is better to trust those you've trusted to become involved in the first place."

Brookins had almost reached a breaking point. "I'm not stupid, Dr. Simms!" he snapped. "And I'll admit quite frankly that I think you could stand an attitude adjustment."

"I'm well aware that you're not a stupid man but that was a stupid thing to say, Mr. Brookins. We here at Project TRAC are true professionals. We prefer not to be categorized. If you have a problem, I'll arrange for you to meet again with Mr. Bouchard. He'll be happy to explain the reasons why we strongly advise our clients to follow our guidelines. It's certainly your call." Simms glared at Brookins and waited.

"I came here knowing pretty much what I was doing so I guess I'll do what you say." He paused and glared back. "At least for the moment."

"We've never had any medical issue but if you show any symptoms like fever or nausea, you should return to us immediately. I sincerely hope that our product is never of any use to you, Mr. Brookins." Doctor Simms stood and made an obvious move toward the door. The unspoken message he sent left Brookins with no choice but to hurry out without another word.

RALPH BROOKINS DECIDED NOT to search for the tiny slit that had allowed Dr. Simms to insert the chip. As the good doctor pointed out, why take any chances on defeating the purpose? "Not even a Band-Aid will be used," Simms said, launching into a brief explanation of a new styptic type formula that anesthetizes the area and then heals it like a shaving cut.

As an intelligent and sharp businessman, he knew that the expense of the procedure and the all-important follow-up were so exorbitant that it would be stupid to countermand the reason for obtaining the implant. Despite the implied challenge from Simms, he had no doubt he could find it. Certainly, there are places on the human body that are never seen by the person inhabiting the skin. Brookins's own sister had been unaware of the changes in a mole under her arm until it was too late. He knew of others who only discovered lethal lumps in odd places months after the growths made their first appearance. As he thought about the human body and its many cracks and crevices where the miniscule device could be placed, he decided that just maybe he wouldn't be able to find it after all.

Better that he not even try and just see what develops. His innate and powerful self-discipline moved the last two hours into the past where it belonged. He turned his attention to the future, his personal safety assured, at least hypothetically, by the implant.

Just above his left wrist, his diamond-studded Rolex covered the less than one-quarter-inch slit. The watch had become second nature to him, no more noticeable than a wedding band worn thin over the thirty-nine years of his marriage. He never removed it during the day, and by the time he took it off later that evening to set it nearby on his nightstand, the slightly red tinge would have faded into a rosy blur, unnoticeable on the mottled skin of a sixty-year-old man.

The Doctor's Second Job

"I'M GUESSING THAT APPROVAL might come as early as 2004 or as late as 2010," Henry Bouchard told Simms during his initiation process. "This is 1992 so you figure it out. Another fifteen years, probably closer to twenty! And even that depends on whether anything happens that will send the ACLU sprinting to the nearest courtroom."

Henry Bouchard, convinced that he would be a multi-millionaire within a year or two, decided that time was a crucial element to the success of his plan. There were so many competitors out there, most of them at least as unscrupulous as he was. He must be the first. Dragging one's feet just because of some stupid bureaucratic regulations didn't make sense. The unique use of an existing product formed the basis for entrepreneurship, and he was not going to allow anyone to steal his idea.

Bouchard considered himself a visionary and it was not difficult for him to observe the direction the world was taking. While some romanticists clung to the notion that man was basically good, he knew that it really didn't matter, even if he did agree with them. When he decided to convince the mediocre Dr. John A. Simms to be his first "inserter," he wished he had recorded his long recruiting speech. It formulated his theory so clearly that the doctor was uncharacteristically speechless.

"The force of good versus the force of evil represents a wonderful philosophical argument," he said. "Unfortunately, the reality of the argument is that there is no argument. Suppose, just for the sake of this non-argument, that only one-tenth of one percent of the population is truly evil. Actually, let's make that one one-hundredth of one percent. The population of the United States is approximately two hundred and fifty million as of the recent 1990 census. That means that we are dealing with more than twenty-five thousand evil people. This is a very conservative estimate, by the way. But you see," he continued, as Simms leaned forward in his chair in conspiratorial fashion, "it doesn't matter that most people are basically good. What matters is that we have more than enough bad folks to wreak havoc with all their good intentions."

His idea appealed to the fear that appeared to be engulfing the human population of the planet. Although the odds are not in their favor, he would point out to anyone who would listen, the bad guys are winning. His plan would use existing technology to capitalize on that human weakness. The simple fact was that every night for at least an hour, the general population was subjected to a string of news stories on the mainstream networks that could frighten even the most blasé. The clichéd literary themes of man against nature and man against man jolted what used to be the old dinner hour, showing in grizzly detail the effects of earthquakes, hurricanes, and tsunamis. Lest the viewers become bored, the producers cleverly interspersed the natural disasters with stories of murder, police brutality, kidnappings, and, of course, the ever-popular errant bombing raids that "just missed" a top terrorist official, killing dozens of "collateral damage" villagers.

Microchip implantation, originally designed for use in animal tracking and on its way to play a major role in medical circles, simply needed some adaptation. Thinner and smaller than a grain of rice, the microchip to be implanted had to be able to send and receive data and be continuously monitored by a system similar to global positioning satellite technology. Ordinary human muscle movement and body heat powered the chip electromechani-cally, providing an endless supply of energy with no dependence on external sources. Once Bouchard and his small band of thoroughly vetted scientists discovered the methodology to enable the chip to emit a strong enough signal to be picked up by lower level satellite, his plan was ready for implementation.

"The technology exists, the evil is out there, and there are plenty of very rich people willing to pay a lot of money to mollify their paranoiac tendencies." Bouchard concluded his speech to the doctor with a dramatic flourish.

"The best part is that they won't want anyone to know what they're doing. Imagine what that information could do to their image. So, we perform a valuable service, and they believe that they are safe from the dangers trailing behind them as they carry out their duties as the captains of industry and commerce."

Dr. John A. Simms needed no more convincing. He fawned over Bouchard as if he were the messiah sent to deliver him from the doldrums of his everyday existence.

As far as anyone outside their company knew, the technology for the tiny chips to be effective beacons for tracking individuals remained years away. Bouchard knew better than to expose the discovery to the vagaries of the FDA's security systems or the government's system of awarding patents. His requirement that Simms keep his own practice seemed odd at the time, but once he began to perform the procedure, he understood the need for the legitimizing of the process. Approval from the FDA was so doubtful in the political climate of distrust and fear after the recent Gulf War and the fall of the Berlin Wall that it was likely that the blessing of that easily influenced body may never be given. They supposedly would not move without the irrefutable proof of sound, scientific evidence, but then that might change if the proper protocols were followed and the proper officials were sent on the proper all-expenses paid vacations. With controlled excitement, Simms agreed to join the medical team at Univac Redux, a cover company for Project TRAC.

Henry Bouchard, the founder and president of Univac Redux, created the acronym for his company's new product and then found the words to fit. Project TRAC was born when Bouchard convinced his newly recruited physician, Dr. John Simms, to perform the first "medical experiment" on Professor Thomas Gomes of the University of Hartford.

His plan to nickname the implants angelic chips originated with the idea that they were, indeed, to be guardian angels of a sort. It was not difficult to demonstrate that an implanted chip could carry all sorts of important medical information and if the recipient should have a medical emergency, his chip could alert everyone to his condition. Like so many acronyms, the four letters indicated exactly what his firm did.

"We'll *T*race the *R*ich with *A*ngelic *C*hips," he explained during his recruitment of Simms. The doctor had been suitably impressed with the ease with which the implants could be inserted. Perhaps, for the first time in his life, he might be part of one of those cutting-edge field studies that would help convince the FDA that quick approval should be given to this new technology. They had already approved the implants for medical reasons but with the controversy over privacy issues, who could know when, if ever, that agency would find the courage to take the next step.

TRAC Begins

HENRY BOUCHARD'S TECHNICIANS WERE an odd pair by all standards. He hired both Travis Connally and Tommy Maggio within a week and they completed their training by the end of the following week. Bouchard ruled first by practicality, placing them into an income category they had only dreamed of. Once softened by his generosity, they were perfectly set up for his next strategy, which, for the required secrecy of the operation, meant rule by harsh intimidation and clearly outlined threats. He asked for no loyalty other than their promise not to discuss any details of their employment with anyone.

"Tell them you work in developing computer software for satellites," he instructed. "Most people will not want to be bored hearing about that."

After their training, Bouchard explained that he would be the only person at the TRAC project both of them would see every day. Each was assigned to a spacious office packed with the sophisticated equipment necessary to their jobs. Fortunately for Bouchard, the computer industry overflowed with the type he needed, people who would enjoy spending the day staring at a computer screen. The technology they found at the project proved much more interesting than any contact with other human beings, and all of them reacted as if they had finally found the job of their dreams.

When Bouchard explained to them that the project was in

its infancy and their workloads might be heavy at the beginning, neither of them was bothered. Their eight-hour shifts would overlap slightly but that they would not see each other at all. They agreed to any schedule that he would develop, allowing him to alternate the graveyard shifts and weekends in what he saw as a fair and equitable manner. Double shifts could be expected at times as the project got started. While they understood vaguely what it was they were doing, only Bouchard could answer their questions, but his obvious reticence soon purged their curiosity. Like the teacher who knows all the answers on the test but doesn't want to supply any hints, he responded to their inquiries with bland shrugs and pointless words that discouraged additional prying. As long as the substantial paychecks arrived directly in their bank accounts each Friday, neither saw any cause to complain.

Bouchard was the first and the last line of communication. They lived easily with that.

"These blips are what we'll call our 'charges' for now," he said, explaining the terminology for the dots on their computer screens. When Bouchard either called or paid an in-person visit to ask them to identify the exact location of one of their charges, they were tempted to ask why but knew that such a request would be futile. Likewise, when one of their charges disappeared from the screen and they dutifully reported it, he would acknowledge the information with a grunt and hang up. Only when he needed clarification about an exact time and place would he walk directly to the office of the reporter to examine the evidence himself.

Alison's Story

SIMMS DECIDED THAT GHB would work the best. Alison would be out for at least an hour and would awaken with no memory of what had happened. The college low-life types who were currently using gamma-hydroxybutrate to commit their so-called date rapes had made the drug so popular that medical personnel constantly received police reports and warnings to be watching for signs of its use. The FDA was about to ban it altogether, which would mean nothing to those mixing the concoction in their basements or garages. John Simms had no intention of using it for that purpose. He and several of his colleagues often discussed in the most disparaging of terms those pathetic men who couldn't seduce women on their own and needed to resort to drugging their dates.

He had set a personal record with Ralph Brookins, inserting the chip and having it operational within fifteen minutes. The aspect of his work with Brookins of which he was most proud was the effectiveness of the placement. His first meeting with Brookins convinced him that this implant would be different. Simms had to convince him that he needn't know where the chip was, even though it was so well concealed that he likely would not have found it anyway. On the other hand, Alison absolutely couldn't be permitted to find it.

He needed one hour. If the drug lasted long enough for a

sexual interlude, an experience the girls did not realize had even happened, surely he could perform the implant in that time. The only question of concern was where. What part of a woman's body is rarely, if ever, seen by the woman herself?

A faint smile formed on his lips when he answered his own question.

ALISON AWOKE TO FIND John Simms staring at her. She glanced around the apartment, trying to shake the discomforting feeling that she didn't belong there. Familiar objects and bits and pieces of furniture swam in and out of focus. It was definitely her apartment. Her sensation was similar to her experience when she endured one of the "twenty countries in twelve days" trips, the kind that every time you awaken, it takes ten minutes to figure out where you are.

"Well, you sure made for an interesting date tonight, Ali. Maybe a little too much wine at dinner or something?" John's words made sense yet sounded foreign at the time. "You've been asleep for over an hour, just passed out like I had slipped you an old-fashioned Mickey Finn.

The dinner they had shared earlier drifted back into her consciousness but the amount of wine she had drunk was not computing. Alison struggled to focus her eyes on the doctor sitting across from her. She sat up and the room spun some more. Back in college, she had too much to drink one time and vowed never to do it again. That night, she had collapsed on the bed on her back and gripped the edges as she rode the merry-go-round so many drunks had boarded before her. John's words were not making sense. She would not have put herself into that position again, but she just couldn't quite bring it back.

"We were just sitting there on the couch and you fell asleep. If I were a different sort of guy, I could've taken advantage of you." Simms laughed at his attempt to bring some humor into the situation. Alison wasn't buying it.

"This is really bugging me, John. I mean, I can't remember

anything after the dinner." Her world was coming back but slowly. "I'd appreciate some help here."

"OK, I'll help you figure this out. It's not all that hard, you know. It's not like you had a stroke or something. I've seen this phenomenon fairly often. It just a combination of things—stress, overwork, fatigue, a bunch of chemicals in your body, including, by the way, a couple of glasses of potent wine and bingo, you go to sleep for an hour or so. Think of it as a poor man's anesthetic. You need to trust me here; in a few minutes, you'll be back to your old self again."

"So, the memory of this evening will come back too, right?" Alison asked the question with an obvious edge, not wanting him to say anything but "of course, dear."

"May or may not, Ali. What's the difference? I was here with you the whole time you were sleeping. I'll swear that you were not abducted by aliens who erased your memory. Just one of those things that happen, so let it go, OK?" John lowered his voice and continued in the soothing, bedside manner voice of a well-trained physician used to calming worried patients. "You'll forget all about this by tomorrow. You took a nap when your body told you to. It is as easy and as simple as that."

"If you say so; after all, you're the doctor. It's just a bit disconcerting but I guess I'll get over it. Thanks for being so understanding and sorry about passing out on you. I'll make it up to you next time." She managed a smile, but the attempt at making it a flirtatious one fell dismally flat.

"I NEED A LITTLE help, Travis."

The sound of John Simms's voice always annoyed him, and this request for help set him on edge. He could understand why Bouchard wanted an inconsequential and invisible sort of doctor for the assignment but why he chose a whiner like Simms escaped him.

"Let's hear it, Simms." He waited for further explanation.

"I'm trying an experiment on my own, and I believe that

Henry will like it. I think we can do this together, and it'll really work out for both of us."

Connally finally answered with one of his patented grunts. "This better be good," he said.

"First of all, it'll be better that he hears about it after the fact. It's always easier to ask forgiveness or extend an apology than be given a flat out no in advance. Come on, I know you're a gambler and I know you like money, right?"

Another grunt, this one more affirmative, encouraged Simms to continue.

"I already did something but a technician has to turn it on." After another minute of listening, Connally reacted.

"You've got to be kidding. You did this without Bouchard's permission? You really are nuts, you know that?"

"All I'm asking is a chance to prove that it has possibilities, that's all. If it's a bust, then we both forget it, but if it turns out how I think it might, we'll both be in line for a more than adequate reward."

The warning bells clanged in his head but the "more than adequate reward" phrase softened them. Travis acceded to John Simms for the first time in their brief history.

"OK. What kind of trial time do you want?" Connally asked.

"Just two weeks; that's all I ask. Then we'll make a decision." Simms was having trouble believing that it was going to be this easy.

"I'm probably as crazy as you are but, OK, let's try it. I'll start it up. What's the number and the code?"

Travis Connally placed the receiver into the cradle and pulled his chair close to the keyboard.

He typed in 0650, Code GERILA. Alison Regan's blip appeared on the screen.

TOMMY MAGGIO WORKED THE three-to-eleven shift enjoying the benefits of having six full hours without Henry Bouchard nearby. His communication with him remained instantaneous, no matter where he was, but there was a certain comfort in knowing that his boss was not within a short walk away. At five o'clock, he knew he could count on the regular intercom call announcing that Bouchard was leaving the building. The ritual of reviewing the contact procedures consumed less than two minutes then Tommy was alone with the technology.

Tommy was two years away from his brief career as an air traffic controller, a job at which he was skilled but emotionally incapable of performing day after day. Less than a month after becoming a full-time controller, Tommy quit. He loved the technology, the whole concept of tracking people who had no idea who you were or even where you were. Bouchard's training sessions gave enough of a hint that this job might involve a similar responsibility without the pressure of knowing that a single mistake could lead to the deaths of hundreds of innocent people.

The day after Travis told him that he had added number 0650, Code GERILA, he received his first call from John Simms. It came in about half an hour after Travis had left the office and the ringing phone startled him. Calls coming into his office were rare, practically non-existent. Simms explained that he was an important part of Project TRAC and that Mr. Bouchard approved his direct contact with the technicians.

"I just need you to give me the location of one of our charges," Simms said. Bouchard's words remained well near the surface of Tommy's mind. He and only he was to be the conduit for all communications about the project.

"I really can't do that, Dr. Simms. You'll have to go through Bouchard. He's got to know about any access to our charges."

"I understand all that, Tommy, and I appreciate your concern. You can contact him right after this if you'd like. I know he'd approve. I'll give you the number and code. How would I know this if I weren't part of the project? Just take a quick look at your screen and let me know where this charge is at the moment, OK? I guarantee it'll be all right." Simms stopped, allowing the vagueness of the project to settle on Tommy.

A moment later, Tommy found 0650GERILA. "The charge is

in the South Hartford Marriot Hotel, Dr. Simms. I'll be hanging
up now and letting Mr. Bouchard know this information as well."

"Yeah, sure, thanks, Tommy," Simms mumbled. The technician didn't hear what followed.

"What the hell is she doing there?" he whispered.

RAISING THE SUBJECT IN subtle fashion was useless so John
Simms charged right into it. Without an answer, he might manage
to get his dinner into his stomach but it would lie there, an undi-
gested lump. He was unable to concentrate on the few patients
he treated that afternoon, wondering what would have brought
Alison to the Marriot. She hadn't mentioned any appointments or
seminars as she usually did so he had no choice but to assume that
his attractive young girlfriend clearly had a liaison on her mind.

"What brought you to South Hartford today? I thought
you were going to be in the office all day?" He watched for her
reaction. People always respond quickly when taken by surprise,
but Alison had just put a sizable piece of the tender filet in her
mouth. She gestured with an index finger for him to be patient
for a moment. He drummed his fingers lightly on the table as she
finished chewing.

"I had to meet with the manager of the Marriot down there,"
she said. "We're working on a contract with them. We need to
get him on board and the window of opportunity presented itself
early today." She kept looking straight at him.

"There was no time to let you know," she added, her eyes
asking the question, one needing no verbalization.

"I was talking to a colleague this afternoon and he mentioned
seeing you down there. I was just curious, that's all. It's not like I
get regular reports on your whereabouts from my spy network."
He smiled.

"I obviously know this colleague, right? Maybe next time I'll
say hello. Anyway, it seems like you're acting relieved, John. As
I'm always telling you, I'm a—"

Simms interrupted. "Just a guy who saw you at one of the
hospital staff parties; you probably wouldn't know him. You

do tend to get noticed, you know. But listen, as you are always reminding me and I know, you're a one-man woman. I really was just making conversation, so let's turn our attention to the matter at hand, namely our dinner." He deftly turned the conversation to the unusual malady of one his patients of the afternoon, allowing the matter of Alison's afternoon activity to drop.

THE NEXT MORNING, AFTER he spent several minutes on hold, Travis Connally answered his call.

"This really has potential. I know that Bouchard will approve. You and Tommy better stay on my side of the ball, Travis," he said.

Alison, Sam, and Parker

SAM OLDEN PREFERRED WRITTEN reports. He didn't relish face-to-face conversations with his superiors, least of all, one of Detective Parker Havenot's stature. Although the door to Havenot's office was wide open, he tapped on the doorjamb.

"Have a seat, Sam. This really shouldn't take long." Olden sat on the edge of the only over-stuffed chair in the office, resisting the natural impulse to sink into the soft padding.

"So, tell me about your interview with Ms. Regan."

"Well," Sam began, his posture as rigid as if he were sitting in a straight-back chair. "If you ask me, there's something to her complaint. Unless I miss my guess, she's not the sort of woman who gets hysterical. Actually, she seems more the opposite; always in control, you know?"

"Will you relax, Sam," Parker said. "I'm just trying to get myself on firm footing. We're talking about a doctor here, and any kind of negative publicity can be disastrous for a professional."

Olden leaned back but stayed rigid.

"If she is so stable and so independent, why do you think she called us, Sam? Did she seem to feel like she was in danger from this guy?" Havenot had determined that he would give this complaint about fifteen minutes.

"Not really, at least that's not what she indicated. She's a real knockout, Parker."

"Not sure what knockout has to with anything." Olden's posture stiffened again. Parker learned early in his career that complaints from attractive women generally assumed more importance than the average with investigating officers, usually because they wanted to spend more time with the women.

"She's been going with him for quite a while," Olden offered. The observation brought Parker out of his seat.

"She's been going with him for quite a while and she's still going with him? What the hell is this all about? Can't she just ask him how he knows where she is all the time? I've got to admit, Officer Olden, that this isn't making too much sense to me."

Sam Olden, on the defensive, squirmed, fighting off his intimidation. "She just said that she was unnerved by it and thought that maybe we could help. I think she probably wanted me to say that we hear this stuff all the time so she could let it go."

"What else?" Parker stretched and yawned, excusing himself. "Sorry to jump on you like that. It's been a long day already."

"The only other thing worth mentioning was that she thought he had changed since she had a sort of blackout at her apartment. He used to keep pretty close tabs on her but since that happened, he seems looser, more relaxed." Olden had regained some degree of confidence.

"A blackout? Tell me more about that."

Sam's poise took one step backward. "I didn't really ask her too much about that. She seemed a little embarrassed by it."

"OK, Officer Olden, I guess maybe I'll visit Miss Regan myself. Thanks for the information."

"I could do a follow-up if you'd like. She seemed comfortable with . . . " He stopped and looked down at his feet.

"I'll look into it but thanks for your enthusiasm. It's refreshing to see an officer so vitally interested in our citizenry, especially the good-looking women." Parker's smile led to a decided relaxation of Olden's tensed shoulder muscles.

"I guess I'll be going," Sam mumbled and proceeded to back into the doorjamb as he fumbled his way out of the office.

PARKER HEARD ALISON'S FOOTSTEPS approach then there was silence. He had called ahead so she should have been expecting him, but her reticence bothered him. She was using the thick peephole in the door to good advantage. The neighborhood seemed to be one where a knock on the door was never a threat. Why the hesitation? He seriously doubted that had he tapped on any other door in this apartment building there would have been any indecision. His intuition that something was wrong disappeared when the door opened.

Sam Olden's description of Alison failed to capture the presence she had. He had his badge in the palm of his hand but she barely looked at it. Instead, she looked directly at him and smiled. She extended her hand and he shook it lightly.

"Come in, Detective. Sorry for the delay but you can't be too careful, you know?"

"No offense, Miss Regan, but this really doesn't look like a neighborhood where you'd have to worry too much." He caught himself staring at her and redirected his attention to the apartment.

"Please, could you call me Alison? I'm not used to such formality." In the space of one minute, Alison Regan made a wonderful first impression on Havenot. "It's not really the neighborhood I'm worried about," she said. "I've just been a little jumpy lately, for no good reason."

"So, Officer Olden . . ." Parker began but Alison interrupted.

"I'm somewhat embarrassed by all this and I only agreed to talk with you because you cared enough to call. To be truthful, I really wish I had never made that first call. I think you'll agree with me after our conversation. I'll make it brief and to the point."

"So brief we're not going to sit down?"

Alison blushed. "I'm so sorry. I even made a small pot of coffee if you'd care for some. I just forgot." She pointed to a recliner in the corner. "Why don't you sit there and I'll get the coffee?"

"Fine with me." Parker took his time sitting down, observing and registering details of the room that the average person would not have noticed for hours. When Alison returned with a silver tray and fancy tea setting, he had just sat down. She offered the coffee and he took it black, ignoring the cream pitcher and the silver spoon begging to dump several sugar cubes in the dainty cup.

"You like your coffee straight up, huh?" Alison asked, her hazel eyes sparkling.

"Only way to drink the high-test version; at least that's what my wife says." He could almost hear Josie whispering in his ear—"no cream and sugar; coffee is meant to be drunk black!" Alison set the tray on the coffee table and retreated to the opposite side of the room, sitting down heavily on a padded hassock in front a huge armchair. She wasn't settling in for a long conversation.

"Tell me about the blackout," Parker said.

Alison gulped a swallow of coffee, surprised by his blunt approach.

"It was really nothing. John explained it and I only mentioned it to Officer Olden because it's a kind of a time marker when I noticed the change." She paused and seemed ready to stop talking altogether.

"The change?" Parker decided to act as if he hadn't heard this part of her story in hope of drawing more of a response.

"I thought Sam would have told you about that too. I've gone with John for quite a while and he's always been a bit possessive, wanting to know where I went for lunch, with whom, you know, that sort of thing. I was actually pretty happy when he stopped being so curious about what I was doing. All of a sudden, he didn't seem to care so much." She hesitated as though waiting to see if Parker was satisfied. He wasn't, but he sipped his coffee in silence and waited for her to continue.

"About a week or so after my episode, he began asking how I enjoyed my dinner at Rudy's or if I found any good deals at Macy's, that sort of thing. Then the other day, he mentioned a business visit I had at a hotel. When I asked how he knew where I was, he'd pass it off as a wild guess and laugh. The hotel visit he said one of his colleagues saw me. It gave me the creeps at first; I'm not sure why."

"Any more of those, uh . . ." Parker struggled to ask the question in a positive tone without sounding cynical of the doctor's terminology. "I think you called it an episode or something, right?"

"No. I haven't but, as John suggested, I've tried to be more relaxed and not get so tired. I've also tried to stay away from that extra glass of wine. Anyway, I appreciate your attention to this but I'm figuring you've got better things to do than calm the paranoia of a silly woman." She drained the tiny cup and stood.

Parker didn't miss the unsubtle cue. One large swallow emptied his cup as well and he was standing before the heat from the coffee faded in his throat.

"It sounds as though your doctor friend explained things pretty well to you but I doubt that he mentioned paranoia, did he?"

"No, he didn't. That's my word. I won't bother you again, Detective. I'll try real hard to be a big girl." She laughed as she extended her hand. Parker shook it, a bit more firmly than at first, then walked to the door.

HAVE NOT LEFT THE NEIGHBORHOOD but couldn't leave his bewilderment behind. Alison Regan had made a positive impression on him, as she obviously had with Officer Olden. He was determined to figure out why she was so willing to drop her request for the police to investigate after gathering the courage to call them at all. Unless his instinct for character had left him, he couldn't believe that Alison was the kind of woman who would overreact. Something must have made her uncomfortable, uncomfortable enough to call the police on a doctor boyfriend.

The simple ethics of the situation told him that he should not spend any more time on the case. After all, if the supposed victim is no longer worried and seems satisfied that her fears are unfounded, who was he to override that? Still, his cop's intuition screamed at him that something was wrong but he couldn't identify it. There were too few pieces of this puzzle, and without a cooperative "victim" there didn't seem to be much choice. By the time he returned to his office, he had made a decision. He picked up the phone and dialed the office of Doctor Peter Capaldi. The receptionist who answered recognized his voice instantly.

"You're in luck, detective," she said. "He just finished with a patient. I'll ring him for you."

"Thanks a lot, Donna," Parker said. "And how are you doing, by the way?" he added, a habitual but sincere question that always made an impression, especially with younger women.

"I'm really good, Detective. Thanks for asking. It's been a while since we've seen you around here. Always good to hear your voice, and you can stop by any time, even to just say hello," she murmured, a slight flirtation in her voice. "I'll get the doctor for you." A few seconds later, he was chatting with the doctor he had first met under most unusual circumstances.

"Hey, Peter, how's the hardworking doc?" He resisted the constant temptation whenever he spoke with Peter Capaldi to throw in a one-liner about the difficult job that gynecologists have, spending their whole day examining women spread out in stirrups before them. "If you've got a minute, I'd like to ask a favor if I could."

The strong friendship that had developed since they first met made his response automatic.

"Not a problem, Parker. What's up?"

"I've got a kind of difficult one here and wondered if there is any way you could find some things out about a fellow physician, strictly underground, so to speak. What I need to know is if this guy is in good standing with his profession. I'd rather not be the one asking questions, as I'm sure that you understand."

Peter Capaldi normally would have dismissed the request out of hand. His profession, always self-protective, was circling the wagons ever tighter with the onslaught of both frivolous and legitimate lawsuits. This situation was not normal. Parker Havenot had a sixth sense about propriety and would not be asking him to do anything to jeopardize his professional standing unless it was important.

"Sure, I can do that but you know me, always the curious one.

What are we looking for here, anyway? If you're free to share, of course."

"Might be a case of harassment but if so it's a strange one. Could also just be a case of a young lady overreacting, not that I blame her in this day and age." Parker fell silent.

"Truthfully, Parker, and off the record, of course, I doubt . . ." Havenot interrupted him in mid-sentence.

"What's this off the record stuff, Pete? As far as I'm concerned, everything is off the record with us." He laughed loudly. "All the stuff I've told you about? I thought I was safe!"

The doctor returned his laugh. "You're absolutely right. Anyway, I doubt that many physicians today would put themselves into that position. Even the most unethical of my noble profession could find plenty of agreeable young ladies without resorting to any kind of harassment. The percentages are much more in favor of entrapment; you know, a setup to get even for whatever . . . could be any number of reasons."

"I love it when people rise to the defense of their colleagues. There's something endearing about that. But I guess you have to trust me on this one. This particular young lady doesn't seem the type."

"OK, Parker. What's the name and I'll see what I can find. But you owe me!"

"You win a free, all-expense paid trip to our cottage in New Hampshire. And I'll even give you a tour of the crime scenes up there. Anyway, the guy's name is Dr. John A. Simms. Seems like a general practitioner, if there is such a thing anymore."

"I'll call you when I have anything worthwhile and we'll meet for lunch. Your treat, of course."

"Naturally! Why not have the poor old detective treating the successful doctor? McDonald's, I presume?"

Both men chuckled as they hung up in unison.

CLARISSE WAS EMBARRASSED. SHE couldn't recall exactly when John Simms asked her to call but it was at least a couple of days. "Better late than never," she told herself.

Josie Havenot heard the phone ringing through the half-open front window and managed to drop her packages and unlock the door. She arrived at the phone just one ring short of the answering machine kicking in. She gasped an out-of-breath "hello" into the receiver.

"Mrs. Wallace, this is Clarisse Shearer at Dr. Simms's office. I'm really sorry to bother you and I know you haven't been patients of ours for a while, but Dr. Simms thought he saw your husband today in the city and he asked me to confirm that he's back from New Hampshire."

"I'm sorry, Miss . . .um . . ." Josie fumbled for her name but couldn't come up with it.

"Shearer, and it's Mrs. and again I apologize. The doctor prides himself on knowing all of his patients, past and present, and he wondered how Mr. Wallace is doing.?"

"Well, Mrs. Shearer, I'm sorry to tell you this but Dr. Simms is mistaken. My former husband is dead, and, just for the record, we've been divorced since the doctor saw him last. My last name is Havenot now but there's no need to change any of your records. My husband and I are both with another physician now." An icy shiver shook Josie as she closed the conversation, remembering the last visit to New Hampshire.

"Brad might not be gone," Gordon Tibideau had said before being shushed by Parker.

"Please thank Dr. Simms for his concern," Josie said. Then she hung up.

She glanced up at the kitchen clock, regretting that Parker was not expected home for at least another two hours.

JOSIE OPENED THE DOOR between the garage and the house before Parker was out of the car. She greeted him with an enthusiastic hug with his first step into the kitchen.

"Wow, I guess you missed me today. Everything's OK, right? Not that I mind but you usually let me get my jacket off before attacking me."

"I've got some things to tell you about, that's all. But they can wait. I'm just glad you're home." Josie broke off the hug. "Would you like to sit down with a drink and relax for a while before dinner?"

"Hmm, now I am curious. But sure, if that's what you feel like doing. Just a little out of character for you, that's all."

"Don't want to be predictable, you know. With Brad, the martini hour was automatic and I had a reminder about him today. Maybe that's what made me think of it."

"Forget the drinks for a bit, Jos. Let's just hear what you want to say."

"Having a detective for a husband is scary sometimes. You always seem to know what is going on in my head." She laughed. "OK, I think it's really nothing but come on, I'll tell you all about it. I have a feeling you just might want that drink after all."

Several minutes later the story of the phone call from Clarisse Shearer had Parker up and pacing about.

"So, you say this is your old family doctor and his name is John Simms, right?"

"We went to him right up to the time of the separation and divorce but I haven't seen him since. I know Brad thought he was great but that was probably because he always told him what he wanted to hear."

"You know how I feel about coincidences, Josie. There just aren't any, but if there were, this would be right up there with the best of them."

THE NEXT DAY, PETER Capaldi called.

"There's not a lot to tell you. From everything I can find out, he sure seems legitimate. The only thing any of his colleagues mentioned, off the record, of course, was how he managed to have such an apparently sizable income from such a routine general practice."

"Well, that sure doesn't sound like it's worth a lunch but I'll live up to my part of the bargain. Put Donna on and I'll schedule it through her. I know doctors are way too busy to arrange their own schedules."

Peter just chuckled. "You are incorrigible, Havenot. You know that, don't you?"

"Yep, I do," he said. "See you soon."

John A. Simms, M.D.

PARKER OPENED THEIR CONVERSATION as soon as his friend sat down. Their instant engagement in a heavy discussion prevented them from noticing the waitress, who materialized as if from thin air and stood within hearing range.

"I need to know what would make a strong, healthy young woman black out for over an hour and not remember anything leading up to it or during it," Havenot announced.

Peter Capaldi, no longer surprised by his friend's blunt manner, sighed, the sag in his shoulders dramatically exaggerated.

"Could you at least say hello before beginning your cross-examination, Detective?"

"You surely didn't think I invited you to lunch, my treat, just because I enjoy your company." Parker laughed. "I need information!"

The waitress continued to hover over them. Neither acknowledged her presence.

"I might need to consult my medical dictionary, something I'd rather do on a full stomach, if you don't mind," Capaldi said, a wide grin lighting his face.

The hovering waitress evolved into the intrusive waitress in a matter of seconds.

"What can I get you boys?" she asked, then added before either of them had a chance to respond, "One of them date rape drugs?"

50

Both men looked up at her and she stepped back. "Couldn't help but overhear what you asked," she said, no apology in her voice. "I saw it all on *Oprah* a couple of weeks ago."

Havenot reacted first. "Two Diet Cokes and then about ten minutes of uninterrupted perusing of the menu," he said, staring at her.

"Thanks," the woman said as she turned her back to the table and hurried off.

"I think you might have just ruined the slim chance of good service we may have gotten from her but she deserved it," Capaldi said.

Parker, determined to put this case to rest in the least amount of time possible, resumed the inquisition of his good friend.

"Let's go back to my original question. We can answer that and then get our order ready before our nosy friend returns. Do you think she might have something, by the way?"

Capaldi thought for a few seconds.

"I'm not an expert on that sort of chemistry. My job is child-birth and all the peripheral female stuff that goes with it. A year or so ago, I attended a three-day conference in Washington and one of the seminars was about those date rape drugs. I didn't go to it but I heard that it was pretty intense."

The waitress returned with the Cokes, putting each of them down with a loud thump.

"You're probably not ready yet, right? It's only been three minutes," she said, gazing blankly at her notepad.

After a hurried glance at the menu, both men agreed to have a simple club sandwich and a cup of vegetable soup.

"It's something like a kind of ray; I can't remember the real name but that's what they said on that show worked the best." She hadn't written anything on her pad. Instead, she just looked at them. "Stuff really works; that's what they said, anyway. I'll get your lunch." She straightened out of her waitress-induced posture and squared her hunched shoulders, proud to have the last word.

The lunch stretched from the intended forty-five minutes into an hour. Peter Capaldi finally ended it, even though fascinated that

Parker Havenot had taken such an interest in what appeared on the surface to be a simple case of a jealous older man coming to terms with the disadvantages of having a younger girlfriend. From what they both referred to now as the "nail caper" experience, Parker's first contact with Bradford Wallace, Peter knew not to question the detective's instincts but had no idea where this particular case might lead. With the promise to do a little research on gamma-hydroxybutrate, he said goodbye to Parker, leaving their waitress smiling as she scooped the generous tip from the table into her pocket in a singular motion.

Brad Wallace: Dead? Or Alive?

FOR THE FIRST TIME since his last mission in New Hampshire, Brad Wallace ventured out to mingle with the general public. He already was comfortable in what he fondly referred to as his hermitage in the kind of neighborhood where people moved in and out without ever having spoken a word to anyone living close by; years could pass between the arrival and the departure of the moving vans without so much as a hello between neighbors. It was just what he needed.

The cumulative effect of the time spent in New Hampshire and in his new environment in the outlying suburbs of Hartford surprised him. His isolation had been good, but the need to resume his lifestyle of dispensing vengeance along with the excitement of the city finally prodded him into chancing the trip into downtown West Hartford. He had been out of circulation long enough that he scrapped his plan to change his appearance by growing a beard, longer hair, and bushy sideburns. He had left Connecticut almost two years before, and when people who knew you believed you were dead, the chances of being recognized dwindle significantly.

Brad strolled along Highland Avenue, not quite blending in with the crowds of businessmen and women heading for Memorial Park and a leisurely lunch but invisible enough. He had just hustled across the Avenue against a red light when he caught a glimpse of a man sitting alone on one of the park benches lining the sidewalk that meandered through the park. Something familiar about the man caused Brad to turn toward him just as he looked up from the half-eaten sandwich in his hand. Eye contact was made but broken immediately.

"Shit," Brad muttered as he hurried on his way to nowhere in particular. "That was Dr. Simms."

His plan for this first outing was simply to get used to being back in the human race. If the outing went well, the next trip on his new agenda would be a visit to Brad, Jr.'s grave. He could only dream of how rejuvenating that trip would be. An added benefit would be a nostalgic trip through the old neighborhood. He tried, without success, to imagine being that close to Parker Havenot, who topped the list of his least favorite people, people from whom he would soon be extracting a degree of justice. Maybe he would even catch a glimpse of Josie.

"Dr. Simms's Office, Clarisse speaking." The phone rang exactly at the opening time of 8:30 but Clarisse had already been at her desk for a full hour so she was prepared.

"This is Parker Havenot. I'm with the Covington County Sheriff's Department." Parker hated the necessary introduction because almost anyone receiving a call from the police automatically thought it would have to be bad news. "May I speak with Dr. Simms, please?"

"He's not in just yet but I expect him any minute. He doesn't start appointments until nine this morning. Can I help you with anything?"

"What's his schedule today, Clarisse? I'd like to talk to him for just a few minutes." Havenot said, ignoring her offer.

"I know he's really booked right up today. It would be impossible to see him. Maybe tomorrow . . .?" she asked.

"Does he eat lunch?" Havenot asked, well aware that he was eating lunch when he supposedly saw Brad Wallace.

"No, that's not possible. The doctor works very hard and his lunch hours are sacred."

"Look, Clarisse, I don't want to be pushy. By the way, do have a last name?"

"It's Shearer, Detective. Why do you ask?"

"Because, Miss Shearer, I don't like to call women I haven't met by their first names."

"OK, but I know Dr. Simms will not be available at lunch. And it's Mrs., not Miss."

The conversation was going nowhere so Havenot put an end to it. "What time is his lunch hour, Mrs. Shearer? And you can tell him I'll take just five minutes of his time but I want that five minutes today."

"He tries to eat between 11:45 and 12:45. And he likes to be by himself." Clarisse Shearer was no match for Parker Havenot.

"I'll see him at 12:40. Tell him his lunch hour will have to be cut a little short today." Parker hung up without giving Clarisse Shearer a chance to say another word.

PARKER WAITED OUTSIDE UNTIL exactly 12:37 then climbed the three flights of stairs to the office of Doctor John Simms. The size of the waiting room brought him to a halt before the door had opened halfway. It was the smallest reception area he had ever seen in a doctor's office. As he pushed the door completely open, he noticed three straight-backed chairs with minimal padding lined against one wall. They were bookended by two laminated mahogany tables topped by a garish lamp with a multicolored shade straight reminiscent of the fifties rather than the early nineties. The requisite doctor's office magazines graced the tables but were in perfect stacks as if they hadn't been touched in weeks. Parker noted that it was halfway through the day and there was little evidence of any patients having been in the room. To his right, an opaque glass-enclosed cubicle reflected his presence. Only a small window allowed visual access to a woman who sat with her back to the waiting room. He approached the window and had to stoop slightly to see through it.

"Mrs. Shearer, I presume?" he asked to the woman's back.

She jumped as if she was not used to hearing a human voice. She recovered quickly and rotated her austere office chair toward the window.

"Yes, I am and you must be Detective Havenot." She mispronounced his name, as did most people who did not know him. He had said it for her earlier on the phone and spelled it out but that had been several hours previous.

"It's actually pronounced as if it has a long 'o' with an 'e' at the end, but don't worry about it. I get called a lot of names in my business anyway."

"I pride myself on names, Detective, and I apologize, but it surely looks like 'have not' to me." She had recovered completely from being startled and now assumed her role as guardian of the gate. "Dr. Simms isn't back from lunch yet but I expect him at any moment. Just have a seat, please."

"Didn't you tell him I'd be here at 12:40?" Parker asked, an edge in his voice. "It's now 12:41."

"I did tell him but since you didn't say what this was about when you called this morning, he just said to tell you he'd be back from lunch as soon as he could." Clarisse Shearer spun her chair back to its original position and began shuffling the few papers that were on her desk.

Parker was deciding which of the chairs in the waiting room looked the most comfortable when the door opened. The detective stopped his search for a chair and stared at the handsome man entering the room. He seemed to be about Parker's age but his obvious Just for Men colored hair look, which should have made him appear younger, had the opposite effect. A toothpick dangling from his mouth ruined his chance of being referred to as polished, although he carried himself with the confidence that doctors so often project.

"You must be the detective. I'm Doctor Simms. I think Clarisse already told you that I don't have much time. I've got afternoon appointments to prepare for. I'm sure you understand." He brushed past Parker's extended hand as he walked across the room toward the door leading into the office area.

Parker didn't move. "We can talk out here if you want. It'll only take a few minutes of your time, which I know is very valuable." He somehow stretched the word very into several more syllables than it required. This meeting was not off to a good start.

"I'd rather you come on back to my office. I'd prefer my patients not be intimidated by the appearance of a police officer," Simms said, as if the detective were wearing full-dress blues.

"Whatever you say," Parker answered, adding a facetious, "you're the doctor."

The interview was over in a matter of minutes. Parker never mentioned Alison Regan.

"I was there when Brad Wallace went down, and I don't see how he could have survived," Parker said. "Are you certain the person you saw was him?"

"This is an uncanny coincidence, Detective. I mean, what are the odds I would see him, then find out that his wife is now married to the guy who investigated his parents's fatal accident years ago. It is a bit much, don't you agree?"

"Yeah, I guess I do," Parker replied. "But you haven't answered my question."

"If I see him again, I'll let you know. That's about all I can tell you. Now, if you'll excuse me, I've got some things to do."

"OK. I'm sure I can find my way out. Thanks a lot for your help." Parker offered his hand once more but John Simms had already turned his back on him. He made his way through the office and waiting room, pausing as the door shut behind him.

"Arrogant son of a bitch," he muttered under breath.

Back in his office, Dr. John Simms also was muttering.

"It was Brad Wallace, Detective, and if I ever see him again, I just might have a use for him."

A Connecticut Black Period

BRAD TOOK A CIRCUITOUS route to his old neighborhood of
Hampton Village. He entered the downtown area, unchanged in
the two years since he had been there. It remained a two-block
stretch of small specialty shops catering to locals and struggling to
compete with the encroaching retail giants sprouting like weeds
on the outskirts of town. He drove in ever-increasing circles on
the streets of the village, a route that carried him past Hampton
Village High School. The fall session was still weeks from beginning but the familiar signs of activity were there. As he passed
the football stadium, he stopped the car and stared through the
wrought-iron fence. Melancholia enveloped him as the memories
of so many happy times crashed over him.

"What the hell am I doing here?" The words came out of his
mouth so loud that he startled himself. He put the car in gear
and began circling again. As he neared his old house, he started
cruising around the blocks in both directions, backtracking like a
wise old buck might do to outwit a hunter. Several passes from a
variety of directions convinced him that he had no worries. The
streets were deserted, most people off to work, play, or whatever
filled the days of the average person in the suburbs of Hartford.
He finally made the turn into Sycamore Drive. Another wave of
gloom swept over him as he approached number 21. His former
home looked exactly the same as it had when he left it. It seemed

as though nothing had changed, as if he could walk up to the door, open it, and be greeted by Josie, offering him a cool martini. The car slowed as Brad let up on the gas pedal; he gazed at the house, searching for answers which were not forthcoming.

"Brad Wallace, you are so totally screwed up that it's hopeless," he whispered. "But, we've got to do what we came for."

He drove around the block at a speed that would not draw attention should any neighbors happen to be out walking. On his second pass by the house, he slowed to a stop at the mailbox, which threatened to be overtaken by a rosebush planted at its base, a rosebush he remembered nursing to health years before. He reached into his pocket and pulled out a single twenty penny nail. After a quick glance around, he opened the box, relieved to see that the mail had already been delivered. He placed the nail between what appeared to be two bills. He shut the door and drove off, continuing his nostalgia trip that included a drive-by of Hampton Village Community Church, where he and Josie had been married almost twenty-six years before. The fragile hold on his emotions fell away once again as he stopped in front of the picturesque New England church, with its gleaming white clapboards and copper-roofed steeple housing the bell that called the worshippers to church every Sunday.

"Shit," he swore as his eyes watered. "I never expected this. I really need some help here."

He slammed the gearshift into drive and stomped on the accelerator, the church disappearing in his rearview mirror as he headed for his primary destination in Hampton Falls—Mountain View Cemetery.

The black, wrought-iron sign announcing the entrance to the cemetery passed overhead as Brad inched his car through the narrow gate. The archangel Michael still guarded the gate, his statue duplicated on both sides of the entrance, mirror images of each other with huge white wings fully extended and intimidating all who might enter with malevolent intent. The original trivial nervousness in Brad's stomach had morphed into a mass of butterflies now flitting around and bumping into each other. It had been a long time since he had a comforting session with Brad, Jr. in this setting. The surrogate gravesite at his house in New Hampshire had been a poor substitute for the real thing.

The anticipation as he left the car was almost more than he could bear. He almost jogged up the path toward Brad, Jr.'s grave but as he drew closer, his pace slowed to a crawl, until he just shuffled his way through the last few feet. He looked down at the marker.

"Goddamn it!" he shouted, producing an echo off the tall trees surrounding the grounds. Weeds and grass had spread over the stone, encroaching to such a point that the words could barely be read. He knelt down, ripping the violating vegetation out by the roots. When he finished, he removed his handkerchief from his back pocket, using it as a whisk broom to brush away the dirt. Tears splashed on the marker as it glared back at him.

BRADFORD J. WALLACE, JR.
INFANT

It was a harsh reminder of the long discussions and dis-agreements that only once escalated into a full-fledged marital argument. The subject could not have been more unpleasant. Do you take up a cemetery plot by burying a stillborn son?

"What difference did it make anyway? You never made it into the world. Six months in the womb doesn't count, Junior, but I've got to tell you that I'm glad she won in the end. If we'd never buried you here, and I couldn't have had my sessions, I'm not sure what I would have done." Brad realized that his voice had risen in volume. He rose from his knees and made a 360 degree survey of his surroundings. There was still no one else in the cemetery.

"And I can't believe they would let you go like this. Doesn't your mother ever come to visit you? Son of a bitch—Havenot! He's made her forget all about you. Well, I just left him a reminder that he'd better pay attention." Brad stood for a few minutes in silence, thinking. Then he squatted down.

"I'm probably pretty messed up, Junior, but I think I'll pay a visit to Dr. Simms, our old family doctor, the guy who seemed to understand me before. I'll let you know what he says about my mental state. Can't tell you how rejuvenating this was and I'll see you again real soon." He was right at home with the one-sided conversation.

Brad returned to his car but instead of turning the key, he sat there for a few minutes, reminiscing.

He had admitted to only one person in his life that he some-times felt slightly out of control. His last appointment with Dr. John Simms ended with a sense of euphoria enveloping him. After admitting to strange nightmares and being outraged over events that he saw as being unfair, the doctor's declaration that he was no different than most of the human population vindicated him. It was then that he knew he could separate his two realms, using his black periods as release valves for his anger and frustrations while the rest of his world viewed him simply as Brad Wallace, a quite normal human being. Following his physical that day, Simms commented on his outstanding reputation as an educator. Just as Brad was closing the door, the doctor called to him.

"I'm really sorry about the loss of your child last year, Brad. Real tough situation."

The simple expression of sympathy had resonated with Brad at the time. Now, remembering it word for word four years later, it sounded as hollow as any of the other clichés surrounding a death. "It is God's will" and "it's for the best" do not supply much comfort in the face of the death of a child, even if that infant never made it past the second trimester.

Brad twisted the key in the ignition, stepping down hard on the gas almost before the engine caught. A slight chirp signaled that a small black tire mark would likely be left behind. He slowed just slightly to maneuver the car through the gate.

"Yeah, real tough, Doctor Simms. As if you had a clue about what tough really is."

As he drove back to his modest rental home, he realized that the doctor's harmless words had catapulted Brad into his first act as an agent for justice. Dr. Peter Capaldi had been the recipient of that one.

All signs of the nervousness and butterflies he experienced when he first approached the grave were gone. He had a mission. Things were about to get much better.

Another Nail Caper

JOSIE ARRIVED HOME FROM her biweekly trip to the Hampton Village Library, the sack of books thrown over her right shoulder causing her to list to starboard slightly as she walked up to the front door of 21 Sycamore Drive. She set the bag and her purse down and glanced at her watch. Even during the Christmas rush, their mailman always arrived within five minutes of his usual time and, in the summer, his customers could count on him being exactly on time. Josie turned and meandered toward the mailbox, inhaling the intoxicating aromas rising from the mixture of late blooming phlox and petunias lining the walkway. The roses entwined around the box added their bouquet as she approached.

"I've got to get out here and trim this sometime," she whispered to herself.

As usual, she found the mailbox stuffed to overflowing with the usual sale flyers, advertisements, and solicitations that swamped the meaningful mail. She pulled everything out and started back to the house, skimming through the stack in search of anything important. Halfway up the walk, she heard a clinking sound as though she had dropped a key or a coin on the pavement. She stopped and looked down. The nail had bounced toward the flower bed but did not quite make it.

"What the heck . . .?" she said aloud as she bent to pick it up. After retrieving it, she hurried up the walk, almost dropping the pile of mail. With one hand, she reached into her pocketbook and pulled out her house key. Leaving her purse and cache of books on the front porch, Josie entered the house and went straight to the closest phone, a wall phone hanging in the kitchen.

Josie had used this phone hundreds of times since she used it to call the ambulance when she lost Brad, Jr., but each time that blurred moment came back to her in vivid and dispiriting ways. Her life changed forever that crushing day.

She dialed the central office of the Covington County Sheriff's Department. By now, the significance of the nail she was squeezing in her hand had taken hold. Her hand shook, matching her quavering voice.

"Parker Havenot, please. This is Mrs. Havenot." Her request came out sounding too formal, but she knew just one of the dispatchers and did not recognize the person who answered.

"I'm sorry, ma'am, but Detective Havenot is out of the building and I don't expect him back for at least another hour."

"That's no problem. Just have him call me as soon as possible, please. It's important but not an emergency." Josie's quivering hands added sweating palms, a combination that almost made her drop the phone.

"Will do, Mrs. Havenot. Is there anything else I can do for you? You sound a little nervous." The policeman's manner changed as he realized that he was speaking with his favorite detective's wife.

"No thanks, Officer. Thanks again for your help." Josie placed the phone back in its cradle, the memory of that awful day when that same phone slipped from her hand cascaded over her like an unexpected rogue wave on an ocean beach.

WITHIN MINUTES OF JOSIE'S call, the dispatcher had Parker Havenot on the line.

"She said it wasn't an emergency, sir, but she sounded upset so I thought I should let you know. I hope interrupting your meeting with this was OK." The officer's nervousness was obvious.

"It's OK, Ben. You did the right thing and thanks a lot for being so concerned. I appreciate it." Parker handed the phone back to the Superintendent of Schools.

"Sorry I've got to cut this short, Dr. Metcalf. I appreciate your time and if it is all right with you, I'd like to follow up on our conversation; that is, if you don't mind."

"Nothing to it, Detective. Always happy to help the local law enforcement. You guys have the toughest job in the world and I admire what you do." George Metcalf smiled and shook Parker's hand.

As he walked across the parking lot to his car, Parker couldn't help but voice his opinion of George Metcalf, if only to himself.

"What a self-serving phony," he said as he got in the car and headed for 21 Sycamore Drive.

Josie heard the car door slam and ran to the window.

"Parker!" She hurried to the front door and greeted him with a hard hug, an embrace she extended to allow the moisture in her eyes a chance to dry.

When they separated, Parker looked into her eyes. His concern climbed in direct proportion to the distress evident on Josie's face.

"What is it, Josie? What's going on?"

Josie went to the kitchen table and picked up the nail.

"This fell out of the mail today. Somebody slipped this nail into our mailbox and it must have been after the mail had been delivered because it was wrapped up in it."

"I guess that settles it, doesn't it? Brad Wallace is not only alive but he wants us to know it. I'll be damned!"

"What should we do, Parker? Do you think we need to be worried? I mean, do you think he might be dangerous?" The questions came in staccato fashion as the implications of what Parker had said became clear.

"I've just got to find him, that's all. He would never hurt you, I'm sure of that, but there sure are others that he might want to get even with."

"Meaning you, Parker. You know you'd be one of the first on his list."

Wallace and Simms Reunited

BRAD WALLACE'S DECISION HAD nothing to do with needing a physical or for any other medical reason, for that matter. He had to know if his old doctor Simms had recognized him in that brief moment. When he arrived back at his house after the visit to the grave, it was just before three o'clock in the afternoon. He made the call. After a few minutes of bantering, he became serious.

"Listen, nurse, I'm a fifty-year-old guy who wants to get physical checkup. How hard can that be?" Brad's irritation at Clarisse Shearer rose closer to the surface.

"Well, sir, as I told you, Dr. Simms has to be very selective as he is the only doctor in the practice and is quite busy. And by the way, I'm not a nurse. Now why don't you leave me a phone number and I'll speak with the doctor and get back to you." Clarisse waited, hoping that she would hear the phone line go dead from the other end.

"Let me explain this a little further. Dr. Simms was our family doctor a few years back and he's really the guy I want to see. He helped me out a lot back then and I'd just like to see him and I'd rather not leave my phone number. No offense but I've discovered that people often don't call back when they say they will."

The extended pause indicated that his persistence might be paying off.

"Can you hold for one minute? The doctor happens to be

available and I'll ask him. What was your name again?" This time, the pause came from Brad's end of the conversation.

"This is probably a crazy question and please don't take it wrong but does doctor/patient privilege exist beginning right now?" Brad asked, already knowing the answer.

"If you give me your name, I'll speak with Doctor Simms. And yes, we do not share any information about our patients, even from the first contact."

"Tell the doctor that this is Bradford Wallace and I really want to see him." Brad heard Clarisse Shearer let out a small gasp before replying.

"I'll tell him, Mr. Wallace. Please hold."

Brad listened happily to elevator music from the sixties for the better part of five minutes, the tunes assuring him that there had not been a disconnect. When he finally heard the music click off, he came out of his slouch in the chair.

"The doctor will see you tomorrow at nine o'clock. Do you know where our office is located?"

"Yes, I do. I'll be there at nine," he said. "And, uh, Mrs. Shearer, that confidentiality thing holds, right?"

"You have no worries, Mr. Wallace. Please trust me on that."

Clarisse set the phone down and looked over at John Simms.

"What in the world is going on with that man?" she asked.

Simms just shrugged his shoulders. "I guess we'll find out tomorrow."

Another Gravesite Visit

PARKER HAVENOT WAS IN full detective mode. After getting Ben Spaulding's call from dispatch and racing home to check on Josie, he made a few calls to confirm that his presence at the station wasn't required. Except for a brief excursion to find their mailman, he spent the last two hours of the day with Josie. After a couple of afternoon glasses of Cabernet, Josie's nerves had settled and Parker began to lay out his plan.

"He was here today, Jos. I spoke to our mailman who acted as if I had lost my mind when I asked him if there was any way for a nail to have become mixed in with our mail. I will guarantee based on what we know, he would have visited the gravesite. Right after supper, I'm going over there."

They were sitting on the back porch with Parker staring off toward the cemetery, less than a mile from their house. He heard a whimper followed by louder sniffles. By the time he reached Josie, she was sobbing.

"Shit, Parker, Brad was here, practically on our front doorstep, and he's supposed to be dead. I mean, I saw him go down..." She drew in quick breath. "Then there you are sitting exactly where he used to sit so he could get a glimpse of the graveyard. Now you're going over there...I'm sorry, but this whole thing is just too fucking much!" Josie's sobs turned louder as she realized what she had just said. "And Parker, I haven't worked on the gravesite for months; it's going to be a mess." She dropped her head down, ashamed of her stammered admission and what it meant.

Parker bent down beside her and took both her hands in his. She shook loose, reached out and grabbed him, burying her face into his chest as her crying subsided into hiccupping whimpers. Parker stood up, lifting Josie up with him, and they wrapped themselves into an all-encompassing embrace.

"I'm going to find him, Josie. You know that. It's just a matter of time. He's can't just disappear down here and he's got to find a way to support himself. I mean, he's supposed to be dead, for God's sakes. He can't collect his early retirement settlement; he can't get a new driver's license; he can't do anything as near as I can tell." Josie's whimpers were now nothing more than soft moans.

"I know you'll figure it out. That's what detectives do, right? And I've heard you're a pretty good one." She was smiling now. "And I'm going with you after dinner and will entertain no arguments about that.

JOSIE AND PARKER SHARED a homemade pizza. Josie kept a supply of shells in the freezer and when they decided to go simple, her suggestion sounded perfect. A few sautéed onions, peppers, mushrooms, and a variety of cheeses sprinkled on top of the always available pizza sauce in the refrigerator created the ideal quick meal. Topped off by a cold beer, the dinner was complete. Shortly before six o'clock, they began their walk toward the Mountain View Cemetery in complete silence. Neither said a single word during the mile trek, each lost in an individual reverie that needed to be honored.

As they reached the entrance, they glanced at the looming angels on either side. Josie paused, reached out to take Parker's hand, and turned him toward her.

"I love you, Parker Havenot," she said, adding the jibe about his surname he had heard so many times. "And you are surely are a have note, not a have not."

"I love you, too, Josie, and we're going to get this thing over

with. I don't like what it's doing to us and everyone around us."
Parker's eyes glistened, a rare occasion. "OK, let's go see what we
can find."

Josie stayed two steps behind Parker as they approached Brad
Jr.'s grave. When Parker arrived at the marker, he turned to his
wife, his eyes revealing the depth of sadness and empathy he felt
for her.

"Looks the same to me as when I saw it last," he said.

Josie crept forward and peered over his shoulder. Her reaction
startled Parker so much that he almost lost his balance.

"It's trimmed," she cried. "Someone has manicured around
the stone."

"It's probably just the caretakers, Jos. That's what they are
supposed to do, right?"

"No," she said, whispering. "We're supposed to keep up the
ground level markers. He was here and cleaned up the site." She
turned and started to walk away.

Parker surveyed the area and decided that nothing could be
done that couldn't wait until tomorrow. "Let's get out of here,"
he said to Josie's back as she was hurrying out of the cemetery. He
caught up with her at the area where a visitor in a car would most
likely park to visit gravesites in the area. The short black tire tread
mark stood in bold contrast to the lighter paving.

"Somebody left in a hurry or a huff," he said, but he might as
well have been talking to himself. Josie had already passed through
the gate and was well down the sidewalk on her way home.

Another Physical

CLARISSE SHEARER LET HIM in when he knocked on the door at 8:30, even though the posted signs indicated that office hours began at nine.

"You're a half hour early. The doctor is very punctual and he'll be here at nine but not before. Just have a seat." The cool reception left no doubt how she felt about his aggressiveness on the phone the day before.

Brad looked around at the sparse furnishings and chose a seat closest to the receptionist. The waiting room was narrow enough that he could read the diplomas and licenses on the wall across from him. Dr. Simms's credentials appeared to be sound but he was reminded of the jokes that circulated within all of the professions. Not everyone graduated at the top of the class; therefore, someone had to bring up the rear in class rank but the diplomas looked the same for everyone. It would be extremely bad taste to ask your doctor, or lawyer, or teacher for his class rank. He briefly wondered where Dr. Simms stood in his class, then he began skimming through the old magazines on the table.

Brad glanced at his watch when he heard the door open. It was 8:59.

"Good morning," Dr. Simms said as he brushed by. He was through his office door before Brad had a chance to respond.

Clarisse stood and went through the rear door that apparently

72

led to the doctor's office. She was gone for about five minutes, during which Brad stood and stretched, expecting to be called in at any moment. He looked at her expectantly when she reappeared.

"It'll be a few more minutes," she said through the small window separating her desk from the waiting room. She turned to her word processor and began to type.

It was Dr. Simms himself who called him into the examination room ten minutes later. Clarisse Shearer was still busy at the keyboard when Brad followed the doctor though the door.

"Have a seat, Mr. Wallace. We can chat for a few minutes before we get started on the physical." Dr. Simms stared at him the entire time required for him to choose one of the two available chairs and sit down.

"I should tell you right upfront, Doctor, I'm not really here for a physical. I just needed to talk to you." Brad noticed that Simms seemed to register no surprise at this announcement. "You probably don't remember this but the last time I saw you, you said a few things to me that made me feel better about some issues I was dealing with and right now I've really don't have many people I can trust so I thought . . ."

Simms interrupted. "While we are being candid, Mr. Wallace, I have to tell you something as well. I know you're supposed to be dead. I thought you were until recently when I saw you crossing the street here in town. I did some checking."

"Checking?" Brad leaned forward, his concern obvious to the observant doctor.

"I had my assistant call your house. We still had the number on file. Your wife, or your ex-wife, I guess it is now, said that you were indeed dead. Clearly, you're not. So, tell me, Mr. Wallace, what are we doing here? Clarisse just told me this morning that you were quite concerned with doctor/patient confidentiality when you spoke with her yesterday. So again, I ask, what is it that you expect to gain here?" Dr. Simms leaned back in his chair and waited.

Brad did not answer immediately, taking his time digesting

what he had just heard. The pause in the conversation stretched into a full minute. Simms continued to observe him, as if convincing himself that this was not an apparition sitting in front of him.

"OK, Doctor. Here it is." Brad's decision had been made. There was no one else for him to approach. "I came here, just like I did back then, because I need some assurance that what I'm doing is right. You gave me that assurance a few years back and I'm looking for it again."

"I can understand that, even if I can't remember at all what I did for you or, for sure, what I said to you. I'm guessing it was pretty good." The inflection in his voice indicated that Simms intended this to be a question and he waited once again for the forthcoming answer.

"You just convinced me that I wasn't crazy for being upset over things that were not fair. I'd recently lost a son; I lost a colleague in Vietnam; there was just too much going wrong with the world. I left your office that day believing that I needed to take an active part in correcting what I could." The words had tumbled out so fast that Brad had not taken a breath. Simms remained silent, waiting for him to continue. "So I did, Dr. Simms. I did, and I need to keep on doing it."

"Well, Brad, I think that just maybe we can help each other. First, I will tell you that a detective came by the other day, following up on my report of seeing you." Brad's reaction cut the doctor short. He came up out of the chair, almost knocking it over backwards.

"Fucking Havenot! That's who it was, right? What did you tell him? Oh, Christ, you didn't confirm, did you?" Brad looked at Simms, who was smiling. He slumped back down.

"He's your wife's husband now, right? Isn't this just the smallest world we live in?"

Simms was still smiling as he assured Brad that he had not confirmed his sighting, passing it off with Havenot as a mistake. When he finished, a slight but tentative smile creased Brad's face.

"Now I'm confused. Where does all this coincidence stuff leave us?"

"I work for a man who believes that the good people of this world don't stand much of a chance against the evil, even though the good might outnumber the evil a million to one. We're trying to make things better for some of the good ones and I think a guy like you who doesn't exist could be of assistance to us. What would you think of earning a living making the world a better place?"

One hour later, after providing a lengthy explanation of the merits of TRAC and other possibilities associated with it, Dr. Simms walked Brad to the door.

"I'll be in touch, Brad. Just stay invisible." They shook hands and Brad left with the same enthusiasm he had the last time he visited with John Simms. From the doorway into the reception-ist's office, Clarisse Shearer watched, her hands firmly planted on her hips.

Henry Bouchard and Brad Wallace

EVEN IN HIS SITTING position, John Simms cowered from the verbal assault. When he set up the appointment with Henry Bouchard, he mentioned that he had just two items to discuss with him. The first of these sent Bouchard into a rage and there seemed no likelihood he would ever get to the second, the reason why Brad Wallace was sitting in the vestibule outside of the spacious office.

"You inserted a chip into an unknowing person, your girlfriend, for what purpose? You really are a fucking idiot, you know that? We've got maybe five years if we're lucky before everyone catches up with us and the government makes all of this legal. We've got to make our money before that happens. Now, you jeopardize that by tracking an everyday citizen who may or may not become aware of what is happening to her! We're paying you enough to keep your goddamned mouth shut. I thought you were smart enough but I guess that was a mistake." Bouchard paused to take a breath, giving Simms just enough time to squeeze in his first line of defense.

"She'll never know, and I thought it could possibly be another revenue stream."

"Revenue stream! You're talking like a fucking accountant. We have enough revenue as it is and the way we make it insures that everyone has a stake in keeping it quiet. What were you thinking, Simms?"

John Simms let out a quiet sigh of relief when a fraction of Bouchard's anger seem to dissipate. "If you'll give me a minute, I can explain. Travis will back me up on this."

The mention of Travis Connally suspended the tension in the air, at least temporarily.

"Travis knew about this? For how long?" Bouchard suddenly seemed interested in Simms's explanation.

"He was involved right from the start. We both thought it would be better to see how it worked before we brought the idea to you." Bouchard reached for the intercom as he waggled a finger at Simms.

"Travis! Get over here right away. I don't care what you're doing, just get over here," he barked into the receiver. Then he turned his attention back to John Simms. "We're going to wait a minute to continue this discussion. I want Connally to hear what you have to say."

The pure silence acted a vacuum, seeming to suck the air from the room. After an interminable three or four minutes, Travis Connally knocked on the door. Bouchard boomed a "come in" and Travis entered. When he saw Simms, he blanched and knew instantly why he had been summoned.

"Do I pay you well, Travis?" Bouchard asked.

"Yes, sir, I have no complaints at all. I love working here. It's been an ideal job for me. Is there a problem?" he asked, directing his attention to John Simms.

"I was just filling Mr. Bouchard in on our little experiment. I thought it had gone well enough to let him know about it now. Remember how we didn't want to worry him until we knew it would work?" Brad looked from one to the other, waiting for a reaction. Neither man said a word, forcing him to continue. "Think of the long-range possibilities, Mr. Bouchard. They are practically limitless. Parents keeping track of their kids, employers knowing who is goofing off, wives or husbands always knowing where their

spouse is, I mean . . ." Bouchard's thundered "shut up!" accomplished its objective. The room fell silent once more.

"Limitless and all totally illegal. What we are doing with
these rich people is not legal. The devices are not approved for
general use and likely will not be for years yet. That's why this is
a secret operation, Simms, and that's why you were chosen. No
one's going to pay attention to a small-time doctor unless he starts
doping his girlfriend and then all of a sudden knowing where she
is all the time. Stupid!" His tirade lost its steam and he addressed
Travis Connally.

"Did you know about this from the beginning?"

"Just after the fact, sir. Simms told me about it about the insertion, but I'll admit that I went along with it. I wasn't thinking
straight, I guess." Travis's eyes darted around the room, avoiding
contact with Bouchard. He knew he had made a mistake.

"Well, we're not going to fire anybody, at least not yet. But
here's what we're going to do," Bouchard said.

Brad Wallace had been waiting for fifteen minutes when a
chastened John Simms came out of the office.

"He can't meet with you today. I'll explain later."

Alison Revisited

WHEN THEY RETURNED HOME after the traumatizing visit to Mountain View Cemetery and the gravesite of Josie's stillborn son, Parker announced to Josie that he would be leaving for work earlier than usual the next morning. The fact that Brad Wallace was brazen enough to not only return to Hampton Village but to come to their home disturbed him on a level he couldn't explain, even to Josie. The nail in the mailbox symbolized the direction that Brad's life had taken years ago while also signaling that he wasn't finished with his warped sense of meting out justice to those he felt had wronged him in some way.

Josie, usually allowing Parker to fend for himself when he decided to go to work early, was up and fixing breakfast when Parker came out of the bedroom after his shower.

"Hey, it's summer vacation for you teachers who only work half a year for a full year's pay. You get to sleep in while I trudge off to the grind." Parker smiled. He'd always admired the dedication of teachers he knew, but since his marriage to Josie, he had come to respect the teaching profession more than ever. He still enjoyed teasing her and her teacher friends about the cushy job they all had. Josie handled the jokes well but could never seem to come back with a suitable retort.

"I get laid off for two and half months every year. I should be able to collect unemployment. You know, we feeders at the public

79

trough might as well collect all we can." Josie's attempt at humor fell flat, as it usually did. "Breakfast is ready; hopefully you have time to eat since I got up especially for you."

They ate in comfortable silence until Josie raised the question.

"So, what are you working on today?" she asked, a natural enough inquiry for a wife but laden with implications from the events of the day before.

Parker had been a detective too long to miss the real meaning of her question. "I'm going to find him, Josie. I can guarantee you that much. But I wish that all I had to do today was to hunt for a damn ghost. I'm really hung up on this Simms thing. It just seems like something deeper is going on there." He paused, searching her face for approval.

"I sometimes wonder if there's not something to those reincarnation theories about meeting the same people in life after life and we travel in the same circles all the time. I mean, Doctor Simms was in my past life with Brad and now he surfaces in this one. He supposedly sees Brad, yet tells you he didn't. He's a central player in one of your cases that has nothing to do with Brad. It's just weird, that's all." Josie laughed. "Just what you need this morning—a crazy wife with crazy ideas sending you off to fight crime and keep the streets safe for the citizens of this fair city."

Parker laughed along with her. "I love you, Josie Havenot, even if you are crazy."

They finished their breakfast and Parker rose to leave. Without a word, Josie went to him and they embraced, an intimate hug with full body contact. "I'll have dinner ready when you get home, unless you want dessert first," she whispered in his ear.

"You sure know how to make a guy not want to go to work," Parker said, "but you can bet I'll be thinking about your home cooking."

They walked to the door, arms draped around each other. Josie waited until Parker's car left the driveway before glancing down the street in the direction of Mountain View Cemetery.

PARKER SETTLED IN AND began sorting through the stack of

paperwork in his in basket. He thought about calling Alison Regan but decided that seven thirty in the morning was not a courteous time to be calling anyone. She had provided her work number but calling her there was not an option until at least eight o'clock. As almost an afterthought, he placed the pile of papers back in the in slot and looked across the room at his personal filing cabinet. As cases closed, were ruled inactive, or, in the worst instances, declared as cold, he would keep any personal notes he had made during the investigation in a private file. Most of these scratchings, as he called them, were on pieces of yellow legal pad paper, often wrinkled, soiled, smeared, or otherwise defaced. All of his official reports and notations stayed with the case file in the archives, but if he ever wanted to refer to his originals thoughts, he knew exactly where to find them.

He got up from his desk, which was cluttered with file folders in varying stages of completion but organized as he wanted them to be. An eight by ten glossy photograph of Josie taken the previous fall at school caught his eye. "I'll find him," he said to the picture and then went immediately to the bottom drawer in the cabinet, labeled simply "WXYZ."

The drawers were not locked, primarily because no one could ever read what he had written anyway, he explained to any of his police buddies who asked why. The WXYZ drawer slid open easily with a slight pull. The first manila folder in the drawer had *Wallace, Bradford* scrawled across the top. He lifted the folder out. It contained just three dog-eared, faded, and maligned sheets of yellow legal paper. Parker put the first page on the only available space he could find on his desk and smoothed it out with his fingers, beginning at the center outward toward the edges. The washed-out background served to highlight the contrast between it and the writing.

The years had not diminished his recollection of the contents. The three headings at the top of the page stood out in print and in his memory. *DATES, EVENTS, WALLACE* separated the page into thirds. Parker had only to look at his first entry to remember what the rest of that page would say. Under date, he had written 1968;

under event, the word Capaldi appeared; under Wallace was a capital Y. He scanned down the page, stopping at the entry for Rich Lane. That entry bothered him the most. Rich was a paraplegic because of Bradford Wallace.

"That bastard never paid for any of these. Now he's back again." Josie's picture stared at him across the desk. "If not for you, then for Rich, Josie." He was talking to himself but sometimes he was at his best as a detective when he did that. With the pages back in the folder, he flipped the Rolodex on his desk to the Rs then dialed Alison Regan's number at work.

AFTER THE USUAL FORMALITIES of the beginning of phone conversations, Parker moved into the reason for the call.

"We can probably do this by phone, Miss Regan, and it won't take but a few minutes, if that. It's really just a couple of quick questions."

Her momentary hesitation told Parker more than a quick answer might have.

"I'm surprised to hear from you, Detective. I thought we left it at my calling you if I had any further issues. And, again, please, it's Alison."

"Yeah, right, uh, Alison. Anyway, have you had any of those, I believe you called it an episode or something?"

"No, I haven't and, as I said, I would have called you. John isn't in any trouble, is he?"

Havenot sensed that something was on her mind.

"No, but why would you think that? Is there something else you wanted to say?" Extended silence was the only answer.

"OK, Ms. Regan, let's ask the second question and then I'll let you get back to work. And I do apologize for the inconvenience."

"No problem, Detective. And the second question is . . ." Her voice trailed off.

"I just wondered if there's been any other incident of Dr. Simms knowing where you were when he shouldn't have. You know, like you complained about before." Parker heard her clear her throat, a sure sign that something was coming.

"Well, he did ask recently what I was doing in the Marriott Hotel south of Hartford when I didn't even know I was going to be there myself until I went to work that day. But he said a colleague, actually, I think it was a friend of his, saw me there. It was all pretty harmless and I really didn't think about it afterward." Something in her voice informed the detective that she had thought about it, maybe even often.

"Thanks a lot, Miss Regan, umm, Alison. I'll promise not to bother you again," he hesitated. "Unless you call us, of course." They hung up with neither saying goodbye.

A Revisit with Simms

IMMEDIATELY AFTER DISCONNECTING WITH Alison Regan, Parker dialed the dispatcher on duty. After filling him in on where he was going, Parker left the building, bound for the office of Dr. John A. Simms. The drive from Hampton Village to the western suburbs of Hartford only consumed fifteen minutes. He used Interstate 84 for the first few miles then veered off into the countryside of Covington County. The lyrics of the old Bob Dylan song popped into his head. Twenty-eight years had passed since the 1964 tune heralded the theme of the turbulent sixties and the development of the east side of Covington County surely made the singer look like a prophet. "The times they are a-changing" was an apt description for the landscape he was driving through. Where forests interlaced with magnificent horse farms once stood, housing developments of every size and description mauled the environment. Within minutes, he crossed the invisible dividing line between zoning districts and the suburbs with their green lawns and manicured properties faded away, replaced by buildings of increasing heights and sizes.

And this is all Covington County. Dylan was right about something else. My old road is rapidly aging and maybe I'd better get out of the new one, he thought as he pulled into the parking lot next to the building housing Dr. Simms's office. It was 8:55 a.m.

CLARISSE SHEARER HEARD THE door open. She leaned forward to see who was entering, fully expecting John Simms to walk in, even if it was five minutes early. She rubbed her disbelieving eyes like someone awakening from a nightmare when Parker walked into the waiting room.

"Is the doctor in yet, Mrs. Shearer?" Parker asked with what he hoped was a disarming smile. It wasn't.

"No, he's not. I don't see how he could have time for you today anyway. He's booked solid. Perhaps if you could come back later in the week . . .let me get the appointment book and we'll see what's available." She started to turn away but Parker's sharp words stopped her. He was no longer smiling.

"I'll be his first customer, Mrs. Shearer, whether it's convenient or not. Now, the sign says office hours are nine to five. I assume that means he'll be here at nine, right?"

As if on cue, John Simms walked into the waiting room. He immediately caught sight of Havenot and for a brief moment looked as if he might bolt back through the still open door. Parker crossed the room in two strides and offered his hand, which was ignored yet again.

"I'll just take a few minutes, Doctor. Mrs. Shearer told me you have a full schedule of patients today so I'll be quick."

Without a word, Simms led Parker back to his office.

"So, what's this all about, Detective? I told you everything I know about Brad Wallace. Just a case of mistaken identity. You said yourself that he was dead so I guess I'm not understanding why you're here again." Simms paced back and forth behind his desk as if contemplating a major decision.

"Wallace is only one of my reasons for being here, Doctor. I'm willing to let that remain where it is for now. The other reason for stopping by is a bit of curiosity on my part. You obviously don't have to answer if you don't want to." Parker paused, waiting for any reaction.

Simms stopped pacing and stood straight behind his chair, his hands resting lightly on the high-quality leather seatback. "I can answer anything you'd like. I'm feeling like a criminal here. I don't often get visited by the cops, let alone by the same cop twice. So, what is it you want to ask?"

"I'm just a little curious how a modest practice like you appear to have allows you to live the lifestyle you do. Do you do some moonlighting on the side or something?" The edge of the intimidation factor in the question was dulled by Parker's soft delivery but it still brought Simms around his desk and into the detective's personal space.

With his forefinger jabbing the air in front of Havenot's face, Simms hissed an answer. "That is none of your business!"

"You're absolutely right. It only came up because your name has been mentioned in other contexts around the department so I thought I'd just check it out. I'll find my way out and thanks for the time."

Parker was closing the office door behind him when Simms caught him.

"What other contexts; what the hell does that mean, Detective?" The doctor's face showed a few red blotches.

"Oh, it's really nothing, just some routine stuff that comes up, you know. Peripheral information, that sort of thing." Leaving Simms staring at him, he slowed as he passed Clarisse Shearer's office. The waiting room remained empty. "Have a cancellation for the early appointment, Mrs. Shearer?" he called to her. Then he was gone.

Moments later as he sat in his car, he wondered if the strategy would work.

"At least it'll get him thinking, and maybe even a little worried," he mumbled.

Back in the doctor's office, Clarisse tapped on the half-opened door then entered. John Simms sat at his desk, staring out the window.

"John," she asked softly, "are you OK?"

He turned and looked at her with the dazed expression, as if just awakening from a nap.

"What was that all about, anyway, I mean, I'm a little curious what the sheriff's department would want with you." Their long employer/employee relationship had been interrupted for several years with a purely physical love affair that cooled immediately when Simms met Alison Regan. The end of the affair meant a return to a business relationship that now included Clarisse's attitude that she held a higher position because of performing such a variety of services for her boss.

"The detective seems to think that former patient I had you check on the other day is still alive, even though he said he had witnessed the death. I've got no idea why he's wasting his time with me."

"Interesting. I didn't mean to pry but I really do care about you, you know."

"Thanks a lot, Clarisse. I appreciate that." He went back to staring out the window while she backed out of the office.

It Must Be Drugs

PARKER RETRACED HIS ROUTE through the burgeoning eastern part of Covington County, shaking his head at the added responsibility of the sheriff's department at a time when budgets cuts represented the norm and hiring freezes in all public services were in effect.

"How the hell are we going to cover all this?" he muttered; then his thoughts returned to the enigma of John Simms, Brad Wallace, and Alison Regan. What was going on there?

When he returned to his office, he dialed Sam Olden's number on the interoffice phone. There was no answer but he knew that he was somewhere in the building. He picked up the all-call intercom, paging Sam to come to his office. As the name echoed throughout the hallways, Parker smiled, knowing that Sam would arrive out of breath, flustered and nervous about being called to report to him. Eventually, when he discovered what Parker wanted and had calmed down, he'd be pleased about the call. In the meantime, he'd be frantic.

When Sam arrived in the predicted state of mind, Parker calmed him with a single sentence.

"I need your advice, Sam." Sam's relief was evident as the tension left his body, leaving him looking as loose as the scarecrow in *The Wizard of Oz*.

Parker outlined the entire situation, including his conversa-

tions with Alison Regan and John Simms. He mentioned Brad
Wallace as an afterthought, concentrating instead on the attitude
and arrogance of John Simms. "Looking at it just from what I told
you, what's it look like to you?" Sam sat up straighter in the chair,
like a marine just being told he was up for a promotion.

"It must be drugs. It sure seems as though Ms. Regan was
drugged; the whole wine fatigue thing doesn't wash with me. If
the doctor used drugs for that, what's to say he's not peddling?
Unexplained income for a professional with easy access to pre-
scription drugs? Makes sense to me." Sam sat back, folded his
arms across his chest with the air of someone who has just said
something profound.

"That makes sense to me as well, Sam. But here's what has me
puzzled. How in the hell does Simms know where his girlfriend
is all the time? I can see the drug part as an obvious answer to the
cash flow but how does it relate to being able to track someone.
Could he hire someone to follow her? If so, wouldn't you think
she'd catch on? Something else is happening and I'll be damned
if I can figure it out." Parker stared out the picture window over-
looking the town commons, mentally scratching his head.

"Well, sir, if you'd like, I could do some research. I love doing
stuff like that. Libraries are my favorite places. Maybe I could
come up with something. Can't promise anything but I could try."

Parker stood and Sam Olden saw that this meeting was over.
"You do that. I'd appreciate it. I just can't spend much more
company time on it because Miss Regan doesn't want it pursued
and I've got nothing to go on with the doctor and drugs except
for his excessive income but who knows, maybe he had an inheri-
tance or something." They shook hands as Sam promised to let
him know if he found out anything that might help.

Brad's List

HIS TINY RENTAL HOUSE at 12 Hopkins Street in Farmington provided a perfect place for Brad Wallace to be invisible. The neighbor on one side was a shut-in who had visitors about twice a week as nearly as he could determine, probably church people doing a welfare check as part of their involvement in a make-a-difference program. The neighbors at 14 Hopkins were never to be seen, as least so far in the time he had spent there. It seemed a neighborhood without life; there were no children playing, no dogs being walked, no friendly klatches of people gossiping on their front steps, and no sign of any outdoor activities like barbeques or backyard get-togethers.

One of the first things he did after moving in was to remove the curbside mailbox that appeared to have suffered from several drive-by baseball bat attacks. The mailman stopped in the first day after the dismantling of the twisted metal frame and Brad assured him that he would get his mail through a post office box. He didn't choose to tell him that dead men don't usually receive much mail.

After the fiasco with Doctor Simms which started out so with such potential, he left no information about where he might be found. "I'll come back to you in a couple of days," he had said. The original plan included only a several month stay in Connecticut, but the bland house and innocuous environment he had found was looking more and more like a good place for a base of operations, even those he planned in New Hampshire. It was, after all, only a three-hour drive, an easy round trip. If Simms was correct and could line up a source of income while he was able to remain anonymous, then Hopkins Street might be his domicile for quite a while.

While he waited for the days to pass before he went to see if Simms could indeed be a positive force in his life, he worked on his list. For the immediate future, there would be no new additions, although he had no doubt that he would be adding names as time went by. His agent for justice status depended on it. He would stay with his standard modus operandi, simply introducing a minor inconvenience into the overall scheme of things then allowing fate or destiny or whatever name the power calls itself to take control. There would always be collateral damage, unfortunately, but that was the way of the world.

He went into the bedroom, which housed a single bed, a nightstand with a gold lamp that could be turned in any direction by its flexible neck, and an antique wardrobe where every bit of clothing he owned was stored. His leather suitcase, a leftover remnant of his professional career and the only part of it he had taken with him to his hermit life in New Hampshire, sat in a corner. He dragged it into the kitchen and lifted it onto the small oak table that was no bigger than two TV trays. An old spiral notebook was the first thing he touched as he reached into the case. He felt around the bottom of the compartment he remembered held all of his writing utensils, pulled out a pen, and scratched out a test on a page of the notebook.

At the top of a piece of paper, he printed in capital letters: THE CONNECTICUT CONNECTION. Then he started to write.

Parker Havenot ★★★
Robert Snyder ★★
George Metcalf ★★
Rich Lane
Steven Capaldi★★★
Josie Wallace (Havenot)
Harriet Long (Stanton)

Brad Lands a Job

"BROOKINS MAKES TWELVE AND with the addition of your girl-friend, we're keeping track of thirteen clients, Simms. I have to admit that it's getting a little wearing for me. I mean, Tommy and Travis are fine and they do what they're told but the hours are getting to them and to me as well." The phone call surprised John Simms and worried him as well until he caught on to the tenor of Henry Bouchard's voice. As Clarisse informed him when she took the call, he sounded pretty calm, not at all angry.

"What are you thinking? Maybe another hire to fill in? You've told me there is no end to the market of people who will do this sort of work and be happy about it." Simms was almost giddy that he was not on the receiving end of a tongue lashing as only Henry Bouchard could supply.

"Actually, I was thinking about it but the thought of going on another search, even for one person, drains me as much as filling in for the boys does." Bouchard sounded tired, his usual bravado lacking in his voice.

"I might just have a solution for you. I know how pissed off you were when I did the unauthorized insert. Maybe this could make up for that, in a small way, at least." The conversation was going better than Simms could have expected.

"Actually, in thinking about that insert, perhaps you have some-thing. I'm revising my estimate downward for how many years

92

we have before my product is not the only one on the market. I'm figuring about 2000, maybe a year or two after that, the technology will explode and we'll be out of business. So, we've got about eight years to, as they say, make hay while the sun shines. Was never sure what that meant, exactly, but it sounded good." Bouchard chuckled, a sound totally unfamiliar to John Simms, who rolled his eyes at Clarisse Shearer sitting across from him. "Anyway, Simms, maybe there is another market for the product. Now what's this idea you have?"

"I've got this patient, actually he was a patient and he just got back in town. He might be the perfect person for your needs because he has no personal attachments and is adamant about his privacy. For all intents and purposes, he's invisible to the rest of the world and has no commitments. I know he could use some supplementary income and he has some very good reasons for keeping to himself. The operation would be secure with him, I'm sure, and he's a smart guy as well." Simms stopped and listened to gauge his boss's reaction.

"Sounds like you're his agent or something, Simms. He hasn't got some kind of hold over you or something, does he?"

"Oh, no, Mr. Bouchard. If anything, I'd say it's just the reverse." Simms sent a wide smile to Clarisse, who had no idea what the conversation was all about but remained in rapt attention in hopes of figuring it out.

"Give him this number and tell him to call me as soon as possible. I'd like to meet this guy. And Simms, I'm no longer pissed, to use your term, at you. Unlike my other enterprises, TRAC is a small operation but profitable and I'd like to keep it that way with the original people I brought on board. We're like family, you know." Bouchard shocked Simms again with a loud laugh. "Thanks and I'll be calling soon. I think we've got a couple more clients lined up." The phone clicked in John Simms's ear.

"Let's hope Brad Wallace makes an appearance here soon," he said to Clarisse, "because I have no idea how to contact him, let alone find him."

LESS THAN A WEEK later, Brad Wallace was one of three technicians in the TRAC offices. The negotiation process with Henry
Bouchard was short and to the point, with most of the conditions
being put into place by the "new hire." Bouchard was happy to
oblige since Brad's conditions worked in his favor as well. The
need for confidentiality clearly did not present any issue for
Wallace, who insisted that any contact he had with his fellow technicians was kept to an absolute minimum. At one point during the
training process, as Brad revealed additional stipulations for his
personal anonymity, Bouchard made one of his rare jokes, only to
realize that perhaps it wasn't such a joke after all.

"It's almost like you want people to think you're dead, Brad,"
he commented, a statement greeted with a strange response.

"Well, Mr. Bouchard, that would suit me just fine," Brad said,
leaving Bouchard speechless.

The nature of the operation, in the mind of its founder, celebrated secrecy and Brad Wallace would fit in with that celebration
just fine.

TRAC and the agent for justice would be a perfect match.

Sam's Research

GIVEN ANY CHOICE IN the matter, Sam Olden would rather spend time in a library than at a movie, a baseball game, or most other forms of entertainment. The exception was his fanatical following of the New England Patriots in the National Football League. Sunday afternoons during the season were inviolate. If the team played at home at the new Foxboro location in Massachusetts, he was there. If they were on the road, he was camped in front of the television. He had just one Sunday before the season opened.

Unless he was working, he usually spent Sunday afternoons in the Hartford Public Library. When Parker Havenot allowed the opening, he offered to do the research but had no idea where to begin. Here was a chance to impress a detective whose work was admired so much throughout the department. Maybe a quiet Sunday afternoon at the library would expose some answers to the basic question at hand.

How does someone know the whereabouts of someone else without their knowledge? The obvious answer in the world of 1992 was that someone would be followed. In the case of Alison Regan, that answer seemed illogical. Why would someone go the trouble of having his girlfriend followed if their relationship was sound, as the doctor and Alison Regan's seemed to be? He decided that his research had to take a more unusual path. He approached

95

Muriel Libby, the research librarian, whom he knew well, and asked the question.

"What would you do if you wanted to know where someone was all the time but didn't want them to know that you wanted to know where they were?" he asked, in such convoluted phraseology that Muriel laughed out loud.

She reigned in her giggles as a few patrons frowned at her. In typical librarian fashion, she came back with an answer and a place to begin without hesitation and without referring to any resources.

"There's a lot of experimentation being done with tracking devices, especially in the areas of farms and ranches where animals can get lost. It's a little different but, in effect, it's kind of the same. A rancher doesn't want his cows getting lost so he wants to know where they are when they're out of his sight, right? I haven't really read a lot about it but maybe there's something to it."

"As always, Muriel, your logic is impeccable. I'll start there."

"The best place to start might be the new program we just installed. It's called Newsbank and it's over there in that corner." She pointed to a work station wedged between two old-fashioned listening centers which appeared to be a display of antique audio equipment rather than something of use in the 1990s. "It's a dedicated computer—you might remember it when it was in print form. All of the articles were on microfiche then. Anyway, good luck and let me know if I can help you with anything." She smiled and sat back down at her desk.

Sam approached the computer with the uneasiness of someone out of his element, even though he had some experience with computers at the office. He came expecting to start with the *Readers' Guide to Periodical Literature,* a format he had learned to use so well back in high school and had used ever since. Once he sat down at the carrel, the computer screen became the center of his world. There were no distractions such as might have been at a table in the main section of the library. "This is going to be fun," he said to himself.

In the blank space labeled Subject Search, he typed the words "tracking devices" using the hunt and peck method so common with people who never learned to type. Harboring no expectations, he was stunned when line after line of articles appeared. He looked over his shoulder to see if Muriel was still at her desk. She happened to be looking up at just the right time and Sam made eye contact and motioned her to come over.

"Can I print some of this stuff out somehow?" he asked as she stood behind him, looking over his shoulder at the screen.

"We've had to put a limit on the number of free pages but if you're willing to pay, you can print all you want. The printer's in a cabinet under the shelf. Just let me know how many pages and I'll let you know how much. Anything else?" she asked.

"Just a huge thanks for putting me on to this. It's amazing!"

"I hear that a lot," Muriel said, smiling.

THE NEXT THING SAM knew, Muriel was tapping him on the shoulder. "We're closing in fifteen minutes, Sam. You probably need to wrap things up."

The vintage school clock hanging over the checkout desk read 4:45. He had occupied that little carrel for over four hours. The green computer screen indicated that he was on page four of five in the article he was reading. It was not one he wanted to print so he skimmed the last page and the signed out. He counted the pages he had printed and reported to Muriel Libby, gripping the pile tightly in his left hand as he searched his pocket for change with his right.

"I've got thirty-seven, so how much do I owe you?"

"Ten are free. The others are five cents each. Apparently you found some useful information?" she said, but the question in her voice was obvious. "I'm really curious, if you don't mind telling me. It might help with other patrons."

"I wouldn't have believed it, Muriel. Heaven help us in the future. People are figuring out more ways to keep an eye on other people . . ." He hesitated, looking for the words. "It might be 1992 but it sure sounds like that George Orwell thing to me, you know, *1984*. Anyway, thanks a lot for your help! I really appreciate it."

Back in his car, he flipped through the pages he had printed. "Hope Parker Havenot will share my enthusiasm," he whispered.

Years Away

ON MONDAY MORNING, SAM Olden arrived at work an hour early. The night before, he had arranged the articles he had printed in chronological order with the most recent on the top of the pile. He also had read them through once again. If Parker Havenot had any questions, he wanted to be able to answer them with authority. For the first time in his memory, he bypassed the coffee pot in the break room, even though Monday was the day that the donation of two dozen donuts arrived from Pop's Bakery, a weekly thank you for what the sheriff's department did for the community. The aroma of the sweet, freshly baked pastries wafting through the door caused a momentary pause in Sam's step but he continued on to his desk.

The envelope with his research from the day before was under his arm and he dropped it on top of the pile of file folders. He picked up the phone and asked dispatch for Parker Havenot's message box. When he connected, he left a succinct and, he hoped, intriguing message.

"Detective," he said, "this is Sam Olden. I did the research you wanted. I think you're going to be very interested in what I found out. Tracking may be easier than we thought."

Parker Havenot, like a majority of the human population, was a captive of routine. Unless there was a special occasion, his arrival at the department rarely varied more than a minute in either direction of eight o'clock. The first thing he noticed when he unlocked his office door was the red blinking light indicating that he had at least one message. He picked up the phone and pressed the play button. Sam Olden's voice came through loud and clear. A brief glance at his desk calendar showed no commitments until 8:30 and he soon had Sam on the intercom.

"Your place or mine?" he said without preamble when Sam answered.

"I'll be right there, Detective."

Parker's door stood open, as it always did. His colleagues often teased him about being the personification of an open door policy. Sam knocked on the doorjamb and Parker waved him in. A chocolate covered doughnut with a huge bite taken out of it sat on a sheet of tissue paper next to a large size Styrofoam cup of Dunkin Donuts coffee in the middle of Parker's desk. Parker noted Sam's surprise at the sight.

"I have a doughnut once a week, Sam, whether I need it or not. I mean, the guy donates them as a debt of gratitude so I feel obligated. Now have a seat and tell me all about it. I've got a half hour. "

Sam handed the envelope to Parker and sat down, still eyeing the doughnut. The detective hefted the packet as if weighing it, then set it on the left side of his desk, the symbolic in basket for him.

"Thirty-seven pages, and there was a lot more. I was amazed at what I found," Sam said, his enthusiasm obvious.

"How about you give me an overview, Sam? I don't really have time to read all this stuff right now but I eventually will. In the meantime, I'd like to know if I should spend any more time on this. So, as I just said, tell me all about it."

Sam had prepared for the request and launched into an exposition of current experimentations with insertions of miniature digital chips, smaller than a grain of rice, into animals. His research discovered a number of companies in the early stages of developing a chip that could be tracked by satellite, but these companies thus far had been stymied by the issue of providing enough continuous power so that the device could transmit a signal.

"Years away," Sam said. "Anything I could find about the companies, whether it was Thermo Life, or VeriChip, or Applied Digital, or Univac Redux, they all repeated the same mantra—years away from practicality. The one that came closest was an outfit called Digital Angel Chip. They're doing stuff with GPS systems but still the same old story—years away."

"What's GPS again? I've heard of that before but don't remember." Parker seemed dazed by the deluge of information coming from Sam.

"Global positioning systems. It seems to be the wave of the future. They made great use of it in Desert Storm the last couple of years but it's a long way from general public use."

"Yeah, I know—years away, right? So, what do you make of all of this? Did you find anything worth pursuing for our purposes or is it just way beyond what anyone could do in little old Covington County?"

"It sure goes far beyond anything we've dealt with before. Here we are working on a puny little harassment case but they're working on cutting-edge science." Sam realized the implication of what he had said and tried in vain to recover. "I mean, what we do is important . . ." He stopped speaking and waited.

Parker's cold stare made plain what he thought of Sam's gaffe. "OK, Sam, I'll look over the material and get back to you with any questions I might have. And I do appreciate your efforts, even if they might not help out our puny little case."

Sam knew it was time to go, even though his half hour wasn't up yet. As he hurried from the office, Parker called to him. "One more thing, if you don't mind. Were any of those companies you found anywhere near here?"

"They were all on that tech corridor up in Boston, you know, the 128 beltway around the city." He thought for a minute. "No, I take that back. There was one in Connecticut, that one sounds like a John Updike book. Something redux. It's in the packet."

With almost ten minutes before his appointment, Parker picked up the packet Sam had left behind. He pulled out the pile of paper and starting skimming the content from front to back. A paragraph heading on the fifth page stopped him.

UNIVAC REDUX OUTLINES FUTURE PLANS

He skipped down to the current address listed for the company. The headquarters for Univac Redux was the two-story building directly across the street from John Simms's office. He could look out his window and see the entrance.

"Interesting," Parker said to himself as he set aside the page he was holding and put the other papers back in the envelope.

Henry and Brad

HENRY BOUCHARD WAS A realist. So far, TRAC had attracted only one of the groups he intended to enlist. He called them the "captains of industry" but the group could be just as easily categorized as a bunch of over-achieving, self-aggrandizing, and paranoid nouveau riche. The word-of-mouth advertising for the project began with Professor Thomas Gomes of the Business Administration College of the University of Hartford. When Bouchard offered him a "get in on the ground floor" offer, Gomes first was flattered then became the first recipient of a chip. His contact list for potential wealthy businessmen in the area was extensive because of his connections between the college and the commercial community. Within days of the declaration that the chip experiment was successful, Gomes had three prospects lined up for Henry Bouchard, prospects who were made aware of the need for confidentiality at every level. Of those original three, Ralph Brookins was the only hesitant candidate but now even Brookins had joined the group of twelve. If the project was to turn Bouchard into a true captain of industry himself as he planned, it had to expand its base into the entertainment and political areas. There could be other markets as well, but he was limited to a small circle of people he could trust to discuss the possibilities.

Bouchard decided to gather a think tank comprised of four people. He knew he could trust John Simms, who was completely

dependent on him for his comfortable livelihood. When the inept
Simms introduced the chip into his girlfriend, Bouchard thought
he was an idiot, but the more he considered it, perhaps Simms
might have opened an unexpected market. Simms would not
want to jeopardize his personal situation. Brad Wallace presented
no threat to security either. The extraordinary request by Wallace
to be paid in cash coupled with his refusal to divulge even basic
contact information had worried Bouchard at first, but Simms had
allayed any trepidation.

"The man doesn't want anyone to know he survived and
we can use that to our advantage if necessary," Simms said, after
detailing the Wallace story. Bouchard decided to take a chance
with his new hire as part of his idea team. It was obvious that Brad
Wallace did not want anyone to know he remained on the planet
except those he himself chose. Professor Gomes would complete
the group. Gomes was so invested already that he had everything
to lose if the project crashed.

BOUCHARD WANTED NONE OF his other employees aware of the
meeting and invited the men to his modest house in the outlying
suburbs west of Hampton Village. Eva Bouchard played bridge
practically every afternoon and Friday was a ladies luncheon
bridge at Twin Gorge Country Club so she would be gone for the
day. Henry didn't inform her about the company coming and he
simply ordered a variety of deli sandwiches delivered should the
men want something besides cheese and crackers and a glass of
wine.

John Simms offered to drive and issued an invitation to Brad
Wallace and Professor Gomes to ride along with him, an invitation which Wallace refused immediately but Gomes accepted.
The time of day was perfect for Brad to take another nostalgia trip
through Hampton Village. Josie would be at school and Parker
Havenot was sure to be at work. A brief stop at Brad, Jr.'s grave
would certainly be in order. It had been a week since his last trip
when he left the nail in the Havenot's mailbox.

THE AGENDA FOR THE meeting consisted of three elements. The items for discussion were so simple that Henry Bouchard did not write them down. The first was the purpose for gathering the four together; the second was a summary of how this project could make rich men of all of them; the third was an exposition of Henry Bouchard's philosophy of life.

Brad Wallace was the last to arrive. Henry greeted him at the door as if he were a best friend who had not visited in years. He led Brad through the hall, which had more square footage than the house Brad was renting. They met the other two men in what Brad guessed was a study, although it looked like a small town library. Books filled the shelves that stretched from floor to ceiling. A rolling ladder like something out of a British detective movie stood in one corner, ready to be pressed into use to pluck a book from a top shelf. A large mahogany table anchored the room, sitting exactly in the center and surrounded by six thickly padded upholstered chairs. Their leather covering matched the table right down to the grain.

Gomes and Simms stood by their chairs, gripping the backs firmly with one hand while each balanced a large glass of what appeared to be red wine in the other. They looked as though they had been waiting a long time, even though the chiming grandfather clock indicated that it was only 12:15.

"I'm really sorry I'm late. You know how that interstate can be." His apology was heartily accepted by Bouchard but ignored by the other two.

"Nothing to worry about, Brad. Can I get you a glass of wine, maybe something stronger?" Brad hesitated but finally accepted the wine. "No problem if you want something else. I noticed that you had to think about it."

"Just thinking of my old martini days, Mr. Bouchard, but I don't do that anymore."

"Well, grab a sandwich and have a seat. I don't expect this meeting to take long."

The well-marked deli sandwiches provided a wide variety of choices and it was five minutes before the four men were finally seated and comfortable. Henry Bouchard, sitting at the head of the table, cleared his throat. When that effort did not carry over the rustling of sandwich wrappings, he stood.

"I suppose you are wondering why I've called you all here," Bouchard announced in a voice that silenced the paper crinkling. The statement produced chuckles as the old gag usually did. They looked up at him, waiting for him to acknowledge the joke. When he didn't, Gomes and Simms took a large bite of their sandwiches and started chewing quietly. Brad Wallace continued to gaze at him with expectation, as if waiting for a dramatic proclamation but none seemed to be forthcoming. Instead, Bouchard took his seat and spoke softly.

"Tommy Maggio and Travis Connally are the only other people who know about the TRAC project but I opted not to have them attend this meeting. I have the utmost confidence that they can be trusted but I think the fewer people who know what might be happening as we move forward the better. Their interest is the technology and they'd probably not want to get bogged down in the business end anyway." Bouchard paused to allow time for the explanation to be digested.

Brad took advantage of the break in Bouchard's opening speech to ask the question that had been bothering him since he was invited to the meeting.

"Not to get ahead of things, here, Mr. Bouchard, but I'm wondering what I'm doing here? I've only been with you for a short time and I'm not sure what I could possibly contribute at this time."

"Quite the contrary, my boy," Bouchard responded, causing Brad to snort out an unbelieving chuckle.

"Sorry, sir, but the boy part threw me a bit. I'm on the north side of fifty. I stay in shape and may not look it but I am." Brad said, adding a mumbled, "but thanks, anyway."

The other three smiled at him but it was John Simms who joined in the conversation.

"I've wondered about that, Brad. It's been a while since I examined you for a real physical but you sure seem to have worked hard at keeping yourself fit."

Henry Bouchard waved his right hand with a dismissive waggle. "His fitness," he said, pointing to Brad, "is an interesting topic but that's not what we're here for."

"You're a part of this team because you seem to have no family, no friends, no loyalties. Your anonymity is somewhat rare, if you must know, and it's a trait that is most useful to us. Now, let's get back to the agenda."

For the next fifteen minutes, Henry held the floor with a stop-only-for-a-breath monologue on why he called this meeting and the expectations he had for it. Basically, the purpose centered around a fundamental business premise. If a business is going to succeed, it needs customers. TRAC had a good start, mining the fears of a number of wealthy individuals whose egos convinced them they were important enough to be kidnapped, held hostage for ransom, or perhaps even killed.

"What I need from you," Bouchard said as he made eye contact with each of those sitting around the table, "are more ideas about how to expand this little enterprise. The technology is in place and is turning out to be surprisingly inexpensive now that I've set it up. When we meet again, I'll expect you all to have some ideas."

Brad, his schoolteacher background ingrained in his behavior, raised his hand and waited to be acknowledged. Bouchard smiled at him and said "Go ahead, Brad." Then it was his turn to wait.

Brad thought for a moment before answering.

"As I understand it from Dr. Simms, you are guessing that you're going to have competition in as soon as five years, right?" Bouchard and the others nodded in affirmation.

"OK, then. I'm not seeing the percentages of even trying to keep TRAC operational. This business doesn't seem to have much of a future." The fidgeting in the chairs and the clearing of throats told Brad that perhaps he should have kept quiet.

Professor Gomes, who had said nothing, not even greeting Brad when he came in late, spoke out loudly. "I'll tell you what the future means. It means we make the best of the years we have and take advantage of the fact that Mr. Bouchard and his associates found a way to power those damn chips before anyone else. It won't matter if they catch up if we've got enough money in the bank before they do." He had risen from his seat and was leaning across the table pointing his finger at Brad.

Henry Bouchard also rose again from his seat. "Sit down, Gomes. Let me explain the economics of this." He bent over and lifted his briefcase onto the table. The locking flap was open and he reached in, extracting a file folder. He passed the folder to Brad. "Take a minute to look this over, then tell me again about the future of this business."

In less than two minutes, Brad understood. He skimmed through the first page, a summary of the services provided by TRAC. The second page in the folder outlined a price schedule for those services. The summary of the monthly charges included options but Brad's eyes were drawn to the first choice. A person could opt for full-time surveillance; that is, if the man or woman wanted to be accounted for on a seven days a week, twenty-four hours a day basis, the cost would be $2,000 per month after an initial fee of $25,000. Brad closed the folder and handed it back to Bouchard.

"It's astounding to me that people would spend that kind of money so that someone can know where they are every minute of every day."

"They think of it like an insurance policy. All twelve of those we have signed on have chosen to be full-timers. If you do some quick math, with just the current clients, our monthly income is $24,000. To these guys, $2,000 is pocket change, fun money, completely disposable income. We pay the three trackers a good wage, as you know, and Simms and Gomes have nice tax-free additions to their income so they're not complaining. It's a win-win for all concerned. Good guys are protected from the bad ones and everyone at TRAC is happy." Bouchard finished with a dramatic flourish, his hand gestures directed at Brad but widening with each word to include everyone seated around the table. "You should count your blessings that you found us, Brad. You've got to admit it's a viable enterprise."

There was only silence as Gomes and Simms waited for Brad's response. It came out as a question.

"What we're doing here is not legal, right?" That brought another long silence.

Professor Gomes was the first to answer. He clearly had taken offense at the statement.

"Look, Wallace, these are grown men making adult decisions. What they decide to do in their private lives should not be the business of anyone else, including the government. Just because a bureaucratic arm of the United States government isn't forward-thinking doesn't mean that the rest of us can't be. This is cutting-edge now but it won't be in a few years. Everyone who has one of these tracking chips implanted has done so of his own free will. Sure, it's illegal for now but a hell of a lot of stuff used to be illegal. What about medicinal pot, which is helping a lot of people in San Francisco but trying to use it here will get you a jail term. When these chips become legal, we'll never be able to compete with outfits like Applied Digital or Gen-Etics so for now we use Mr. Bouchard's technology to our advantage."

With that, Bouchard silenced Gomes for the second time. "Let's hear from Dr. Simms. He's been pretty quiet up to this point. What do you think, John? Are we doing some good here or are we no better than the bad guys?" All attention shifted to the doctor.

"Everyone knows exactly what they're doing. We spell it out to them in plain English and I surely don't see what harm we are doing. This is not a case of situational ethics. As you pointed out in your sales pitch to me, Mr. Bouchard, the percentages favor the good people but the evil ones are winning."

"That's a fine speech, Doctor, especially the part about situational ethics. Now, why don't you fill Brad and Tom in on what you're trying on your own and see how they feel about it?" Bouchard's eyes flashed but he quickly controlled his anger before anyone but Simms noticed it.

"I thought, I mean..." Simms stuttered. "You said that was between us for now." A few beads of sweat formed on the doctor's upper lip and his face took on a faint tinge of pink.

"Go on, John, tell them about 0605, Code GERILA." Bouchard's request came out in a soft voice, but for Simms, there was no mistaking the underlying edge.

Five minutes of stammering and stuttering later, Simms managed to complete his reasoning for using Alison Regan as his personal experiment. According to his story, his motivation for taking such an enormous risk was purely for the sake of the TRAC project. Thomas Gomes and Brad Wallace stared at him, disbelief obvious in their slack-jawed expressions. Silence once again washed over the room as the news was digested.

Henry Bouchard stood and declared that the meeting was over. The others stood as well and started gathering up the remains of their lunches. The sound of the crumpling sandwich wrappers seemed to set Bouchard off. He stopped then with a loud shout.

"Don't worry about that stuff; I'll take care of it." He had their attention.

"Don't forget your homework assignment. We need to figure out how to expand our client base but we can't afford to jeopardize the project. Insecure older men trying to keep track of younger girlfriends doesn't seem like a viable market, in my opinion. John here would admit that he made a mistake, despite his protestations that he did it for the good of the cause. I'm just telling you that I want no more surprises."

The three men looked like the three stooges as they bumped into each other in their haste to get out of the house. When they finally reached the front door, Bouchard called to Brad.

"Can we talk for a moment, Brad, if you have the time?"

Brad hesitated, looking at the others, then responded. "Sure, Mr. Bouchard. Be happy to."

The conversation lasted all of five minutes. The major question Henry had for Brad served to allay some of the concerns but not all.

"You've got to admit that your situation is unique, but the anonymity works in our favor. We've got what amounts to a mom-and-pop operation in our field and the TRAC program is crucial to where we are going. I just need some assurances from you that you'll stay loyal."

"I've got everything to gain and nothing to lose by being loyal. I'd say it looks like maybe Dr. Simms is more of a risk than I am. From what he told me, you and I are philosophically on the same page, the good and evil in the world and all that . . ." Brad let his voice trail off.

"We very well might be, Brad. I appreciate your candor."

Josie and Parker

THINGS WERE SIMPLY NOT right. Parker Havenot's senses as a career detective screamed at him but he couldn't figure out any connections. His first dilemma was simple. What was he doing in the midst of this? His second was also simple. What was he going to do about it? His solution, at least in the immediate future, was to do what he always did since Josie had entered his life. He would present his issues to his second wife who had come to be such a pillar of singular rationality in his life and see what she would make of them. Her personal involvement could be an issue in itself but Parker's confidence in her judgment easily overcame that concern.

Josie and Parker set as a priority to make two hours on Friday evening their own. Social invitations, work commitments, family duties, and household chores did not and were not allowed to interfere.

On good weeks, they were together by five o'clock. On busier weeks, it might not be until seven. It didn't matter. When the door shut with both of them in the house, it was their time. Sometimes, they made love within the first few minutes of seeing each other. Other times, it was a glass of Merlot on the deck, usually wordlessly unwinding, then, depending on what kind of day or week it had been, it was a stress-relieving, intimate connection that produced a positive glow for the rest of the weekend.

Parker had been in possession of Sam's research for an entire work week, struggling to decide what to do with it. On Friday afternoon, he left the office earlier than usual, hoping be home before Josie. To his surprise, her car was in the garage as he pulled into the driveway. His surprise multiplied tenfold when he opened the front door and found her standing there in a robe that revealed enough of her body to make him gasp. There would be no glass of wine on the deck until later that evening.

"I NEED TO ASK your opinion of something," Parker said later when they finally got around to the Merlot. The deck provided an extraordinary view of the setting sun as it glinted off the towering oak trees surrounding Mountain View Cemetery to the west.

"Do you want to wait until my legs stop shaking? You about wore me out, you know that, don't you?" Josie's laugh emerged as one of her patented full-throated guffaws that she quieted when she saw the expression on Parker's face.

"Not bad for an old guy," Parker said, trying to match his wife's playfulness but failing.

"I'm sorry. You look like something's on your mind. I didn't mean to interrupt." Josie had spent more than her share of contemplative moments on the deck, looking out in the direction of Brad, Jr.'s grave. Since she married Parker, those times were less frequent but his distracted state allowed a momentary reminiscence to sweep over her. She recovered from it but not before he noticed the change in her body language.

"Are you OK, Jos? Now it's you who looks like you've got something on your mind." He left his lawn chair, circled behind her back, and began kneading her shoulder blades and neck with his thumbs.

"Sometimes we can still see over or through the cracks of the walls we've built to shield us from the past. That's all. Now, I can't wait to give you my opinion, even if I have no idea what you're going to ask me."

Parker stopped the mini-massage and turned his chair around so they were facing each other, knees almost touching.

"Do you remember the coincidence I mentioned when I found out that your old family doctor was John Simms, you know, my case of the young woman who worried about her boyfriend always knowing where she was and that the boyfriend was none other than Dr. Simms?" He paused. "Hold on a second, will you? I've got something to show you—be right back." He was up and through the French door into the house before she could answer.

Josie, mystified as to where this conversation was going, just stared out to the west, watching the sun settle through the trees and finally dip below the horizon. Parker reappeared as the final rays faded from the sky and dusk enveloped them. He was carrying the folder with all of Sam Olden's research.

The evening eroded to nightfall during Parker's lengthy explanation of the research in the folder. Josie listened without interruption, the drama of what she was hearing engaging her every bit as much as *Jurassic Park,* which she had just finished reading. The combination of suspense and science in the book was matched by the articles about implanting miniature chips, tracking people by satellite, foiling kidnappers, and other threats to the famous of the world. She never sat back in her chair the entire time Parker was speaking. When he finished, he closed the folder and looked at her through the darkness.

"I think it is possible, even with the 'years away' proviso placed by most researchers on the probability. What do you think? As you remember Dr. Simms, did he seem like the kind of guy to be involved in something like this?"

"I would say no possible way. The only thing believable I find in the whole story about him is having his girlfriend followed somehow. As I told you before, Brad always liked him but I would have stopped going to him if our marriage hadn't exploded and forced the issue. Frankly, he always gave me the creeps. Never did anything specific; just a gut feeling. It's a girl thing. But you're talking about real intrigue here." Josie hesitated, realizing how fast she was talking. "I guess I'm giving you too much information but, as you know, I'm never shy when asked for my opinion."

"So," Parker said, "if you were the crack detective and had the information I've just provided, what would you do?"

"I'd do what any good school principal would do to track down the truth. Go right to the source. Go see what the folks at Univac Redux have to say. You said it's in the neighborhood of the doctor's office, right? Maybe you could stop in again and say hello to him for me."

"Thanks for listening, Jos. That's pretty much what I was thinking of doing. Proves the old saying about great minds thinking alike or something like that."

"Actually, Parker, I teach my students that the saying is a fallacy. Great minds never think like anyone else. That's what makes them great minds."

Parker's Dilemma

AFTER A LONG WEEKEND of contemplating options other than the one discussed on Friday night, Parker finally came to a decision late Sunday afternoon as he and Josie sipped cocktails once again on the deck. It was a conclusion applauded by Josie and allowed both of them to sleep soundly through the night, a significant event as Josie faced her first day at school on Monday. Even without the students, the first day back with the usual repetitious meetings, administrative pep talks, and new guidelines for every possible situation made for an exhaustive day, making a good night's sleep a prerequisite to staying sane.

Both Havenots were up earlier than usual, Josie because of the excitement of a new school year beginning soon and Parker because of the excitement of visiting the home of Univac Redux. A healthy breakfast of organic rolled oats and a piece of toast had them ready for the day's adventures. Heading into her twenty-eighth year of teaching didn't diminish the excitement for Josie; different classes, different student combinations, and the resulting change in personal chemistry always generated enthusiasm for educators, especially those of the quality of Josie Havenot.

Parker walked her to the door, hugged and kissed her, and sent her off to school with the admonition so many parents would be voicing over the next several days.

116

"Have a good day and behave yourself! Can't wait to hear how it went," he called to her. She smiled broadly and waved.

"Why do I think your day might be more exciting than mine?" she said as she pulled her seat belt across her lap.

AFTER JOSIE LEFT, PARKER thumbed through the folder. The references to Univac Redux were about the fifth layer in and he soon had the name of the CEO in hand. The question centered around the best way to handle the contact. Should he call Henry Bouchard directly and arrange for an interview or just arrive at the facility unannounced?

"Unexpected is always good," he said to himself, as if he thought any differently.

He gulped down his last few sips of coffee and was off to meet with one of those captains of industry he kept hearing about.

The car ride passed quickly, much of his thinking processes about Bouchard and Simms and Wallace short-circuited by thoughts of Josie. He glanced over to the passenger seat. The yellow legal pad sheets from his previous connections with Brad Wallace stared back at him, mocking him like a subtle aside in his life.

"Should've stopped that whole damn mess right then and there," he grumbled as he drove into the parking lot of the corporate headquarters of Univac Redux. "Now I've got another one."

He had been in many company parking lots before but this one struck him with its shabbiness. Faded white lines did a poorer job of delineating accepted parking spaces than the weeds sprouting up in cracks extending in lightning bolt fashion through the blacktop. Only a few cars dotted the lot and he took a space close to the front door.

A large neon sign over the door blinked a not very subtle welcome.

WELCOME

TO

THE NEW WORLD

UNIVAC REDUX

"What the hell does Univac Redux mean, anyway?" he asked himself.

The reception area for the two-story building appeared to discourage visitors rather than welcoming them. The first chamber Havenot entered looked like a bomb shelter built during the Cold War. The cinderblock walls of the eight-feet-square room were coated with a metallic gray paint. No decorations adorned the walls other than a sign directing visitors to push what looked like an old-fashioned doorbell button for service. A single windowless metal door appeared to be the only exit other than the door Parker had come through. He began to regret his decision not to call for an appointment.

As directed, he pushed the button and waited. A full minute passed before he heard the sliding sound of a deadbolt being released and a loud click as the handle on the door turned.

"What can I do for you?" A tall man, likely in his early thirties with a frown etched in his face, entered the room and stared at Parker. His demeanor could only be described as grim.

"I take it you don't get many visitors," Parker said with a twinkle in his eye.

"Actually, we do but they are always expected, which you are not. Now, how can I help you?" He seemed to be studiously avoiding any chance of introducing himself.

"I'm Parker Havenot with the Covington County Sheriff's Department. I'd like to speak with Henry Bouchard." He didn't miss the smirk that formed but quickly retreated from the man's face.

"You do know that Mr. Bouchard is the CEO of our company, right?" Without giving Parker a chance to respond, he continued. "As such, he is a very busy person who doesn't meet with anyone without an appointment." He reached behind him, searching for the doorknob while continuing to glare at Havenot. "If you'll give us a call later today, perhaps we could set up a time for you to come back." He had found the knob and opened the door partway.

"Actually, Mr....uh...whatever your name is, that's not satisfactory. If Bouchard is here, I want to speak to him. If he's not, then I'll speak to the second in command." Parker reached into his pocket and produced his credentials and a business card. "Take this to whomever you need to and tell them I'll be waiting."

With a sneer, the man grabbed the offered materials and disappeared through the door, which slammed behind him, producing a vibrating echo in the small vestibule.

WHEN THE DOOR OPENED again five minutes later, Parker was greeted by another tall man, somewhat older than the first but with a smile warming his face. While his first contact with a human being at Univac Redux would have made him think the place was full of automatons, this gentleman exuded a refinement and confidence that voided that first impression. Parker extended his hand and Henry Bouchard reached out to meet it, even patting him on the back with his left hand in the familiar gesture usually reserved for good friends.

"So, Detective Havenot, I'll admit to being a little curious as to what you would want from us but I guess I'll find out soon enough. Follow me, and we'll talk in my office." Bouchard led the way, and the environment on the other side of the entryway fortress was like the difference between Pluto and Earth. The cold, harsh vestibule was replaced by brightly lit office areas, filled with live plants, colorful paintings, and employees hard at work. There was no sign of the man who had greeted him when he first arrived.

Henry Bouchard's office occupied a second floor corner of the building, picture windows offering a view that would have been spectacular in a New York skyscraper but here it simply opened out to other similar edifices, including, Parker noted, the medical building that housed John Simms's office. On the way through, Bouchard whispered something to his secretary, who, almost before they were seated, arrived in the office carrying a tray with coffee and Danish pastries.

Havenot opened the conversation with an apology for appearing without an appointment that his host dismissed as not an issue.

"I know you're a busy man, and I appreciate your taking the time to see me. I guess I'm lucky to have made it through that first stage. Your man surely wanted to stop me right at the entrance."

"Gavin becomes a little possessive of this place and of me; he's worked for me for a long time. He said you really didn't give him a lot of choices. And you're right; I am a busy man so if you could let me know what it is you need, I'll see if I can help you out." Bouchard's patience began to disappear.

Parker launched into a summary of the research of Sam Olden, mentioning the names of the chief competitors of Univac Redux and what kinds of research they were conducting. He finished with a compelling statistic. "Research costs money and both federal and private grants seem to be drying up. It looks as if up to 80 percent of the funding for your kind of company is drying up. I just wondered what will happen if all that money goes away." He left the question hanging.

When the pause lasted long enough, he changed the subject to a safer topic. "Where did you ever come up with Univac Redux as a name for this company?"

Bouchard responded immediately. "Univac was really the cutting edge of computers—probably put the word computer into the dictionary. It's an acronym for universal automatic computer, first developed back in the early fifties. We like to think we're on the cutting edge in a lot of ways now. The redux part I threw in because of patent restrictions, plus I thought it was kind of clever; you know, a return to the good old days of innovation. As our motto says, welcome to the new world, Detective." Bouchard leaned back in chair, steepled his fingers together, and smiled, his face a mask of self-satisfaction.

"So, what kind of things do you have your guys working on now? I saw some references to miniature computer chips in the folder my colleague gave me. Maybe that's the wave of the future." Parker watched for any reaction. There was none. "One of the companies even seems to be close to developing a way to put medical information on the chips. Fascinating stuff. You could live in Timbuktu and have a specialist in New York reading your medical charts. Competition must be stiff. Do you have any people looking into these chip things?"

Bouchard stood up. "I still don't have a handle on why you're here," he said. "This is all very interesting but just what exactly are you after?"

"Well, the truth is that I'm just trying to stay abreast of the latest technology and, outside of a bunch of high-tech outfits up on the beltway around Boston, you're it, as far as I can tell. Plus, you're in our jurisdiction now so I need to be aware of what it is we're supposed to be protecting. Now, I've taken up enough of your time. You've been very gracious." Parker got up to leave. "You probably need to have someone walk me out—maybe that cute secretary will do it. And thanks again."

"Thanks for your interest in what we're doing, Detective, and I'll have Pam walk out with you." The two shook hands again.

"By the way, do you?" Parker asked.

"What do you mean, do I?"

"Those chips; do you have anyone working on them? From those articles, there'll be all kinds of uses for them. They're like the size of a grain of rice. They're already using them to track farm animals. But you already know that, right?"

"Yeah, right." They had reached the door and Bouchard called to his secretary. "Pam, would you escort the detective to the door?"

The door closed on Parker's back. Henry Bouchard leaned heavily against it from the other side.

LATE THAT AFTERNOON, PARKER dialed his home phone, certain that Josie would not be home. He left a simple message saying that he wanted to continue what had been an intriguing day up to that point and he would be a little late getting home. Then he made another phone call.

Alison Regan heard the phone ring but the effort to get to it from the shower didn't seem worth it. The answering machine could do its job. After toweling off, she wrapped herself in the fluffy angora robe that John Simms had given to her for her birthday, feeling a little decadent as the material sensuously caressed her naked body in interesting ways as she walked. The regular beeping from the answering machine reminded her of the call. She went straight to it and pushed the play button.

"Miss Regan, this is Detective Havenot. I'm just about to leave the office and wondered if you had about five minutes. I should be at your door at about six-fifteen. If this is not convenient, just don't answer your door and I'll go away. Thanks."

"Shit!" she exclaimed, then raced to her bedroom to get dressed.

PARKER TAPPED ON THE door and this time Alison opened it without hesitation. She ushered him into the living room with no preliminary greeting. They sat in the same chairs as they had on his last visit.

"I'd offer you a drink but I expect John to be along any minute and I really would rather not try to explain what you are doing here. So, what's up, Detective?"

"I understand completely, Miss Regan. I've already met Doctor Simms and I'd also prefer not to explain myself. It's really only one question then I'll be on my way." Parker noticed her anxious look toward the clock.

"This is going to sound a little strange but just consider it. You don't even have to answer now if you don't want to. I feel bad dropping in on you like this but it was convenient as I was passing by and . . ."

"Detective, please!" Alison's frazzled exclamation stopped Havenot cold.

He blurted out the question and it sounded so foolish that he blushed as he finished asking it.

"Is there any possibility that someone might have planted a bug on you or something you wear all the time without you knowing it?" Parker looked at her.

She gazed back at him, her expression perplexed and disbelieving. "A bug? You came here to ask me whether I'd been bugged? I've got to tell you that I'm disappointed in you, Detective." She was already on her feet and halfway across the room, ready to guide him out the door.

Chagrined, Parker tried to recover some sense of dignity. "Please keep an open mind, Miss Regan. Stranger things have happened. There is technology available . . ." An exasperated Alison interrupted again.

"You've got to go, and please, Miss Regan is getting a little tiring. Just make it Alison. The formality is killing me." She opened the door with a secretive glance down the hall. Parker hurried through, relieved to see that John Simms was nowhere in sight. "Let me know if you think of anything I might want to know about," he said over his shoulder.

Alison sighed and shut the door.

Parker and Alison

ALISON REGAN SPENT EACH night of the week after Parker's Havenot's visit tossing and turning, unable to get to sleep. With each succeeding night, the problem progressed from a minor frustration until Wednesday night when it became total irritation. Thursday morning, she struggled to get out of bed, guessing that she had a total of two hours sleep and most of that could only be classified as fitful. When she looked in the mirror, her haggard, exhausted reflection convinced her that something was wrong. As she thought back over the sleepless nights, the hurried conversation with the detective seemed to be the culprit. The annoying yet intriguing questions kept popping up, effectively preventing any chance of uninterrupted sleep. She hadn't allowed him to finish his explanation as to why he was there. With John expected at any time, she couldn't have anyway. Havenot had mentioned something about technology; what was that all about? Did he know something about why John was aware of her movements? The whole situation with her doctor boyfriend had gone beyond the bizarre.

By the time she forced down a piece of toast and a cup of powerful black coffee, she had decided to give the detective another chance to explain himself. The idea of a bug was ludicrous yet there was something about the possibility that unnerved her. She needed to clear this up and the sooner the better. She went

124

into the drawer where she tossed the business cards that were constantly being shoved into her hands. Parker Havenot's hadn't yet made it deep into the mix. She pulled it out and put it in her pocket. She'd call him from work later that morning.

THE DISPATCHER REPEATED THE name. Parker could not believe that Alison was calling. Thoughts tumbled through his head. When he left her before, he was certain that he would be the initiator of any future contact. His suggestion that somehow she might have been bugged had been met with, as he jokingly told his colleagues, thundering apathy. It did sound rather absurd when he said it. Why would she be calling? He pressed the blinking light on line 2.

"This is Havenot. Can I help you?"

Alison's response was curt and to the point. "Do you have any time today, Detective? I'd like to come in to your office, if that's possible. Nothing urgent, except I haven't slept very well since I saw you last. Probably just take a few minutes."

Lunch hour was the only time that matched both of their schedules. At exactly twelve o'clock, Alison walked into the central office of the Covington County Sheriff's Department. At exactly twelve-fifteen, Dr. John Simms placed a call to Tommy Maggio, asking where the charge with Code 0605GERILA was located.

ALISON OPENED THEIR MEETING with a lengthy apology for everything, starting with her first call to the department through to her dismissive attitude toward Parker the Monday evening before. Parker listened and several times sought to interrupt but Alison was not having it. He gave up and waited until the telltale sag of her shoulders said that she had drained her energy.

"Apology completely unnecessary, Alison, but if it will make you feel better, I'll say apology accepted." His smile had the effect on her that it had on most of the female population who knew him.

"Thank you. But I have just one other thing to say then you can explain the stuff you didn't get to explain the other day."

Parker responded with a nod.

"This whole idea of bugging me freaks me out, if you must know. I mean, that's science fiction kind of stuff; plus, it's got to be illegal, right? Even if they could do it, it's against the law, right?" She caught herself slipping into a rant and reined it in.

"You're absolutely right—it is against the law to electronically eavesdrop on somebody but this kind of bugging is not the traditional kind." For the next ten minutes, Parker outlined the research of Sam Olden. Alison interrupted once when he mentioned that Sam was responsible for all the information.

"I really liked Sam," she said, a slight blush coloring her cheeks.

"Yeah, well, he liked you too." Then he finished his lecture on the rice-sized electronic chips that several companies were trying to perfect.

"They'll be able to be inserted anywhere under the skin and then send out a signal to a satellite than can then be relayed to a ground station. Violà! Someone knows where you are all the time."

"They can do that?" she asked.

"No, but it's not for lack of trying. Most say it'll happen in a matter of a few years or more. Hey, in keeping with my reputation as a thoughtful person, this is a great time to think of this but would you like a soda or coffee or water or something?"

Alison nodded a no thank you. "I think I've bothered you enough for now. At least I should be able to sleep now that I know I can't be bugged for a while, at least. Thanks for your patience with me and I'll let you know if anything strange happens." She stood to leave but Parker stopped her.

"You may have to run the gauntlet," he said, tipping his head toward the officers who had mysteriously decided to eat their lunch in the reception area outside his office. Sam Olden was among them.

"I can handle that, Detective. I've had a lot of practice."

Parker watched her leave, all of his colleagues' eyes on her gently swaying rear view. She paused, turned, and sent a wide smile in Sam's direction.

The Lake Camp

JOSIE AND PARKER PLANNED to spend much of the weekend preparing for the next, the long Labor Day weekend which they would spend at their camp in New Hampshire. It was to be a reunion of sorts. With Parker agreeing that it would be a great idea, Josie invited the remaining members of the original magnificent seven to join them. The last time they were all together at the cottage, Rich Lane had the incident which left him a quadriplegic. With Tyler Spence and Brad Wallace gone and Harriet Stanton still teaching at the University of Chicago, there would be just four of them, five including Rich's wife, Becky. It could be like old times in a small way.

Jess Grogan and Jack Hopkins, still bachelors but thoroughly enjoying that status, told Josie that they wouldn't bring any "womenfolk" along so as not to cramp their style, as they so delicately put it. The Havenots would use the occasion to replace the memories of Brad's abortive attempt to sink the *Winnipesaukee Belle* with some happier ones. No doubt once the reminiscences about their early days of teaching in Hampton Village started flowing, there would be no stopping them.

Several days of pre-school meeting days had Josie anxious to start but the new superintendent's plan to have those meetings two weeks before the opening of school seemed to drain some of her enthusiasm as she looked at a whole week of being home between those motivational days and the beginning of classes. The weekend at the cabin would give her something to look forward to.

Saturday morning, menus and lists of food and supplies were drawn up with an extensive shopping trip planned for the early afternoon. More often than not, Josie and Parker followed their Friday night ritual, using Saturday afternoon to devote an hour or two to spending some time together, their euphemism for having a relaxing and sensual interlude. Josie concluded that with some careful planning, that remained a possibility until the phone rang.

JOSIE ANSWERED WITH HER usual warm greeting which she taught to her students, although it likely never became quite the habit with them that it was with her.

"Havenot residence. This is Josie." When Josie hesitated, Parker looked at her quizzically through the kitchen door, his expression asking "what is it?"

The woman's voice trembled, as if she were making an emergency call. "May I speak with Detective Havenot, please?"

As Josie listened, she motioned to Parker to come into the kitchen. "He's right here," she said, shrugging and handing Parker the phone.

Parker used his weekend, off-duty greeting which was a simple "hello" and waved a finger at Josie, indicating for her stay right there.

"This is Alison Regan, Detective. I'm so sorry to have called you at home but your card had the number and when you weren't at the office . . ."

There was silence on the other end as Parker waited. He could hear Alison breathing. "It's OK, Alison. It's not a problem. Now, what's up?" He glanced at Josie, returning her earlier shrug.

"I really think I have to talk to you. And soon. John knew I was at the sheriffs' department yesterday."

FORTY-FIVE MINUTES LATER, ALISON made her second visit to the central headquarters of the Covington County Sheriff's Department within the last twenty-four hours. The officer at dispatch motioned her right through the doors, pointing to Parker's office where, as usual, the door stood wide open. Parker heard the soft footfalls of her running shoes on the marble floor and rose from his desk to greet her. Her appearance shocked him. She wore faded jeans and an oversized Boston Red Sox tee shirt which hid the substantial curves her dress had shown so well the day before. Her long red hair was pulled back in a ponytail and the lack of any makeup gave her skin a pallid cast. It was as if she had made a deliberate attempt to cover her natural vibrant beauty. Her eyes were red and swollen, as though she's either been crying or had not slept at all.

Parker steered her to the nearest chair then pulled another chair over next to her.

"Are you all right?" he asked in a whisper, a tone of voice which her aspect seemed to dictate, both in body language and facial expressions.

"Not really," she said, her eyes filling. "He knows, he just knows everything that I'm doing and I don't get it. How can he? How is it possible?" She pulled an already damp handkerchief from the back pocket of her jeans and held it up to her eyes.

"Did he hurt you in any way? I mean physically? Hit you, grab you, shove you, anything like that." As he was asking her, he also was checking for obvious signs but with no makeup, it was clear there were no bruises, at least on her face.

"He caught me by surprise, Detective. Just out of the blue, asked me what I was doing at the sheriff's office around lunchtime. It freaked me out more than anything he's done before." Alison began to tremble and her voice quavered. "I told him about talking with you and he went crazy, not crazy with me, but just jumped up and started pacing around the room, saying stuff I didn't even understand." She paused to dab at her eyes again, giving Parker a chance to interject a question.

"Did you mention anything about my wondering if you could have been bugged?" Parker cringed, anticipating what she was going to say.

"As I told you, he caught me completely off-guard. I think I might have said something about that. Not only was I freaked out but I was pissed off." She stopped, blushing. "I'm sorry. I don't usually use words like that."

"Not a problem. I pretty much have heard just about everything from anybody. Can you remember anything specific you might have said? It could be helpful." He watched her closely as she fought to regain her composure. She seemed like a person who kept things under control.

"I might have said something like, 'what are you doing, having me followed or bugging me?' but I'm not exactly sure. Whatever I said, he stared at me like I had two heads then he just bolted, without another word. I haven't heard from him since."

"I think you should head on home and get some rest, Alison. Let me handle this from my end. I don't think I'd let him in your house until I can figure out what is going on."

"Don't worry about that. He's persona non grata for me from now on." She put the wet handkerchief in the front pocket, leaving a small corner showing so it could be pulled out on a moment's notice. "Thanks for meeting with me; I couldn't have made it through the weekend without telling somebody. You've been very kind." As he had the day before, he watched her walked away; she stood straighter and taller than when she came in.

The Fallout: Monday Morning

JOHN SIMMS WAITED UNTIL Monday morning to make the call. Since Alison told him about talking with that detective, he hadn't been able to think of anything else but he had no idea what to do about it. After more than forty-eight hours, he still didn't but being proactive instead of passive seemed to be in his best interest.

Tommy Maggio was twenty minutes into his shift when the phone rang. He listened without interruption as a distressed John Simms made his request and then assured him he would complete the disconnect as soon as he could. Simms protested, wanting it done immediately.

"OK, John, as soon as we hang up, I'll get it done," Tommy said. He didn't; instead, he dialed the dedicated number that Henry Bouchard had supplied during his training. The order could not have been clearer. It was to be used only in case an unusual and unsolvable situation arose. To Tommy, the request by Simms constituted an unusual situation, although he could have solved it by refusing to carry out the wish. He and Travis Connally often discussed their mutual mistrust of the doctor and turning off one of their charges on Simms's say-so seemed dangerous at best.

Bouchard didn't answer until the sixth ring; Tommy's anxiety increased with each one. This was a first in two ways. He had never called the number and he had never done a total disconnect on a charge. There were a few times when Bouchard asked him to do a temporary removal at a client's behest, but here was Simms, not Bouchard, wanting a permanent one. Simms obviously was on the team at a high level but something was not right.

"This is Bouchard. What's the problem?" The formality of the greeting did nothing to settle Tommy's nerves and he blurted out his predicament.

"Dr. Simms just called, sir. He wants me to disconnect 0605GERILA permanently. I just thought I should check with you first. It seems a little odd . . ." Tommy faltered, not knowing whose side he should take. "I mean, if it's OK, I'll go ahead and do it."

"You were right to notify me and I appreciate that you're on top of things. Don't do anything until I speak with Dr. Simms." An abrupt and adamant hang-up left Tommy's ear ringing.

Bouchard dialed Simms's office. Clarisse Shearer answered but before she could launch into her perky but phony greeting, he told her to get John Simms on the line. "Our hours begin at 9 a.m." she protested but Bouchard was having none of it.

"I don't care what he's doing. Get him on the goddamn phone!" He could hear the receptionist gasp before stammering an answer.

"Yes, sir." Ten seconds later, Simms answered.

"What the fuck are you doing? First you do an unauthorized insertion and set up a client-ignorant track, now you call directly to the trackers' office to have the damn thing turned off. All this on your own! What are you thinking? This isn't a personal game we're playing here." Bouchard drew in a deep breath, more a combination of breathing and sighing at the same time.

"She talked to a sheriff's department guy, a detective. I figured we'd better shut her down." Simms knew it sounded like a lame excuse but he had no other one handy.

"What are you not telling me, John? You're holding something back and I don't appreciate that sort of thing." Henry Bouchard struggled to keep from screaming into the phone.

"OK. Here's the bothersome part. The detective, his name is Havenot, and he's the same one who came here asking about Brad Wallace. If he somehow gets involved and finds out about Brad . . . I didn't know what to do."

"The bothersome part? You don't know the half of it. For one thing, you stay the hell away from the girl until we figure out what to do about her chip. And you said his name is Havenot, right?"

"Yeah, it's Parker Havenot. He married Josie Wallace, Brad's ex-wife."

"Oh, for God's sake, this is ridiculous. He's the same guy that came to talk to me early last week about what it is we do at Univac Redux. Shit!" For the second time in two conversations, he slammed the phone down, leaving John Simms holding a dead line.

Labor Day Weekend, 1992

PARKER CALLED ALISON REGAN early on Monday morning as a courtesy and found her in good spirits.

"I slept soundly both nights since I spoke with you, and I heard nothing from John all weekend. I think he knows that we are no longer a couple." Her effervescent personality managed to come through the phone line.

"I just wanted to check up on you and let you know that I probably won't have a chance to follow up with Simms about our conversation until the beginning of next week unless you feel it is crucial. Couple of court appearances then beginning Thursday, I'll be out of town, but our dispatch can get in touch with me if you need to talk to me."

"It really not a crisis, Detective. You've been a big help already and I'll be fine. But thanks anyway and thanks again for meeting with me on Saturday. Hope you're planning a fun weekend! Bye." She hung up before Parker could reply.

BECKY AND RICH LANE ARRIVED at the Havenots' house exactly on schedule but, as usual, Jess Grogan and Jack Hopkins called to say they were running late. The plan to turn the holiday getaway into a five-day weekend came together just as Josie had hoped but her idea to carpool for the trip to New Hampshire was squashed by Parker. While he was able to arrange his schedule to have Thursday and Friday off, he wanted his own car at the cabin in case of an emergency in the department. Labor Day weekend seemed to create its own set of problems for police, even in the relatively quiet neighborhoods of Covington County.

Jess and Jack finally pulled into the driveway at 9:15 and announced that they also wanted to drive themselves. "No offense intended, but we might want to do something more exciting than the old married couples," Jess explained, his smirking smile making him look like one of his teenage students who'd been caught in a forbidden public display of affection in the school library stacks. It would be a three-car caravan for the trip to the Lakes Region of New Hampshire.

The late start worked to their advantage as the morning rush hour on the interstate highways was over. Three and half hours later, the entourage turned onto Route 109 and headed east, passing through Gordon Tibideau's hometown of Mapleboro and hit the first traffic jam of the trip in Stoneham where pedestrians in crosswalks have the right of way. They inched their way down the hill into the quaint tourist town, bustling with desperation as vacationers tried to fill every last minute of summer with some kind of activity. Cars, campers, motorcycles, and trucks with boat trailers backed up for a mile in both directions as jaywalkers darted and legal walkers ambled across the street as if it were a blacktop playground.

Finally, they pulled into the gravel parking area above the cabin. Jess and Jack jumped from their car first, racing down the path toward the house then disappearing around the corner. When Becky exited the van, their shouts from the dock carried to her, echoing through the huge pine trees surrounding the property and sounding like Boy Scouts who had just been dismissed from formation. She moved around to the sliding doors of the custom-designed vehicle and had Rich and his wheelchair aligned with the lift before Parker and Josie came to assist. All were smiling as their two friends came bounding back up the path, a little breathless.

"Just like I remember it, Josie. Really, really neat," Jess exclaimed. He looked over as the lift holding Rich's chair clumped on the gravel. His enthusiasm immediately was tempered as the memories of the day of Rich's accident flooded his mind. In his inimitable way, Rich Lane sensed the discomfort and set everyone at ease.

"Well, well, here we are once again," he announced. "It's so good to come back to a place with such fond memories."

Everyone stared at him. He had their attention.

"Before we go any further, let's get this over with, and this will be the last time I want it mentioned this whole weekend. Everyone agreed?"

Parker tried to interrupt. "How can we agree—we don't even know . . ."

Rich shushed him. "Hear me out, please." His friends gathered closer. "This is a happy place for me. We all know what happened; fucking Brad Wallace dumped me off the skis and put me in this chair. I can't believe he meant for it to be this bad."

Josie approached him and put her hand on his shoulder. "Rich, we really don't have to go through this. Let's just forget about it." She put her hand to her mouth, as if wanting to shove the words back in.

"Whoa! Forget about it! I'll pretend I didn't hear that, my dear. Now, I'll finish and then we will enjoy the weekend and that's an order. Brad's gone and for that I'm sorry. But, as Parker has mentioned, he thinks Brad saw himself as just an agent, aiding fate and destiny. Setting things in motion. What I don't want is his ghost intruding, ruining this little reunion. Now, Parker, can we agree on that?"

Josie glanced at Parker. He raised his eyebrows and nodded.

"Sure. That makes perfect sense." He looked at the others, who were nodding affirmatively also.

"Good. That settles that. Now can you guys get me down this hill so I can enjoy a cold beer on the deck while you all do the unpacking and all the other work? You know I would help if I could move."

"You're an amazing guy, you know that?" Parker said as he gripped the rear handles of the chair and Jess and Jack each grabbed a handgrip on either side of the front. They picked their way down the well-worn path and soon had Rich on the deck, staring out at Lake Winnipesaukee, where Brad Wallace had supplied him with his unwelcome version of destiny. It was only then that he answered Parker.

"No. Actually I don't think I'm so amazing at all." Then Becky appeared with his beer and held it for him as he guzzled it, their years together allowing her to time his swallows perfectly.

As soon as they were alone for the first time, Josie and Parker agreed on something else. It was going to be difficult to tell their friends about Brad's survival.

SUNDAY EVENING, AFTER THE final barbeque of the season, the six friends were joined by Gordon Tibideau, who normally would have been patrolling the lake on the last big weekend of the season. When Parker called and asked him to come to the cookout, he joked about how much his supervisor would love losing his ace lake patrolman for Sunday afternoon on Labor Day Weekend. With so many boaters pulling their crafts from the water on Sunday to get an early start on the traffic the next day, Gordon allowed that perhaps he could join them for a nightcap. Parker wanted him there for two reasons and he knew it. First of all, they had not gotten together during the weekend and both missed the connection, but more importantly, Gordon could fill in a few of the missing pieces of the Brad Wallace mystery and lend some moral support to his good friend.

Josie finished serving the drinks just in time for everyone to sit in silence, awestruck once again by the beauty of one of Lake Winnipesaukee's renowned sunsets. The lake had calmed after the hectic activity of the day, and the sprinkling of clouds on the horizon heightened the effect of the reflections on the water. Audible sighs escaped from the group when the sun began its final plunge, disappearing in seconds and creating the illusion of sinking directly into the lake. Rich commented that he felt as though they were watching a fireworks display with all the oohs and aahs, bringing chuckles and smiles all around.

Parker reached for Josie's hand. After a mutual squeeze, he cleared his throat loudly enough that the others looked at him.

"I've got something I have to tell you and I've been waiting for just the right moment but there hasn't been one. And this isn't even a good time but you're going to hear it sometime so you might as well here it now." The relaxed composure brought on by the drinks, the sunset, and the pure joy of being with long-time friends vanished, replaced by uneasiness as Jess stood, Jack started tapping his feet, and Becky slid her chair even closer to Rich.

No one said a word until Parker continued. "Brad's not dead," he announced. "He somehow survived and is probably living somewhere in Connecticut." He told them the whole story, calling upon Gordon to supply details about the fruitless search for Brad's body and their visit to Brad's house and finding the newspaper. Josie's described finding the nail in the mailbox and discovering that Brad, Jr.'s gravesite had been trimmed. Parker ended it.

"That's where it stands right now. I'm really sorry to put a damper on the weekend but Josie and I thought you should know."

Dusk encroached on the deck, the timing coinciding perfectly with the pall of melancholy settling over the gathering. The stunned silence held for several minutes, each of them alone with their thoughts. Then Rich broke the spell.

"This is too weird. I just found out that an old friend who I thought was dead is actually alive. Why the hell am I not happy about it?" His voice broke, then became more intense. "Not only am I not happy but I'm thoroughly pissed off. I thought we were rid of the bastard. Let's go in, Becky."

Without a word, Becky stood and spun Rich's wheelchair around and pushed it up the handicap ramp. When she got to the entrance, she turned, shrugged her shoulders, and made her way into the house.

"I'm back on it on Tuesday," Parker announced to the three friends remaining on the deck, two of whom still seemed to be in shock.

AFTER A LONG WEEKEND of perfect weather, Labor Day dawned overcast and damp with the threat of a cold rain falling later in the day. Summer in the deep forests, pristine lakes, and stunning mountains of New Hampshire casts an almost magical spell over the natives and the tourists, but the reality of the approaching harsh winter usually followed shortly after the last weekend of the season. Neither a night's sleep nor the weather served to improve the mood of the Havenots' guests. Despite a hearty breakfast of eggs, bacon, hash browns, and toast dished out by Josie, the usual friendly bantering was missing. The ghost of Brad Wallace had intruded on the weekend but in a far different way than Rich or anyone could have predicted. The teachers in the group normally would have clung to the last day before the new school year like a child squeezes out every extra minute before bedtime, but Jess and Jack came out of their room with suitcases and backpacks in hand.

"We're going to get an early start; you know, beat the traffic, especially with the weather," Jess offered, averting Josie's glance. "But we'll eat breakfast first," he added, the sizzle of bacon and its aroma permeating the kitchen.

A few minutes later, Becky appeared, full of apologies. "Rich is anxious to get going," she explained, then moved closer to Josie. "He's still pretty upset; maybe confused is a better word, as are we all," she whispered. "It's a little strange finding out that the memorial service you recently attended turns out to be for a person who isn't even dead."

Parker's arrival at the table was greeted with mumbled "good mornings" and the rattle of forks on plates as breakfast was devoured. He noticed the luggage stacked at the back door and drew the correct conclusion.

"Looks as though people are bailing out early. That's probably a good idea. Three-quarters of the people in New Hampshire for the weekend will be on the road with this weather," he said with a smile. No smiles were returned. Something had to be said.

"Look, folks, it's apparent I made a mistake telling you about Brad without having an ending to the story. I've upset you and I apologize for that. However, the old saying about shooting the messenger might apply here. I thought you'd want to know." He didn't smile this time.

The looks of chagrin around the table matched the mood. Rich spoke first.

"We're the ones who should be apologizing, Parker. You did the right thing. It's just such a shock. I don't think any of us blame you for anything. It's like wanting to know about a friend's terminal illness. You need to know but you sure don't want to." He chuckled and the sound of it relieved the tension as surely as a pin prick lets the air out of a balloon. "If I could, I'd give you a hug," he said.

An hour later, Josie and Parker found themselves alone in the cabin. After a quick cleanup, they packed and were on the road toward home, she to prepare for the first official day of school and he to find Brad Wallace and figure out what to do about John Simms. Their thoughts about the next day didn't interfere with a lengthy conversation, consuming most of the drive home. Some of the discussion focused on their friends' reaction to the news that Brad likely was alive and well and living in Connecticut, news they seemed to accept about as well as they would accept the news that Elvis was alive and well and living like J. D. Salinger in Hampton Village. Most of the ride was consumed with Josie's curiosity as to what Parker would be doing on Tuesday morning. There were issues on every front. Where was Brad? Was there a connection between Brad and Simms? Where did Univac Redux enter the picture, if at all?

"And finally," Josie asked with a mischievous grin, "how is my brilliant detective going to connect all the dots. Alison Regan, Brad Wallace, John Simms, and Henry Bouchard are waiting for you. As the heroine in all those movies we watch always says, 'be careful,' as if there was another choice."

Tuesday

PARKER ONCE AGAIN ARRIVED at the office one hour before he was expected. His first phone call rousted Alison Regan from her bed. When she answered a sleepy "hello," he didn't bother with the formalities.

"Any problems since last we spoke, Miss Regan?" he asked.

When she realized who was calling and the bluntness of the message, she laughed out loud. "It's seven o'clock in the morning, Detective," she said, placing a sarcastic emphasis on the word detective. "Thought we agreed to be a little less formal, but, to answer your question, no, I haven't had any problems. John hasn't been in contact with me at all, not that I expected him to be. I guess I could ask you the same question but I won't."

Parker asked for and received her permission to interview Dr. Simms once again, stressing that he would keep her involvement to a minimum. She agreed without hesitation. "As long as you keep me in the loop," she added as an afterthought.

The cliché about most of humanity being creatures of habit contains a substantial amount of truth. Parker counted on Doctor John Simms being one of those creatures. He signed out with the dispatcher at 11:45, allowing just enough time to arrive at the doctor's office at 12:15. His previous experience told him that Simms would be at lunch.

As he approached the door, he was faced with a decision. He

was prepared with an explanation for the visit should the doctor, for whatever reason, not be at lunch but he wanted the element of surprise to work in his favor with Clarisse Shearer. Using tactics that come from years of police work, Parker slipped into the waiting room without making a sound. He left the door ajar and crept across the room. The receptionist sat at her desk, a brown bag lunch set out in front of her. She had just put her coffee cup down when he tapped on the window. Startled, she spun her chair around and came out of it virtually in a single motion. When she saw Parker standing at the window, she stopped and stared. Her stare turned to a glowering gaze as she went directly to the door and confronted him in the waited room.

"What are you doing here, Detective? You didn't even call. Has common courtesy not occurred to you?" Clarisse flushed scarlet, her face tight-lipped and pinched.

"I wondered if the doctor happened to be in. Something's come up that I need to ask him about." Parker watched for any sign of a diversionary maneuver.

"You know this is his lunch hour. Maybe I could save you the trouble of making an appointment to see him. What is it you wanted? If you have to see him in person, I could get you in sometime later in the week." She smirked as if knowing that she had the upper hand.

Without answering, Parker reached into his inside jacket pocket and took out a creased five by seven photo. He kept it folded, waiting for some response. When there was none, he unfolded it and slid it back and forth along his pant leg to smooth the crease, keeping it face down.

The waiting finally caught up with Clarisse. "What is that?" she asked.

Parker positioned the photo so that he could expose it to her all at once and watch her reaction. When he was satisfied that it was time, he turned the picture over.

"Have you seen this person recently?" He cradled it in both hands at shoulder height and watched for any sort of reaction.

She looked away from the photo immediately. "Have you never heard of physician/patient confidentiality, Detective?"

"So, you have seen him recently. How long ago, if I may ask?" Parker had dropped his interrogational tone, his voice now in friendly conversational mode.

"I didn't say that. Now I'm going back to my lunch. Please call later to make an appointment to speak with Doctor Simms." She executed a partial pirouette and marched toward her office.

"Does the doctor do any work for a man named Henry Bouchard, by any chance?" Parker shouted just as the door was closing. The question stopped her and for a second, the door paused. Then, it slammed with a vengeance.

As Parker left, he noticed that she had not gone to her desk but headed directly into the doctor's examination room. He strode to the stairs and a minute later was sitting in a covered bus stop on Highland Avenue with a perfect view of the office building he had just exited. As he expected, Clarisse Shearer came hurrying out shortly, heading toward John Simms's favorite park bench.

"THEY'RE ON TO US."

Henry Bouchard regretted recruiting John Simms almost from the first insertion, when he practically dissuaded the client from having the procedure because he was so nervous. He had become more confident with each one but he seemed to be developing similar paranoid tendencies to most of their users. Now this phone call . . .

"Calm down and tell me exactly who and what you are talking about." Bouchard listened intently as Simms related the details of Parker Havenot's visit to Clarisse Shearer. A reasonable enough explanation could be found for showing her the photo of Brad Wallace. Ten minutes of research had told him that Wallace had not been declared dead because his body had never been found in that New Hampshire lake. Since Havenot and Wallace's wife were now married, it was understandable that the detective would have an interest in that.

"So, he has a photo of Brad that he's flashing around. That doesn't mean that he is, as you say, on to us. Now, what else have you got?" Bouchard's famous lack of patience crept into his voice.

"He asked if I ever did any work for you. Where in the fuck would that come from? He's got to be fishing but how could he ever put our two names together?" Simms's anxiety rose to a level to match Bouchard's impatience when there was no response forthcoming. He could almost hear Bouchard thinking.

"There are two common denominators here, Simms."

The doctor cringed at the level of disrespect. What other doctor gets called by his last name? "And they are . . . ?"

"Brad Wallace and your girlfriend. It's that simple. And guess who the common denominator between those two is?"

AFTER HIS PRODUCTIVE VISIT with Clarisse Shearer, Parker decided a call to his favorite gynecologist was in order. Her textbook reactions to his questions told him everything he needed to know. People tend to forget that non-answers are often better used to ferret out the truth than evasive ones. The uncooperative receptionist provided him with the motivation to move forward.

Peter Capaldi would be busy with patients until at least four o'clock. Parker spent the afternoon catching up with mounting paperwork on his desk as he waited for the return call. He shifted his work from the in basket to the out basket and his desk assumed some semblance of order. The folder with Sam Olden's library research lay exposed in front of him. Never wanting to be unprepared, he decided to read the material again before talking with Peter. All of the articles were printed out on eight and a half by eleven sheets and, as he skimmed through the articles that he knew well, he noticed a small piece that he hadn't read before.

The headline read COMPANY OWNER KIDNAPPED and Parker figured that Sam had made a mistake including it. The article, with no byline but with a Mexico City location, described the kidnapping of an executive of a company specializing in development of miniature computer chips designed to locate stolen automobiles. The CEO of the company was quoted in the second paragraph. "We will be devoting considerable attention to finding out a way to track stolen human beings after this," he said, closing with the familiar cliché. "We're years away from that," he concluded.

Parker closed the folder but set the article aside.

"What if Univac Redux isn't?" he said to himself.

At ten after four, his intercom buzzed. "Dr. Capaldi for you, sir, on line 1."

"Heard somebody put some nails in your tire," Parker said to open the conversation, a reference to the incident that originally brought them together years before, an incident fresh in the detective's mind after Brad's recent delivery to their mailbox. It was Havenot who figured out that it was Brad who tried to administer his warped sense of justice to the doctor whom he blamed for the stillbirth of his infant son.

"Not very funny, Detective. That wasn't exactly a memorable event in my career." Peter chuckled. "Actually, I guess it was kind of funny—an adolescent prank played by a grown man."

"He knew exactly what he was doing with those so-called pranks—in truth, it was a pretty sick series of incidents. But, anyway, I've got what may be a nice job for you, should you choose to accept, of course," making it sound like something from *Mission Impossible*.

In a short time, Peter Capaldi realized what his friend was asking. Like any good listener does, he repeated the request to make sure he hadn't misunderstood.

"So, you're going to bring a beautiful young woman into my office and my sole job is to search her body for some sort of device, which might be implanted anywhere. She doesn't know where this thing is and we're not even sure if there is anything there. I spend a lot of time examining women, Parker, but my nurse is always in the room. You're saying the nurse won't be necessary. Do you want to pay my malpractice insurance this month? So, is that basically it?" Before Peter finished with his description, Havenot began to laugh. It did sound ludicrous, at best, and plain crazy at worst.

"I've saved the best part for last." Havenot was still laughing at hearing his proposal repeated back to him. "I haven't told her what we want to do yet." They were both still giggling when Parker promised to get back to him as soon as possible, then hung up.

ALISON ARRANGED A SMALL plate of cheese and crackers and had just poured a glass of wine when the phone rang.

"Hope this isn't a bad time. I'm just trying to get something set up before the day is out."

"My day is out already, Detective. What can I do for you now?"

Parker led her through the entire scenario, even mentioning in a vague way the possibility that her former boyfriend might be involved in something far more nefarious than just stalking her. He was getting used to long silences on the phone lately but this one extended well beyond anything close to normal. He thought maybe she had used her finger to disconnect the call but there had been no click.

"I'll do it," she whispered into the phone. "I can't believe what you're asking but I'll do it, if only for the fact that maybe John could do the same thing to other women. If what you are saying is true, I hope there are laws on the books to cover it. When is my doctor's appointment, Detective?"

"I'll set it up for after working hours tomorrow if that's all right with you." He felt that he had to say something else, out of gratitude if nothing else. "You'll like Dr. Capaldi. I've known him for a long time."

"You've never been to a gynecologist, have you?" He could almost see her smiling on the other end of the line. "Just let me know when and where and I'll be there." She hung up.

Turning Point

HENRY BOUCHARD REFUSED TO believe that anyone on the outside could have determined what the TRAC division of Univac Redux was doing. While he knew, as he explained to Brad Wallace, that the company he owned was small compared to those in the 128 corridor outside of Boston, he also knew that the few full-time research scientists he employed were among the best and most loyal in the country. They were the ones who discovered the methodology to power the chips; they were the ones who realized that the GPS satellites were the best system to use for tracking purposes; they were the ones who hadn't let their best kept secrets become known to competitors. To them, and only to them, the "years away" claim of other companies was a convenient myth.

The mandatory morning meeting with everyone connected to the TRAC program would serve as a reminder of just how important it was to the company as a whole that the project remain confidential. He planned his business style pep talk primarily for the scientists, throwing in current buzz words and phrases as industrial espionage, government overreach, and bureaucratic red tape slowing the wheels of progress. Bouchard had a reputation as an effective motivator and he was at his best. When the meeting, which was really just a one-man speech, concluded, the room came alive with excitement. Animated conversation spilled over into the hallways as the scientists returned to work. Tommy

Maggio, Travis Connally, Brad Wallace, John Simms, and Thomas Gomes, instructed to remain after the meeting, all moved forward to the vacated seats.

"We have twelve charges right now, and I anticipate that the number will grow to at least double that as people find out how effective the program is. The way things are heading in this country, we'll soon be like Mexico where even the middle class live in fear of being kidnapped. It's big business down there now and I see no reason for it to get better." While everyone else was sitting, Bouchard stood, his superiority not in question. He noticed Tommy waving his hand like a teacher's pet in a classroom, eager to be recognized.

"What is it?" Bouchard growled at the interruption.

"We actually have thirteen charges, sir, with the one Dr. Simms added." He looked at Simms, who reacted as though he had been shoved by the playground bully.

"We're deciding what to do about that right after we finish here. My question is this. Can we handle more charges with the personnel we have? You folks have been great but I don't want to push the issue."

This time, it was Travis Connally who answered. "It won't be a problem, Mr. Bouchard, unless Simms decides to add more." Simms had just recovered from the first verbal shove when this one struck him.

Before the doctor had a chance to react, Bouchard dismissed the trackers but asked Brad to stay behind. "Thanks for your input," he said, "and thanks again for your great work. Could you close the door on your way out, Travis?"

John Simms waited until they were gone and then jumped to his feet. "I don't have to take that. Those guys know that I . . ." He noticed Bouchard staring at him and holding out his hand, palm up like a traffic cop.

"Yes, you do. Now sit down and tell us what you suggest we do about 0605GERILA."

PARKER HAVENOT THOUGHT IT best if Alison have an escort

to her appointment with Peter Capaldi. Since he had made the request, he appointed himself her guardian for the early evening. When he called to tell her that he would be picking her up for her examination, she adamantly refused. "Just tell me where it is and when I'm supposed to get there. That's all I need to know. Oh, and by the way, how long do you think it will take?"

Peter Capaldi couldn't have counted how many exams he conducted over his stellar career as a GYN. He figured it must be in the thousands but he never had performed an all-body search for anything, let alone some sort of nebulous device hidden beneath the skin. He let Parker know that he wasn't going to spend much time, especially without his nurse in the room.

"Dr. Capaldi thought it might take ten minutes, if that," Parker said. He gave her the address of Capaldi's office and said he would see her around six o'clock. "I'll wait for you at the entrance to the building."

BRAD COULD SEE JOHN Simms's point. Alison Regan might be the cause of the failure of TRAC. If he were truthful with himself, Simms was the cause with his own stupidity and jealousy but he had joined the team, buying into Bouchard's philosophy. There were evil people in this world and they were winning so you did what you could to stop them, even if meant protecting some who did not deserve it.

He glanced at his watch. It was only ten thirty and he did not have to report to work until twelve. Josie would be at school and Parker was certain to be at work or off doing some protecting of his own. It would be a good time for a visit to Brad, Jr.'s grave. He was badly in need of some refreshing.

With little traffic on the road, the trip from the offices of Univac Redux to Hampton Village took just fifteen minutes. He saw no need to be as cautious as he was the last time he drove through his old neighborhood and did not circle any blocks before maneuvering his nondescript Ford Escort sedan straight down Sycamore Street. As he passed his house, his gut clenched at the memories but this time he did not slow the car, heading directly toward Mountain View Cemetery just a mile ahead. The familiar entrance beckoned him with an urgency he had not felt before, the stone archangels on each side appearing to wave him in as if they were expecting him. He parked in his usual place and took a cursory scan of the surroundings. There were no other visitors in sight.

Over the years since he had buried Brad, Jr. and his parents, the cemetery had expanded. Where the grave had been on the last row, it now lay surrounded by stones and markers of every size and description, but Brad could have walked right to it with his eyes closed. He arrived at his infant son's grave, anticipating that he would have to do some grass trimming again as the late summer had produced a copious amount of rain. Instead, the edges of the familiar marker were evenly cut, obviously with a tool of some sort, unlike his hand trimming during his first visit. "Someone's been here to see you, son. I wonder who that might have been," he said in conversational tone. He reached into his back pocket, pulled out a handkerchief, and spread it on the ground. He knelt down on one knee then started his first soliloquy since what he was calling his return from the dead.

As it had so often in the past, the accustomed blackness descended and he began to speak.

"I've still got some work to do, Brad," he said, his head bowed to the grave. "I thought it would start with your . . . " His composure vanished; his shoulders sagged and he brought his hand to his eyes, trying to stem the flow of tears. When he recovered, he managed to finish the sentence. ". . . Your stepfather, I guess he would be, but that may have to wait. We've got a more immediate problem to solve. We'll just do what we've always done. Try to start something in motion and let the rest take care of itself. I feel bad about Ms. Regan but something's got to be done and someone's got to do it. I guess it's just that simple, right?" Brad rose from his kneeling position and his knees made a series of cracking sounds. Once again, he checked the cemetery for possible visitors as he smiled down at the stone. "Not as young as I used to be, son, but young enough to still accomplish something."

Twenty minutes later, he was at his console at TRAC when the phone rang. It was John Simms. His voice indicated that he was in his usual panic mode.

"Something's happening tonight, Brad. I just spoke with Alison at work with some excuse about leaving something at her apartment and asked her if I could stop by this evening. She said that after tonight, she might know if she'd ever let me near her again. I have no idea what that means but it's not good."

"We'll just make sure she doesn't go anywhere tonight after work. Then we'll figure out what's going on. I'll take care of it but I'll need someone to cover for me here." Brad already had a plan in mind, one that would make Havenot take notice, as if he hadn't already.

"I'm sure Bouchard can get Maggio or Connally. I'll handle that part. Just let me know what you're up to."

"Will do," Brad said, although he had no intention to do so.

At 6:15, Parker started pacing. To others passing by, he looked like an average husband trying to find just the right birthday gift for his wife, idly window shopping in the stores on the street level of Capaldi's office building. Nothing in any of the windows registered as he kept searching up and down the street for Alison Regan. He gave it five more minutes then went back into the building. As he approached the single elevator, the door opened and Peter Capaldi stepped out.

"She's not coming," he announced. "She just called to say she had car trouble and can't make it."

"Shit!" Parker's exclamation earned him icy glares from two women walking across the lobby. "What kind of car trouble? Can I go pick up her up? Why didn't she call a cab or a garage or something?"

Peter recited the conversation exactly as he remembered it and it wasn't until he got to the last part that his eyes registered a moment of disbelief. "She said she was pretty shaken, Parker, because she had not one but four flat tires when she went to her car to come over here."

"Son of a bitch!" The two women had reached the automatic door, but instead of going through it, they turned with hands on hips and stared at him. He was oblivious to them. "That's a Brad Wallace MO. What in the hell is going on here?"

"I don't know but I do know you're going to get me kicked out of my building it you don't calm down. Why don't we go back upstairs and talk about it?" Just then, the elevator door opened; it was empty and the two men hurried in.

The trip to the third floor gave Parker time enough to walk several circles around the perimeter as if he was searching for a way out. When they finally reached the doctor's office, he had calmed considerably but still Peter had never seen him so agitated. When he asked to use the phone, the doctor just shrugged. He pulled a rumpled piece of paper from his inside jacket pocket and was dialing even before he had smoothed it out. When Alison answered, he simply said, "we'll be right over," then hung up.

"I want you to come with me so I can fill you in on over twenty years of Bradford Wallace, some if which you know but an awfully lot that you don't. Then we'll see if we can talk Ms. Regan into having her exam after all. It just became more important."

THE FIFTEEN-MINUTE CONVERSATION DURING the ride to Alison Regan's apartment convinced Peter Capaldi that his detective friend was right. They were dealing with a psychopath. Parker provided a chronological catalogue of the spiraling descent of Brad Wallace into a dangerously unhealthy mental state.

"You didn't start it but you were the first to bear the brunt of his frustrations with an actual physical act," Parker started out. "According to Josie, he's always had an explosive side when he feels things that are happening are totally unfair."

Peter interrupted with an observation. "You're referring to him in the present tense. I thought you told me he drowned himself in that big lake up in New Hampshire." Havenot dismissed the claim in his usual succinct manner.

"He's not dead, nowhere near it." For the remainder of the ride, Peter Capaldi sat quietly and just listened.

"It really started, according to Josie, at least, with a buddy of his." Parker launched into the story of Tyler Spence, an idealistic teacher friend of the Wallaces, who was drafted and subsequently killed in Vietnam. "After that, Josie lost the baby, which, of course, you know about. She said he blamed you entirely for that and he nearly killed you with his nails-in-your-tires prank. I'd have to say that was probably the worst. I watched him visit that grave one day and it seemed like he was having a conversation with it. Weird . . . "

Parker continued the catalogue, including the traffic deaths of Brad's parents caused by a drunk driver. "He managed to take care of Robert Snyder, using yet another variation on the tire theme, just popping the valve and anonymously letting the police know that the drunk driver who killed his parents was drunk and on the highway again. The list goes on and on but this guy progressively got worse, believing he was making things right."

Out of the corner of his eye, he could see Peter shaking his head. "The guy led two lives—great educator and small-scale vigilante. That is, until after his forced retirement when he was ready to sink a damn boatload of people, just to get even with the superintendent and a few others who he believed had screwed him."

They pulled into the parking lot of Alison's complex. Her car was unmistakable. It was the only one sitting on four flat tires. Parker backed into a space near her forlorn Subaru and flipped off the ignition. He turned to face Peter.

"There's a lot more to tell but you can guess where this is going. Somehow, I think he survived and I don't think his near-death experience in Lake Winnipesaukee changed him a bit. If anything, he's more dangerous than ever."

They exited the car and Parker went directly to Alison's car, leaving the doctor staring after him. He knelt down by the front wheel and unscrewed the cap of the valve and a faint brief hiss of air escaping told him what he suspected would be the case. The valve was missing. He didn't even bother to check the others.

"It's the same thing he did to Robert Snyder, the guy I told you about, the one who killed his parents," he said when he returned to Peter Capaldi, who remained in place, gaping like someone who couldn't believe what he was seeing. "Let's go see what Ms. Regan has to say."

ALISON STOOD IN THE foyer, apparently having seen them arrive from her window and likely observed the detective examining her car. Parker introduced Peter, the occasion not calling for formality but his personal principles dictated that the introduction be proper.

"Dr. Peter Capaldi, Alison. This is the doctor I told you about."

Alison extended her hand and completed the introductions herself. "Alison Regan," she said, then with a forced smile, "I don't usually have two such distinguished visitors at the same time. Of course, the detective didn't give me much choice when he called. Come on up." She escorted them to her apartment. Parker noticed her fishing in her pocket and extracting a set of keys fit for a janitor of the building. When they got to the door, she unlocked the deadbolt first, and then the built-in knob lock. She sensed the reaction behind her and called over her shoulder.

"A girl can't be too careful, you know. Sit anywhere you'd like. I'd offer you something to drink but I'm sure you'd rather just get down to business."

For a moment, there was some awkward fumbling as they looked around the room. The three most likely seats formed a nice conversation arrangement but neither man seemed to want to be seated on the love seat with Alison. She assured them with a smile that they weren't in any danger and Peter finally sat down.

"So, what do you make of this, Detective?" It did not take a trained law enforcement interrogator to see through her bravado. Alison Regan was worried. She asked the question while sitting straight up and she did not relax while waiting for an answer.

"There are a good many coincidences that seem to be going on and not all of them involve your Dr. Simms." Parker realized the mistake immediately but it was too late.

"He's not my Dr. Simms!" Alison bristled. "And if he had anything to do with this, I hope to God he goes to prison."

Parker's experience assumed control and his calming voice

had the desired effect on Alison. "I'm sorry; that just sort of slipped out. We don't think Simms flattened your tires but I'm not sure I could say in good conscience that he had nothing to do with it."

"He seemed pretty much the same as always when he called earlier today . . ." She stopped when Parker came out of his chair.

"You talked to him today?" The intimidation factor in his voice combined with his looming presence standing over her forced her back into the soft upholstery of the love seat. "Did you mention anything about what you were going to do tonight?" He sat down but on the edge of the chair.

"No, not really." The hesitation in her voice contradicted her. "Well, actually I did mention that after tonight, I might know whether I'd ever see him again, something like that. He pisses me off, Detective. That's all. I'm sorry."

Peter Capaldi sat watching this conversation careen back and forth as if he were watching a tennis match. He was entirely out of his element and becoming more uncomfortable by the second. When Alison left the sofa, he did also. What she said sat him down again.

"Here's what we'll do. You'll drive me to Dr. Capaldi's office and we'll do the damn examination tonight. You said to let you handle this, Detective, but if something's going on that involves me and my personal safety, I'd like to know about it."

Parker smiled. "Is that all right with you, Dr. Capaldi?"

The doctor smiled in return, glad to be back in his comfort zone. "Fine with me," he said.

THE EXAMINATION TOOK LESS than the anticipated ten minutes. Peter Capaldi wasn't a dermatologist but he knew about the female anatomy. Before examining Alison, he asked her if she ever did any unofficial scans for the early signs of skin cancer and self-exams for breast cancer or any unusual lumps. Satisfied that he would not find whatever it was that Parker was looking for in any obvious places, he asked her to put on the modesty gown with instructions to knock on the door when she was ready. He left the room and waited outside with his detective friend who obviously was enjoying this much more than he was.

"You owe me big time, and not just a cheap lunch, either."

"What, I arrange a physical exam with a beautiful young woman and you're not happy with me? I thought I was doing you a favor."

Before Peter could respond, a loud knock echoed throughout the waiting room.

"So, you said this thing could be the size of a kernel of rice, right?"

"Yep. Good luck and no dawdling." He smiled but the doctor did not.

Parker, standing the whole time, had leafed through about half of an issue of *Sports Illustrated* when the door opened. He peeked over the magazine to face a shocked doctor, his face tinged pink, warming to a full-fledged blush. He held out his right hand, still gloved, his fingers bent inward as if protecting an injured hummingbird.

"Here it is, Parker. I don't believe it, but here it is." The transmitter lay in the lifeline cutting across Capaldi's palm.

"A fortune teller would have a field day with this. Looks like a major event in your life."

"How the hell can you fool around now? Sometimes I worry about you!"

"Joking around at a time like this keeps me sane, if you must know. Now where can I find an envelope or something to make sure I don't drop it and lose it?"

The door opened and Alison stepped out, looking haggard. "Could you take me home now, please?" was all she said.

Still cradling the chip in his hand, Peter went into the examining room and came out with a plastic bag and a paper towel. He spread the towel on a table and gently set the chip down.

"It's in your hands now. Just unbelievable . . ." He was still muttering when the door closed behind him.

Parker wrapped the towel around the precious transmitter, folded each edge, then put it in the bag.

"Come on, Alison, I'll take you home."

The Chip

PARKER DETAILED THE EVENTS of the evening to Josie, thinking that sharing them might relieve some of the tension surrounding them. He was mistaken. After a night of fitful sleep, he awoke with a jolt at 5:30 in the morning and immediately snapped the night table lamp on. He pulled open the top drawer and felt around among its few contents until he found the plastic bag. After dropping Alison at her apartment and confirming that everything was secure, he decided not to make the trip to his office to put the chip in the safe. It may turn out to be evidence but at this point there wasn't any break in the chain since he was the only one who had possession. Still, having it in his house created an inherent tension. The rest of the tension arose out of his quandary as to how he was going to handle the next step.

THE EARLY MORNING CALL on his unlisted private phone unnerved Brad. Only Henry Bouchard and John Simms knew the number. He had told them not to call it unless there was a dire emergency. Simms's request to come to his office right away had an edge that left no room for asking why. Even with the morning rush hour traffic, Brad walked into the office in record time.

"She didn't go anywhere, at least not in her car. I didn't hang around to check but my well-educated guess is that she was homebound the entire night." Brad, thinking of Havenot's reaction, had chuckled as the air blew out of the tires on Alison's car. Now, as he explained his method of keeping her at home to Simms, a creeping doubt slithered into his consciousness and he needed to voice it. The flat tires may not have kept her home at all.

Travis Connally was on the twelve to eight shift at TRAC and a minute later, Simms had him on the phone. Without any greeting other than "this is Simms," he ordered a report on 0605GERILA.

"We actually had a problem with that charge last night, Simms."

The strain between the two men was continually exacerbated by the lack of the simple courtesy of calling him doctor and Simms let him know about it. "For the last time, it's Doctor Simms, and what the hell do you mean, you had a problem with the charge?"

"It went offline. Transmission power started fading about eight o'clock or so and was gone fifteen minutes later. Since it's your charge, I'm sure you can fix it, Simms."

John Simms lost the minimal control he had of his temper. "Just give me the last location, if it's not too much fucking trouble. And I'm sure Mr. Bouchard will be interested in your uncooperative attitude."

"Power fade began in a building downtown, houses shops and offices, then was gone completely on a Sycamore Drive in Hampton Village. Didn't get a number. And by the way, Simms, Mr. Bouchard isn't exactly a fan of yours." Travis slammed the receiver down.

"Where the hell is Sycamore Drive in Hampton Village? You have any idea?"

"I'm afraid I do," Brad said.

PARKER WENT DIRECTLY TO the evidence storage room. He had practically kept his hand on the bag in his pocket the whole time he was driving to work. It was a relief to have an official bag passed to him and he labeled it: *Chip removed from rear buttock area of Alison Regan, John Simms case. Friday, September 11, 1992. Evidence collected 9/10/1992.*

The officer in charge sealed it and signed his name. Parker

walked back to his office at a leisurely pace, considering his next move.

BOUCHARD HAD TO BE informed. If the chip was in the hands of the detective, TRAC would be in jeopardy. The critical question, at least as far as John Simms was concerned, was who would do the informing?

"You seem to have a connection with him; I'm not sure how or why but there's no doubt it's there. He'll take the news better from you." Simms couldn't imagine his conversation with Bouchard. Brad Wallace ignored his plea with a dismissive "you got yourself into this now you can get yourself out of it."

"I can't tell him something like this over the phone. I'm going to drive over to his office and make it face-to-face. If we go together, it'll be easier."

Brad glared at him. "This thing is about to fall apart and I'm not getting caught in the middle of it all. Havenot's a smart guy with a good memory. He knows by now that I'm responsible for that woman's tires. It's time for me to go back to being dead. Tell Bouchard I appreciate what he's trying to do but as of now, I'm out of it. I've got other things to do. He owes me some money and he can get it to me the normal way, if he wants to. You folks won't be seeing me again."

He turned and walked out the door, leaving a dumbfounded John Simms staring after him.

PARKER KNOCKED AND SHERIFF Jim Corbett, who lived up to his nickname of Gentleman Jim after the famous boxer, called for him to come in. Since Parker had joined the department, the two had formed a comfortable bond, never close friends but with the mutual respect that comes from two competent and talented lawmen doing their jobs. Parker's experience in the Major Crimes Division of the Philadelphia Police Department provided a resource unequalled in Covington County and surrounding areas while Corbett's ability to juggle rural crime needs and an unwieldy political structure earned his detective's admiration. Gentleman Jim could not have been prepared for the issue his ace detective was about to present. It was not going to be a short story and Parker closed the door behind him. His expression and demeanor had the sheriff reaching for the phone. He informed dispatch to hold his calls until further notice.

THE SHERIFF KNEW MOST of the background of the story so Parker began with the bizarre weekend in New Hampshire at the beginning of August that ended with the apparent death of Brad Wallace. He guided his colleague through the maze of discoveries during the weeks since then that led him to the conclusion that Josie's ex-husband was not dead. The sheriff listened, never asking a single question during that section of the narrative. However, he couldn't keep quiet when Parker began his explanation of the possible connection between John Simms, Alison Regan, Brad Wallace, and Univac Redux.

"Parker, my friend," he said, a salutation that always preceded some difficult questions. "I respect the hell out of you but you're asking me to believe in what can't even be called a startling coincidence, more like an impossible one. Look, without belaboring the point, here are the players based on what you've told me so far— an unethical and insecure doctor, the doctor's paranoid girlfriend who's being followed all the time, a man who is on the verge of being declared dead, and a large corporation which may or may not be engaged in illegal activity. And these are all connected." The sheriff grinned, his point made. Parker grinned back at him.

"Do you want to hear the rest of the story? It'll make your day."

Gentleman Jim nodded. "Of course! This is the most fun I've had in a long time."

Parker commenced to tell him about the appointment with Peter Capaldi and Alison's tires, mentioning that Brad Wallace seemed to have a juvenile thing with flattening people's tires. He ended by describing his sole piece of physical evidence that could change all of the improbabilities into possibilities.

"Seriously? You actually have one of these things in your possession?"

"Came right out of Ms. Regan's backside. Apologies for being crude but she's been amazingly cooperative."

When the two men finally emerged from the office, the curious eyes of the other officers followed their progress down the hall toward the evidence room.

HENRY BOUCHARD TOLD HIS secretary to keep Dr. Simms with her until he called back. After a brief call to Professor Gomes, he allowed Simms into his office. The grim set to the doctor's face did not bode well.

"Gomes is coming right over. I'm not sure what this is about but the fact that you showed up without an appointment tells me that it must be important and I want Gomes in on it." A long, uncomfortable quietness descended, Simms left to gaze around the well- appointed office while Bouchard sorted through some file folders on his desk. The silence was broken when the intercom buzzed. A few seconds later, Gomes and Bouchard sat staring at Simms.

"It's your meeting. Want to tell us what's on your mind? Perhaps before you do, you should know that I had a call from Travis a while ago. Seems they lost contact with one of the charges. But, anyway, go on, Simms."

At the last comment, the doctor shifted in his seat, fighting off the urge to squirm. The other two men noticed a change in his decorum, as if he had suddenly acquired a degree of dignity that had been lacking. He had obviously made a decision. He squared his shoulders and cleared his throat.

"I have no idea what happened but it appears that the sheriff's department has somehow gotten a hold of the chip that I inserted into 0605GERILA."

"That would be Ms. Regan. Why don't we cut the bullshit here? You're telling us that one of our tracking chips is in the hands of law enforcement, right?"

"That would appear to be the case." Simms hadn't quite finished his sentence when Gomes jumped to his feet and approached him with balled fists, his cheeks reddening with rage.

"Appears to be the case, huh!" he shouted. He turned to Bouchard, who was witnessing the scene playing out before him like a disinterested observer. "We are fucked, Henry, and it's all because of this wimp. I'm telling you, we are screwed over."

Bouchard stepped in only when Gomes appeared ready to attack.

"Sit down, Thomas, and save the theatrics. Dr. Simms is the one who, as you so aptly put it, is fucked. There's been only one unwilling participant in our experimental research, which is what TRAC is about to called, and that participant is a victim of the unscrupulous Dr. John Simms. Univac Redux is a reputable company doing respectable research and we are under no obligation to share specifics."

Henry Bouchard remained seated in his observant mode. His voice came out in a hissed whisper.

"Get out of here, Dr. Simms. And don't look back. I don't like the language but it is so appropriate. You are fucked!"

THE SHERIFF AND DETECTIVE walked briskly to the evidence storage room and signed out the package which Parker had deposited recently. They passed the processing lab on the way back to Corbett's office. The sheriff motioned Parker to stop for a moment; a minute later, he emerged carrying a case.

Back in the office, Parker opened the package and removed the plastic bag. He spread open the paper towel on the sheriff's desk, revealing the miniscule transmitter. Corbett opened the case and removed a microscope and a pair of tweezers. He gently picked up the electronic device and placed it on the display stage. "Plug that cord in, will you, Parker?" He waited, then flipped the light switch.

As he looked through the dual eyepiece, he adjusted first the coarse focus then the fine focus knobs.

"I'll be damned. You've got to see this." He shifted over to allow Parker room to get to the microscope.

"Wow," was all he could say as he hovered over the viewer.

"CANCEL EVERYTHING I HAVE for today, Clarisse," John Simms said as he breezed through the empty waiting room. He said it as if his was a fully functioning medical practice. He disappeared into his office before she had a chance to respond. There was nothing on the morning docket and only a smattering of appointments for the afternoon. The tension trailing after him kept her from following him. After a few minutes, she ventured in, tapping lightly on the door then entering. She was just in time to see him hurl the phone across the room. The cord brought it up short and kept it from smashing against the wall. Alarmed, she began to back out of the room, but he called her back.

"I just called the number an hour ago and now it's disconnected. How can they do that?"

Clarisse's boss looked ready to burst into tears.

"New technology," she said. "The telephone company can turn phones off without even leaving their central offices." She didn't realize that his question had been rhetorical.

"I've got no allies now, not that I was sure Wallace ever qualified for that distinction, but at least I had something on him."

Clarisse had no idea what he meant but chose not to inquire further.

"WE'LL SPEND THE DAY putting the case together," Gentleman Jim told Parker. "By late this afternoon, I'll have the warrants. We'll act on this first thing on Monday morning."

Parker rewarded Corbett with his broadest smile. "This will be fun," he said. "I'll be thinking about it all weekend."

A Doctor Disgraced

SHERIFF JIM CORBETT AND Detective Parker Havenot met for coffee in a small shop on Highland Avenue near the medical office of Dr. John Simms.

"Enjoy the weekend, Parker?" Jim Corbett asked.

"Oh, yeah, but I think I might enjoy today even more."

The aroma of the freshly baked cinnamon buns overwhelmed them and both succumbed to the temptation, extending their stay well beyond what they intended.

Corbett had two warrants in his pocket. John Simms would be placed under arrest on one count of use of a date rape drug, a felony charge for which he could go to prison for up to twenty years. On the same warrant, he would be charged with a more nebulous crime, the so-called invasion of personal privacy by stalking. Although Connecticut had the harshest punishments of all the New England states for stalking, the statutes contained convoluted language involving many different provisions and the sheriff did not hold out much hope for that charge ever being prosecuted. No provision of any law said anything about inserting a tracking device under someone's skin without their knowledge. This was new territory. The second warrant had Brad Wallace's name on it but neither expected to execute that one on this trip.

After discussing what part each would play in the upcoming scenario, they left the shop at 8:45. Five minutes later, they sat side by side in the waiting room, while an apprehensive Clarisse Shearer paced in her cubicle. When they arrived, she tried to call the doctor to give him advanced warning but without success. As expected, the elevator carrying John Simms creaked to a stop outside the door at exactly 9:00.

When he opened the door and saw Havenot standing there, he blanched. When he noticed the second man behind him, it appeared he might run. It was the proverbial "deer-in-the-head-lights" look and the detective caught it and slipped behind him, cutting off the only exit. Sheriff Corbett stepped forward and introduced himself. He reached into his pocket and produced the arrest warrant. While John Simms stood there, perspiration streaming down his face, Gentleman Jim read the charges on the warrant and asked if he understood them. The doctor seemed unable to find his voice and only nodded. Parker then stepped around to face him while the sheriff assumed the exit duty.

The detective reached into his shirt pocket and produced a well-worn three by five card and read Simms his rights. Clarisse had come out into the room but stayed away with the back of her hand pressed against her mouth as if to prevent a scream from escaping. The whole process consumed only two minutes or less but John Simms had not yet uttered a single word. When the sheriff came up and asked him to hold his hands out behind him, he finally found his voice.

"Is that really necessary?" he asked, as Corbett slipped the handcuffs on. "What will people think?"

"I guess they'll think you did something wrong, Doctor," the sheriff replied. "But this is standard operational procedure and I've got no choice since one of the charges is a felony."

Clarisse recovered her voice at about the same time. "What's going on, John? Should I call somebody?" Then, in a shrill voice, "What shall I do?" That plaintive cry aroused Simms from the stupor of his shock.

"No need to do anything right now, and don't worry, I'll be back in no time." The pained expression as they made eye contact did not inspire confidence in her.

The two officers framed Simms between them and hustled him out of the building.

BRAD WALLACE WATCHED AS John Simms was unceremoniously dumped in the back seat of the unmarked police car. From his vantage point in the sandwich shop across the street, he could see that Simms was handcuffed. Simms was a first-class jerk but he didn't deserve that kind of treatment. All he wanted was to keep track of his girlfriend. He figured that once they had their cargo safely ensconced in a jail cell, the next stop would be Univac Redux and Henry Bouchard. When the car pulled away, he crossed the street to the payphone he had used to cancel his phone service. He knew Bouchard's personal number and he spread out a selection of coins on the shelf under the phone. A brief hesitation before the number connected allowed just enough time to drop in the required change. A series of clangs, dings, and assorted other noises preceded the connection. Finally, the phone rang and Bouchard picked it up before the first ring had stopped.

"They've arrested Simms," Brad said. "Just thought you might like a heads up."

"Thanks. He screwed up and now he's going to pay for it. What about you, Brad? What are you going to do?"

"Don't really know for now."

"Well, stay in touch. We might be able to help each other someday." Bouchard disconnected.

THE BOOKING PROCESS FOR John Simms occupied most of the morning. After it was completed, Parker walked down the hall to Jim Corbett's office and peeked in the door. The sheriff's eyes shifted from the paperwork in front of him. The question in them was clear. "What now?"

"I know you've seen more of me in the last twenty-four hours than you cared to, but do you want to get some lunch before we visit Univac Redux?"

Their plan included a surprise afternoon visit to the company headquarters. Henry Bouchard was sure to be there and they agreed it would be better if he didn't have time to plan how he would handle an official call. It would be a casual information gathering expedition.

Corbett accepted the lunch offer. They met in the new Panera Bread restaurant that the sheriff wanted to try. As they had in the morning over coffee and melt-in-your-mouth cinnamon buns, they discussed the strategy for the supposedly impromptu meeting with Bouchard, this time enjoying a first-class noontime meal. It was to be a classic good cop, bad cop routine with Gentleman Jim siding with the local businessman while Havenot harassed the hell out of him. Neither had any idea where the afternoon would lead.

BOTH OF THEM HAD their credentials in hand when the door opened. They were greeted by Gavin, the same man who had set a record for rudeness when Havenot had last visited the premises.

In choreographed fashion, both extended their right arms and opened the palms of their hands, revealing badges in leather cases.

"We're here to see Mr. Bouchard," Parker said, forming his mouth into a thin, grim slit.

After a staring contest worthy of dueling adversaries in an old western movie, Gavin turned on his heels and left without a word.

"That went well, don't you think?" Corbett said with a smile. "I assume that he'll be back, right? And you're correct about feeling like I'm in a nuclear bomb shelter. Real welcoming place they have here."

The door swung open and a voice barked. "This way!" They followed the sound. Nothing had changed since Parker had been there. They were led through the bright office area and Jim Corbett whispered to Parker. "This actually looks pretty normal to me."

Their guide knocked on the dark mahogany door with an ornate nameplate centered between two elaborately carved panels.

HENRY BOUCHARD
OWNER & CHIEF EXECUTIVE OFFICER

"Leaves little doubt who's in charge . . ." Corbett whispered another aside, bringing a fleeting grin to Parker's face.

The door opened and, as before, Henry Bouchard smiled warmly when he saw Havenot. "Well, Detective, to what do we owe the pleasure of this visit? And you've brought a guest along." He turned his attention to the sheriff. "An honor to meet you, sir. I recognize you from your photos in the newspaper." He shook hands with both men then directed them to take a seat. "So, what can I do for you?" he said as he walked around behind the huge desk, establishing a buffer zone between them.

As planned, Parker spoke first.

"Do you employ a doctor named Simms or a man named Brad Wallace?" Without any preface, the questions should have caused at least a ripple of confusion. Both lawmen noticed that it did not. Bouchard had an answer ready.

"Dr. John Simms was on a team of researchers we have, yes. But I've never heard the name Wallace before. Should I have?" Havenot and Corbett exchanged looks. Either Bouchard was telling the truth or he could make a living as an actor.

"I'm sure you wouldn't mind if we checked your employee records," Parker said, adopting his grim face again. Then, it was the good cop's turn.

"Come on, Detective, I'm sure Mr. Bouchard knows his employees, even one who would be pretty far down on the food chain in the company." He looked directly at Bouchard, as if seeking confirmation.

"I take some pride in knowing who works for me, even those who, as you so indelicately put it, are further down the food chain." His deeply furrowed frown showed his annoyance with the phrase.

Havenot assumed the lead once more. He had not uttered a civil word yet.

"Let's talk about Dr. Simms. Was that a slip of the tongue or did you use the past tense to describe his employment?"

"I don't do slips of the tongue, Detective. Dr. Simms's employment here should be in the past tense." The frown seemed frozen in place.

The good cop stepped in to rescue what was a deteriorating situation.

"We're all on the same page here, just trying to figure out what the hell is going on," Jim Corbett said. "We're not accusing you or your colleagues of anything but some things need to be clarified. Truth be told, Simms is the real reason we are here."

He shifted his attention to Havenot. "Show him what you've got, Detective."

As Parker drew the plastic bag from his pocket, Bouchard inched closer, the implacable frown replaced by a mixture of curiosity and concern.

"We thought you might help us with this," Parker said. Creating as much suspense as possible, he deliberately removed the paper towel from the bag. In a prearranged move, Corbett moved nearer and held out his hands in from of him, palms up as if to catch a drink of water from a running faucet. Parker placed the towel in his hands and with movements designed to test the patience of Bouchard, unfolded it. Bouchard watched, his fists clenching and unclenching at his sides.

"Shit!" Bouchard exclaimed when the chip was finally revealed.

"Care to tell what you know about this?" Havenot asked.

Henry Bouchard's composure slipped for an instant but he recovered quickly. After an indignant "Where in the hell did you get this?" he retreated once again behind the bastion of a desk and sat down. Havenot reversed the unfolding process and when the chip was safely back in the bag, he and Corbett did the same.

"We are a research and development company. We conduct many experiments in our facilities and what you are holding is one of them. If that device came from John Simms's girlfriend, then what you have is the reason that he is no longer under contract to us."

The questioning expressions and dead silence forced Bouchard to explain what he meant. He unleashed a stream of consciousness monologue that left him out of breath but clarified the major reasons for the lawmen's confusion. They abandoned the good cop/bad cop routine in the face of the explanation.

"So, Mr. Bouchard, you're telling us that this device is part of an experiment and all of the participants except for Alison Regan know what they are part of." It was the first time that Parker addressed him by name on this visit.

"Simms abused his authority. There is no law against a company carrying out a research project. Haven't you seen offers in the newspaper for people to take part in studies? That's what ours is, Detective. It is a research study and everyone involved is given a privacy guarantee. They're also required to sign an exclusionary promise. You've heard of industrial espionage, right? Our relationship is as sacred as any doctor/patient relationship. The doctor in question used our experiment for personal reasons. That's probably why you arrested him. Now, if you'll excuse me, I do need to get on with my day." He moved from behind his desk with confident strides and escorted them to the door. "If I can do anything more for you, please let me know."

Parker prevented the door from closing like a door-to-door salesman, shoving his foot against the jamb. "What about Brad Wallace?" he asked.

"I told you before. Never heard of him." He turned his back, leaving them no choice but to leave. They crossed the room to the exit, many curious sets of eyes watching them.

It wasn't until they were in the car that either spoke a word. When they did, they said virtually the same thing in unison.

"How in the hell did he know that we had arrested Simms?"

Wallace's List

AFTER WATCHING HAVENOT AND another policeman escort John Simms out of his office building, Brad made the call to Bouchard then hurried back to Farmington. His stomach churned, the image of the doctor being humiliated fresh in his mind. Since his return to Connecticut, he had accomplished nothing. If his survival after the abortive attempt to deliver a degree of justice on the big lake was to mean anything, he had to get to work. The supply of cash from his work with TRAC would finance his efforts for the next few months. What he needed was motivation and he knew exactly where to get that.

The folded piece of paper remained on the kitchen table. He opened it and read his list. He reached for the pen and began to make revisions. When he finished, he read through it again.

~~THE CONNECTICUT CONNECTION~~ Justice Deserved
Parker Havenot ★★★   Steven Capaldi★★★
Robert Snyder ★★Alison Regan ★ ★
George Metcalf ★★
Rich Lane
~~Steven Capaldi ★★★~~
Josie Wallace (Havenot)
Harriet Long (Stanton)

Satisfied with the revised list, he folded it and put it in his side pocket.

"This'll be a start," he said aloud. His next stop would supply the inspiration to get to work.

"Just like old times, my boy," Brad said as he knelt by his infant son's grave. "Your psychopathic dad is back." The Mountain View Cemetery was once again deserted, as it seemed to be every day during the week. Brad idly perused his surroundings. "I guess people only grieve on weekends," he muttered. He removed the list from his pocket.

"Here's where I need your assistance, Junior. But before we start, I have to say that it's hard to believe that you would have been in your twenties by now. That's one of the reasons I moved Capaldi to the top of the list. He really started it all. He got off with a minor inconvenience all those years ago." Brad gazed across the grounds in the direction of his old house, lost in an unpleasant reverie for a full minute before he came back.

"Anyway, I wanted to share this with you and see what you think. I think these are some folks who deserve to have some help with their fate. Let's see if you agree."

After Brad read each name, he would pause, conjuring up pictures of each person along with a catalogue of wrongs they had inflicted on him. In a religious or spiritual setting, the exercise might have provided a healthy outlet for frustrations and displeasure with one's fellow human beings because it would be followed by a fervent call for forgiveness, the next step in any healing process. This wasn't a spiritual setting and he wasn't asking for forgiveness. The images flashing through his mind enlightened him as clearly as a lightning flash illuminates a pitch dark stormy night. His priority asterisks on the list needed some alterations.

When he finished with the list, he held it in both hands, as if he could absorb power from it by osmosis. "Havenot, Lane, Josie, and Harriet can wait until a New Hampshire opportunity presents itself. For now, we'll concentrate on the locals," adding, as if for emphasis, "no more adolescent nail pranks."

After another scan of the cemetery, he rose to his feet. "This is the only place in this world where I feel like I'm sane," he said to his son's marker.

Steven Capaldi

DR. STEVEN CAPALDI WAS the first. More than two decades had passed but to Brad Wallace, the memory of that first attempt at making a difference could be brought to the surface as easily as if it had happened yesterday. John Simms had told him then during his yearly physical exam that he was perfectly normal; he did not stand alone in his rage at the unfairness of life. He couldn't do anything about the loss of his good friend and colleague, Tyler Spence, in the shameful Vietnam War or the nation losing leaders like Martin Luther King and Bobby Kennedy or racial injustices and lynch mobs. His visits to his son's grave, where he could vent his frustrations and rage, turned into therapeutic sessions, pieces of time when he could unburden himself. He started calling them his black periods, not because they were bleak but because they surrounded him like a virtual room darkening shade, shutting out the light of reality that threatened to overwhelm him. It was during one of these early periods that he realized that there were issues he could address, wrongs he could right, and events he could control. As Dr. Simms told him long ago, he was perfectly normal. Controlled rage and even-handed justice, he decided back then, had to prevail. Peter Capaldi, Josie's gynecologist who should have prevented the loss of Brad, Jr., escaped with minor injuries the first time. More than twenty years later, Brad would see that this encounter would have a different result.

AFTER JUST ONE SCOUTING trip driving around Hartford, Brad found the busiest Midas shop in the downtown area. A day after he watched John Simms marched out of his office, he returned to the shop. He entered the parking lot and drove to the end of a row of cars, as far away from the office entrance as he could get. He assumed an air of naiveté as he entered, looking like a typical mechanically challenged customer. A girl of about twenty-five greeted him enthusiastically. She could have served as a model for one of those calendars so common in automotive establishments, a wide, seductive smile on her face, long blonde hair, a blouse opened three buttons down, and jeans that were so tight they looked like they might have been painted on. Her name tag read Miranda and it was pinned exactly where most men's eyes would be drawn first.

"What can I do for you, sir?" she asked, leaning forward over the chest-high counter.

"I probably need to talk to a mechanic. I'm not even sure what to ask."

"Why don't you try me; I know a lot more than you might think," she purred.

"OK, but I don't want to waste your time. It's probably silly. I think I have a leak in the brake line or something. There's some fluid on the garage floor." Brad smiled. "I'm a class A dummy when it comes to cars."

"Tell you what we'll do. Let's go look at your car and I'll see if there's anything obvious. If so, we'll make an appointment. If not, we'll still make an appointment." She came out from behind the counter and pranced out the door. Brad followed and asked an innocuous question as they walked to his car.

"What if it's a pin hole, like from a stone or something? Is that possible?"

His casual question brought forth a diatribe on the danger of brake lines as she cited several horror stories from her experience with Midas. A partial cut in the steel brake lines was most dangerous because you would have brakes at first, but when they were applied, the pressure would increase and the fluid would leak out.

"How could that happen?" Brad asked, innocence masking his intent.

"Those old murder mysteries aren't that farfetched," she said. "You know, where the cuckolded . . ." She hesitated. "Is that the right word?" she asked, her eyelids fluttering. Brad nodded and she continued. "Where the husband kills his wife and lover and makes it look like an accident? Perfectly possible, even with today's cars and steel lines. Just a little snip with a good pair of wire cutters, and there you go."

He regarded her with appreciation. "You sure do know your business." The compliment created a full-fledged blush that made its way from her neck to her forehead in record time.

Five minutes had passed and Brad had all the information he needed from Miranda. He shook her hand, apologized that he had an appointment, and promised to return by noon.

"But I haven't even looked at your car yet," she complained.

"Later. I promise." He drove off. He glanced in the rearview mirror. Miranda's right hand was raised in a hesitant wave, looking like she had just waved to a friend only to realize that it was a complete stranger.

"I wonder if fate will still be on the doctor's side if he has no brakes," he said to the disappearing Miranda in the mirror.

Brake Failure

THE CALL CAME LATE in the evening. When Josie finished her school responsibilities for the next day, she joined Parker on the sofa in front of the fireplace. The combination of the first cool evening of the approaching fall season and the first fire had the expected romantic effect. The top layer of the couple's clothing had already been discarded when the phone rang. The temptation to ignore it was overcome by Parker's sense of responsibility to his job and Josie's encouragement for him to answer it. She knew immediately that it was not good news.

"It's Peter Capaldi," Parker said. "Car accident. I'd better go. They took him to Hartford County. They didn't have a report on his condition." Josie came over to him and hugged him.

"Of course," she said. Then he was gone. A minute later, she heard his car pull into the driveway. The door slammed but the engine was still running. Parker hurried through the front door as if on a mission.

"What's going on? Did you forget something?" Then she panicked when she saw the tears in his eyes. "Parker! You're scaring me. What is it?"

He took her hand and led her to the sofa. Then he reached for her other hand and forced her to face him. "I've got to ask you something and I need you to tell me the truth."

"Have you ever known me to do otherwise?" She tried a smile but the effort was a dismal failure.

"I've told you some things about my first marriage to Hannah but there was one incident that seemed the final blow to any chance it would succeed. I got about a half mile from here and the memory of it came back with a vengeance. It was just like tonight. Hannah and I were having a rare quiet night at home when a phone call interrupted us. It was the third night in a row I'd gotten a call about a homicide. They were pretty frequent in downtown Philly. I could've said no but I didn't. She didn't want me to go but I did." A single tear escaped and trickled down his cheek. "Here's the bottom line. If you want me to stay home tonight, I will. I couldn't stand to lose you, Jos." Now both cheeks were moist but he clung to her hands, ignoring the dampness.

"That was your job, Parker. I wouldn't have objected then but this is different. Peter's a friend of yours and he and his wife need your support. I'd be disappointed in you if you hadn't reacted the way you did. Now get going before I kick you in the butt!" A full-blown smile lit up her face.

He let go of her hands and stood up. "You are too much, Mrs. Havenot. I'll see you as soon as I can."

"HE'S STILL IN SURGERY."

Mary Capaldi struggled to get the words out. "The doctors have been encouraging and they all know Peter. They'll do their best but it's just so upsetting." Parker reached out and embraced her in an awkward hug. While his friendship with Peter Capaldi had deepened over the years, it was only since he married Josie that the two couples had begun to see each other socially. He didn't know Mary that well but his concern showed in the worry lines around his eyes. "He'll be OK, Parker; I just know it."

"I'll go down to the snack shop and get some coffee for us. Cream and sugar?"

"Just black, please, and thanks a lot for coming. I really appreciate it."

After two hours in the surgery waiting room, the door finally opened. A doctor who could have doubled for television's Dr. Kildare entered. Mary sobbed when she saw the grin on his face. "He's fine; he's going to be just fine. A couple of broken bones that we took care of and no internal injuries. He'll have to explain away a couple of black eyes, too. He'll be in recovery for an hour or so then you can see him." He shook her hand and winked at Parker on his way out.

"If you don't mind, I'd like to hang around and see him for a couple of minutes," Parker said.

"It looks like his front brakes failed. He worked later than usual so it was dark but he's traveled that road home a thousand times. We'll know more tomorrow when we get a good look at the car." His explanation to Josie included his initial response when Peter tried to describe the accident.

"I think somebody tried to sabotage your car. Do you have any unhappy patients these days, Peter?" he'd asked the doctor.

"No, not that I know of, certainly none like that crazy one years ago. But he's dead," Peter had answered.

"Brad! Oh, Parker, you don't think that…" Josie stuttered to a halt.

"Depending on what we find with the car, it might be time for another visit to John Simms and Univac Redux."

Neither one slept well for the remainder of the abbreviated night.

Capaldi's Car

PETER CAPALDI'S CAR SAT in the sheriff's towing lot, which served a triple purpose. It was a graveyard for abandoned vehicles, usually left by the side of a highway by disgruntled drivers finally tired of throwing money into a hopeless cause. It was a temporary storage facility for automobiles that suffered the indignities of being booted when their scofflaw owners allowed the parking tickets to accumulate to a ridiculous level. The doctor's car rested in a specially gated area, corralled by an eight-foot cyclone fence topped by spiral barbed wire slanted inward within the confines of the compound. The cars in this section had either been used for criminal activity or were the victims of it. There was no chance of anyone tampering with the evidence in this enclosure. Were anyone to manage a doubtful entry, their escape would be even more unlikely.

As soon as Parker arrived at the office the morning after Pater's accident, he contacted the mechanic in charge of the lot. With the usual hesitancy of someone who worked at the bottom of a bureaucracy, the mechanic told Parker that he couldn't look at the car without permission, in writing, from Sheriff Corbett himself.

"This accident is going to be given high investigative priority so I don't see the harm in you taking a quick look. It'll just be between us, for now." Parker was frantically searching through

180

the staff directory for a name to go with the voice on the phone. He just couldn't come up with it and calling someone by name improved the chances of getting a favor tenfold.

"Look, Detective, I'd love to do you the favor. I know your reputation and all that . . ."

Parker knew this request wasn't going anywhere. "Thanks a lot for your help." The name still hadn't come to him. "I'll be back to you."

He called central dispatch. The sheriff was not due in until about eleven. "Court appearance," he was told.

"Shit," he mumbled.

His next call went to Covington County Court Records. They opened at eight and the chances of one of his friends answering were good. He wasn't disappointed.

"Millie, I need a favor and you are the only one I'd ever asked to do this."

"You say that to all the girls, Parker, and we're all onto you. It's only because you're so cute that we comply with your requests. Well, that, plus you apparently do a lot of good things with our information. What do you need?"

Ten minutes later, a secretary tapped on Parker's door. She held a two-page fax in her hand. "This just came for you from court records. Cover letter said you needed it right away." She dropped the document on his desk. He picked it up, began reading, and sent a belated "thank you" at her receding back.

Parker finished reading the first page when the intercom buzzed.

"This is Dave down at the towing lot."

Parker smiled. "Dave," he said to himself. "That's it!" Under the mechanic's gentle coaxing, he issued a solemn promise that no one would ever know that Dave had not only looked at Peter's car but had reported what he found to a detective. He grabbed a yellow legal pad from the corner of his desk and listened, jotting down about five lines of notes.

After a final admonition from Dave, Parker thanked him but not before asking why he changed his mind.

"You aroused my curiosity and the car was, like, right there, so why not?"

The phone hadn't stopped rocking in the cradle when the intercom rang again. It was Jim Corbett. "Understand you've been looking for me. The court thing was postponed. What the hell else is new? Why don't you come on over and we can chat? No one expected me back this soon anyway."

For the moment, Parker wanted to reflect on what exactly Dave's discoveries meant.

"Give me ten minutes and I'll be down."

He left his desk and closed his door, a foreign experience to him when he was in his office by himself.

The notes stared up at him as if they had a life of their own.

1. Cursory but effective examination by Dave
2. Front brake line "nipped" (Dave's word) on both right and left sides
3. Emergency brake and rear brake lines not damaged (Dave—that kept the crash from being worse—30% braking power)
4. "Nips had to be intentional" —Dave (swore me to secrecy again on that one)

There was no question what the notes meant. He was on his way to see Jim Corbett in five minutes instead of ten.

No sooner had the 7-11 cashier snipped open the bound stack of the afternoon edition of the *Covington County Herald* then Brad grabbed the top copy. He handed the acne-afflicted teenager a quarter and told him to keep the change. The adolescent scowled, muttered an unintelligible response under his breath, and reached into his pocket. He handed a nickel to Brad, saying, "you probably need this more than I do." Dumbfounded, Brad took it without a word and went right to his car.

When he taught his advanced current events class in the social studies department of Hampton Village High School, the intellectual seniors challenged his knowledge base daily. Those amiable challenges required Brad to read as widely as possible and he perfected the headline-scanning technique that his students often struggled to master. The front page of the *Herald* carried no news of any fatal accidents and his perusal quickly led him through the major news items of the day. With each disappointing page, he slid further down in his seat. On the last page of the local news section, he finally found the object of his search. It was a filler item, just a paragraph long obviously taken from a police radio scanner because there was little detail.

The headline read simply: DOCTOR INJURED IN CRASH. The story of Peter Capaldi's accident on the country road created a déjà vu moment for Brad. The similarity of the account of the last accident he had arranged for Capaldi years before disturbed him to the point that his hands shook, rattling the newspaper. Once again, the injuries sustained did not appear to be serious or, at least, not life-threatening, the brief article indicated.

Fate or providence or destiny surely seemed to be on the doctor's side.

"You're one lucky bastard, Capaldi!" he fumed, as he crumpled the entire newspaper into one big ball and tossed on the floor in front of the passenger seat.

Robert Snyder

OVER TWENTY YEARS BEFORE, Robert Snyder spent just fifteen days in prison for the vehicular manslaughter charges in the deaths of John and Sandra Wallace. The class C felony carried a maximum of ten years in prison but the social and political turbulence of the late sixties made some judges wary of imposing harsh sentences. When Detective Parker Havenot delivered the news that a plea bargain had been arranged, Brad accepted it with apparent good grace, but it left him seething inside. Snyder's was a first offense and his lawyer coached him well. As he addressed the judge, Bob was the picture of humility, expressing his deep remorse. His voice dripped with sincerity when he promised that he would be an upstanding citizen if only given a chance. He was sentenced to ninety days in jail, but seventy-five of those days were suspended. Havenot had warned Brad that the sentencing would be disappointing but Brad chose to be in court anyway. He could not believe what he was hearing as the judge announced that the drunk driver and killer of his parents would be allowed to serve the fifteen days on weekends so that he was not required to miss work. After a refreshing black period at his son's grave, Brad developed a plan to make certain that Robert Snyder's life was at least somewhat interrupted.

THE YEARS HAD NOT been kind to the development at Water-ford West. Robert Snyder's house at 202 Pineland Road joined the others in what seemed a race to disintegration. Years before, when Brad had cruised through the neighborhood, the lawns showed the distinct signs of children, with driveways littered with bicycles and wagons and basketball hoops hanging from garage roofs. Now it was obvious that many of the homes were empty nests. Rusting swing sets and lopsided storage sheds dotted most back-yards. An occasional house showed signs of regular maintenance but peeling paint and missing roof shingles appeared to be in style. Brad had searched the Covington County phone book he found in his rental house and discovered that Robert Snyder still lived at 202 Pineland Road. As he drove into the cul-de-sac at the end of Pineland, the memories of the day he followed Snyder home after his sentencing surfaced. The familiar sense of outrage at the injustice made his vision blur. For more than twenty years, Robert Snyder moved on while his parents lay in their graves, consigned to an eternity of rotting indignation. He slowed as he approached the house. An old pickup truck rested on blocks in the front yard, a block and tackle tripod hovering over the hoodless engine com-partment. There were no other vehicles visible on the property.

Brad stopped his car and got out, stretched, and wondered what he was doing there. A curious scenario was sure to develop if he knocked on the front door and Robert Snyder, in the flesh, answered. As he weighed the wisdom of approaching the house and considered other options, the door creaked open, startling him.

"Can I help you?" an attractive brunette called out.

Brad almost bolted but he recovered quickly.

"I'm wondering if there is a Robert Snyder living here. I'm an old friend of his."

The woman came down the cracked concrete steps and walked toward him. Brad retreated a few steps and leaned against his car. She continued her approach until she was close to invading his personal space. A slight aroma of coffee and cigarettes drifted to him. He guessed her age to be late-thirties, about the right age, but her appearance clashed with his picture of what a wife or girlfriend of Snyder might look like. The loose sweatsuit she wore still managed to accentuate her figure. Brad began to look for an escape route.

She smiled and extended her hand. "I'm Sheila," she said.

The ingrained socially acceptable response overrode logic. "Brad Wallace," he responded without thinking. Instantly, he regretted it.

She allowed her hand to drop to her side when he didn't return her offer. She just stared at him, waiting for further explanation. When none was forthcoming, she assumed the lead. "You said you're an old friend of Bobby's? I don't remember him ever mentioning your name."

"We've kind of lost touch over the years. I'm passing through on business and on a whim I thought I'd try to look him up," he said with what he hoped was a disarming smile and lying as smoothly as he ever had in his life.

"Well, he does live here. I've only been with him for a few months. Do you want to come in for a cup of coffee or something? I don't get to see many of Bobby's friends and it might be fun to visit with someone who really knows him." She balanced the invitation with a mix of friendliness and flirtation.

Brad began to work his way around the car to the driver's side. "I've got to be going, but thanks anyway. And tell Robert I'll catch up with him another time." He fought the urge to run. Sheila would be sure to remember him.

"Huh," she said, giggling. "I've never heard anyone call him Robert before."

Brad reached the other side of the car and practically dove into the driver's seat. He threw a half-hearted wave in her direction as he drove off.

Sheila returned to the house and immediately wrote down his name so she could tell Bobby about his visitor. Next to his name, she wrote "Grey Escort, Mass plate WMB2578."

"Bobby'll be so proud of me," she said into her coffee cup later.

JIM CORBETT WAS CONVINCED. There had to be something to the Brad Wallace thing. The current argument that nothing is original anymore converted to the belief that everything is a cliché. The disavowing of coincidence has been used so often that in and of itself, it is a cliché.

When the sheriff met with Parker Havenot to lay out the plan to protect those who needed protecting in the Brad Wallace case, coincidence became the operative word. Somehow, John Simms and Brad Wallace knew each other. Simms worked for Henry Bouchard. Did that mean that Wallace also knew Bouchard in spite of his adamant denial? Why would he deny the existence of Wallace? The coincidences in the case mounted with each passing day. It was time to get this resolved.

The first item on the agenda for their meeting addressed the most important issue—keeping innocent people from getting hurt. Parker's answer to that point was profound in its simplicity.

"We don't have resources enough to assign personnel to guard Ms. Regan, George Metcalf, Robert Snyder, and Peter Capaldi. I propose that we warn them. Wallace has not shown that he's willing to use traditional methods to harm people. Even the stuff he did up in New Hampshire on the lake was bizarre. We'll just tell them to be more aware of their surroundings until we find him."

"Well. It's a little late to warn Capaldi but I agree. That should be our first step and I think we should do it soon." Jim Corbett laced his fingers together, put his hands behind his head, and leaned back in his chair. "So, who does what? And, by the way, I'll say this even if you don't want to hear it. You and Josie are probably on his list, too."

"If it's all right with you, I'd like to handle the warnings and I'd like to start this afternoon. I'm stopping by to see Peter later this morning then I'll try to contact the others by this evening."

"Fine with me if it works for you."

The two men moved on to the second item on the agenda. Both were in agreement on the methodology of handling the perplexing problem of finding Brad Wallace.

"We put the screws to Simms and Bouchard," Jim Corbett said. "Nine o'clock tomorrow morning, we'll meet right here and pay them another visit."

Warnings

PETER CAPALDI TRIED TO sit up straighter in the hospital bed when Parker walked through the door. He groaned with the effort and slumped back down. His eyes, as predicted, had developed circles of black, blue, and yellow which migrated into both cheeks. Ice had prevented massive swelling but his face looked as though it had been used as a punching bag by Muhammed Ali.

"The sheriff told me to come over here and tell you to be careful." Parker grinned when his friend coughed out a snort. "Glad to see you sort of up and about."

"Mary and I appreciate your coming over last night," Peter said with a nasal twang. "Can't tell you how much." It was evident that talking was an issue.

"Just listen for a change then I'll let you get some rest. Your patients are going to be pretty unhappy to have someone else giving them the exams you're so good at."

The doctor let out another snort.

Parker related in general terms what had been found with his car. Peter tried again to sit up straighter, as though his posture could make what he was hearing more believable. The detective ended with a brief explanation of the plan to try to find Brad Wallace.

When he finished, the doctor was shaking his head.

"Fucking guy sure can hold a grudge, can't he?" His smirk couldn't cover the tears that welled up in his eyes.

189

"We'll find him. Now you rest and take care of yourself." He touched Peter lightly on the shoulder then hurried out the door. Once out in the hall, he wiped his eyes with the sleeve of his jacket.

PARKER LEFT THE HOSPITAL and returned to his office to set up appointments with the remainder of his list. His first call went to Dr. George Metcalf, Superintendent of the Hartford School System. As the bureaucratic system performed at its best level, he was transferred from one secretary to a second, then to the business manager's office, where he was put on hold. A minute later, that secretary returned to ask, rather stiffly, "to whom would you like to speak?" It was at that moment that he lost any pretense of patience.

"This is Detective Parker Havenot of the Covington County Sheriff's Department. If I am not connected to George Metcalf in the next thirty seconds, I'll be over there in person and I can't guarantee what will happen. Do I make myself clear?"

"Please hold." Fifteen seconds later, Dr. George Metcalf was on the line.

"Sorry for the delay . . . uh . . .officer," Metcalf stammered. "Is there something I can do to help?"

Without introducing himself yet again and allowing the superintendent's mistaken salutation to stand, Parker addressed him formally. "Dr. Metcalf. Would you check your calendar for tomorrow? I need a few minutes of your time."

A befuddled Metcalf, taken aback by the request, asked for a minute to check. When he came back on the line, he had recovered enough to try to take control of the situation.

"I'd like to know what this is about. I'm a really busy man and my schedule is pretty full. Did you say you're with the Hartford Police Department?"

Parker Havenot did not deal with arrogance well. "First of all, I'm a detective with the Covington County Sheriff's Department and we've met before, and secondly, I'm not going into details on the phone but we think you might be in some physical danger. Now, do you think you could squeeze me in tomorrow or not?"

Metcalf lapsed into his befuddled state once more. "Physical danger . . .I . . .don't understand." He was stammering again. "How's one o'clock in my office?"

"I'll be there." Parker hung up.

AT FIRST, ALISON WAS happy when the detective informed her that she was the catalyst for the arrest of John Simms. Then, she began to think about a trial or even a hearing before a judge, both of which would require her testimony, and her bravado decreased in subtle but real increments. Had it not been for the four flat tires, she would have dismissed the possibility that someone might try to harm her. When Parker Havenot called to set up an appointment to speak with her, a niggling shiver of fear fluttered through her stomach, but she agreed to meet with him late the next day without asking the obvious question. Why?

PARKER WAITED UNTIL JUST before he left for the day to phone Robert Snyder, expecting that he would be home from work by then. With the same address and phone number, he assumed it had to be the same man he visited in a jail cell over twenty years before. He was waiting to be sentenced for killing Brad Wallace's parents while driving when he could hardly stand up. A female voice bid him a cheery hello.

"Robert Snyder, please. This is Parker Havenot of the sheriff's department."

Sheila's tone lost all semblance of cheerfulness. "He's not home from work yet. Can I give him a message?"

"Do you know if he'll be home early tomorrow evening? I'd like to swing by and speak with him for a few minutes."

The long hesitation indicated the woman's dilemma. She answered Parker's question with one of her own and the quavering voice revealed her reluctance to hear his reply. "Is he in any trouble? I mean, I can't imagine it but a call from the sheriff, you know . . ."

"No trouble at all, ma'am; just a routine matter that won't take more than a few minutes, if that." Sheila's sigh radiated palpable relief through the phone line.

"Yes, sir, he'll be home. We pretty much hang around the house most evenings. Is it OK if I tell you him you're coming? Maybe even what it's about?" she asked, hoping to get a hint.

"You can tell him that I'm coming but I'd rather give him my message in person; that is, if you don't mind." Parker threw in the final comment to diffuse her concern even further. "I should be there around seven and thanks a lot for your help."

The "goodbye" in her voice matched the cheery "hello" that had started the conversation.

The Morning Visits

PARKER WAITED IN JIM Corbett's office. At exactly nine o'clock, the sheriff arrived with a bag of Dunkin Donuts glazed doughnut holes and two huge containers of coffee.

"I figured we could use some sustenance. I have a feeling this is going to be a long day." He laughed as Havenot shook his head. "Actually, I do this every Friday, sort of a tradition. What we don't eat will be gone within a minute after I set it on the table in the break room."

Parker thanked him for the coffee and reached into the bag then passed it to Corbett. They each downed two of the pastries while sipping their still steaming coffee without a word passing between them. The sheriff excused himself, grabbed the bag, and headed for the break room. When he returned, they smiled at each other as the sounds of dozens of scuffling feet heading for the doughnut holes reached them through the open door. They settled in to plan their day.

John Simms made bail before noon on the day of his arrest. No official was present to argue about his release. The judge announced that such a respected professional surely was not a flight risk and there was no logical reason to deny the bail request. He set it at a nominal minimum and a call to Clarisse Shearer brought her to the courtroom within an hour. Neither man saw any reason why he wouldn't have returned to his office to continue his practice. "Such as it is," Parker pointed out.

"So, we just drop by again. I don't see any reason to make an appointment. Same can be said of Bouchard. Seems like he lives at his office. Why don't we just take a trip and see if we can find Brad Wallace?"

"I've got an appointment with the superintendent at 1:00 so I've got all morning."

As EXPECTED, THE DOCTOR was in. Also as expected, his waiting room was empty. However, the same formidable obstacle to seeing him remained firmly in place. Clarisse Shearer's loyalty was impressive; in a profession where loyalty to one's comrades was paramount, the two law officers respected that. When she discovered through her window who had entered, she rushed out to greet them before they were two steps into the room.

"The doctor's busy. Unless you have some sort of an official document, a summons or something, he doesn't have to talk to you." She stood in front of his office door, figuratively in a spread eagle defensive position which shouted that no one was going through that door without walking over her first. She also had been schooled in legalese since their last visit. Parker's impatience threatened to take control. The irritation vibes filled the room, impossible for Jim Corbett to ignore. He stepped forward, effectively shielding Parker from sight.

"Look, Ms. Shearer, this is an unofficial visit. Dr. Simms could be very helpful to us and if he is, it could go a long way toward helping him as well. We don't want to cause any problems for you or your boss. Really. Please." He would have crossed his heart and hoped to die if he thought it might help. Parker peeked around him, trying to determine if it was safe to come out.

Clarisse, whose body had been radiating tension to such a degree that even her hair seemed clenched, relaxed ever so slightly. "I can't promise anything but I'll ask him. It's all I can do." Like a schoolteacher admonishing a recalcitrant student, she shook a finger at the sheriff. "Wait here," she said, adding a sarcastic "and it's Mrs., not Ms."

FIFTEEN MINUTES LATER, PARKER and Jim Corbett left a smiling Clarisse behind. The doctor had been cooperative far beyond their wildest expectations. The information he supplied sent them off to see Henry Bouchard with guarded optimism. There was little question that he saw some possibility of escaping his legal problems if he collaborated with the authorities. The effusive praise he heaped on his receptionist in their presence for her allegiance and strength in this difficult time made both of them smile as they left. No doubt remained that Brad Wallace was alive and well and operating in their backyard. The problem with the information which Simms provided was simple. He didn't know where Wallace was living and he had no contact information.

"If I can locate that phone number, I'll be sure to call you. It was disconnected when I called him so I just filed it away somewhere."

"Where in the hell is he?" Parker asked when they reached his car. Since Corbett could have asked the same question, it just hung in the air in rhetorical glory. "It takes a court order to get anything out of the phone company and he probably got the phone under a different name anyway."

"Maybe Bouchard will know."

"One would think. If someone worked for you, you'd know where he lived or how to get in touch, right?" Havenot asked without enthusiasm.

FOR THE SECOND TIME, Brad Wallace watched the sheriff and his detective leave the premises of John Simms, but unlike last time, they didn't have Simms sandwiched between them. After they were safely out of the area, he decided that it was time for another short pilgrimage to Mountain View Cemetery to get some advice. Something was going on and he needed to know what it was.

He followed the usual routine. The school year had just begun so Josie's presence in the neighborhood would not be an issue. Since his return to Connecticut, he had not seen a single person at the cemetery on his visits but he approached more cautiously than ever.

Once again, Mountain View was deserted. He parked in his usual place and walked more briskly than usual to have his conversation. It had taken years but he could now stand over the grave without thinking about what lay beneath the surface. A few times before his self-imposed exile to New Hampshire, his experiences at the site had paralyzed him. Now, they offered him what he described as the spiritual equivalent of the refuge and strength of God sought so desperately by devoted churchgoers.

He spoke in a conversational tone and rhythm.

"It was a big mistake, actually a crucial one, Junior." As he usually did, he sank to one knee, as though giving a pep talk to one of his teams back when he coached. "Visiting Robert Snyder's neighborhood and then being caught by his girlfriend was foolish but we can't go back, can we? The Capaldi accident didn't work out the way I'd planned either. Havenot's probably suspicious. But here's the real quandary." He lowered his voice to a conspiratorial level and bent closer to the marker.

"Two people know that I was not food for the bottom feeders in Lake Winnipesaukee. One's out on bail with a court case coming up. He has the most to gain by exposing me if he gets asked the right questions. The other is much more powerful and even offered to assist me in any way he could." Brad stopped speaking and waited, as if listening for a response. After a few minutes of yoga-like contemplation, he stood. "Thanks a lot, my boy." Unbidden tears sprang into his eyes.

"We would have had a great time together, son," he said. "And I agree. Maybe Mr. Bouchard would appreciate another phone call."

Brad stopped at the first gas station he saw that had a public phone. Henry would be prepared for the detective and the sheriff.

THE OFFICES OF UNIVAC Redux hadn't changed but the manner in which they were greeted differed. Once again, Gavin answered the bell but instead of making them wait while he received approval for their entrance, he ushered them directly to Henry Bouchard's office. Havenot and Corbett made eye contact and nodded to each other. All signs indicated that they were expected.

As cordial as Henry Bouchard had been on their first visit, his greeting this time hovered between chilly and cold. Without offering his hand to either of them, he retreated behind his massive desk. They waited to be offered a seat. The offer never came so the three men stood staring at each other until Parker finally broke the spell.

"We're trying to track down Brad Wallace. It's very important that we do before he hurts someone. We know . . ."

"Look, Detective," Bouchard interjected. "This is getting old. I told you I don't know a Brad Wallace and even if I did, I'm under no obligation to share any employee information with you." It was Jim Corbett's turn.

"Follow this logic, sir, if you will," the sheriff said. "John Simms worked for you, correct?" He plowed on without waiting for an answer. "John Simms says that Wallace did some work for you and that maybe you would know where we could find him. Therefore, we're here to ask you where he is. Are you able to follow that or would you like me to spell it out in plainer language, like obstruction of justice terms?"

Jim Corbett had Bouchard's complete and focused attention.

"Simms told you this? And you believe a guy who's out on bail and facing a felony charge? Ludicrous, simply ludicrous." Bouchard remained standing but placed both hands on the back of his chair for support.

"To put it simply, yes. We have no reason not to believe him. So, what have you got for us?" The two policemen moved closer to the desk and adopted an expectant posture, one that seemed to give Bouchard no choice.

"He was perfect for our project; he seemed to have no past, no friends, no family, nothing. Security would not be an issue with him. It was like he didn't exist. His only condition for employment was anonymity. He was paid in cash as an independent contractor; we had no contact information—no phone, no home address. I'll admit it was a little strange but, again, perfect for our needs. I think we still have the information for depositing his pay. You're welcome to that but that's about all I can do. You can wait in the reception foyer and I'll have Gavin bring it out to you. "

The conversation clearly was over, at least from Bouchard's point of view. Jim Corbett fired the last salvo.

"You lied to us about Wallace and I'm thinking that maybe that's not all. We'll probably be back and fairly soon." The two men left the room and proceeded on what was now a familiar path through the business offices of Univac Redux. Gavin, the mysterious greeter and apparent bodyguard of the CEO, joined them in the foyer in less than a minute.

"Mr. Bouchard said you should have this." He handed Havenot a piece of paper with a number of a Federal Express box at a pack and ship establishment in West Hartford. They would need yet another court order to get any information there. As they sat in the car fuming over the stonewalling tactics they had encountered, Bouchard was dialing a familiar number. Informed that John Simms was gone for the day but sure that she was lying, he sent Clarisse Shearer reeling backward into her chair with his message.

"Tell Simms he has ruined everything and then tell him that he is thoroughly fucked!"

He scribbled a note on a legal pad and called for Gavin.

"I have a delivery for you. The address is on the envelope. Take it there right now and just hand it to the guy who answers the door."

Gavin glanced down at the envelope. He'd have to check his map of the West Hartford area. He knew Farmington but Hopkins Street didn't mean anything to him.

BRAD OPENED THE DOOR, but kept the chain in place. Gavin said nothing but slipped the envelope through the crack. Brad accepted the proffered envelope then watched as the messenger scurried down the sidewalk. He guessed immediately who had sent it. No one knew his whereabouts until he spoke with Bouchard earlier that day and they had reached a simple agreement. Comrades in arms, Bouchard had called them. Brad would continue to let him know of any developments with Simms that might impact TRAC. In return, Henry would contact Brad if it appeared that Havenot was getting closer.

He sat at the kitchen table, opened the envelope, and read Bouchard's neat printing.

Best get out of town now!
Take care of Simms on your way out if possible.
He's ruined us.

The Afternoon Visits

EVERYTHING PARKER KNEW ABOUT Dr. George Metcalf, chief of the sprawling Hartford City School District, came from newspaper articles, mostly concerning his political hobnobbing, and from Josie, who passed on information obtained from Brad before his "early" retirement, which was actually a no-choice, take-it-or-leave-it offer he couldn't refuse. Crossing Dr. Metcalf or making him look foolish in public was not good for one's career. Brad had been virtually his second-in-command for a number of years but his professional integrity became a liability under Metcalf. The superintendent knew how to play the game of upper-level politics; his leadership had much less to do with education than it did with keeping his bureaucracy intact.

Dr. George Metcalf lived up to the buffoon status which Parker had granted him based on his limited knowledge and hearsay. Exactly on time for the appointment, Parker introduced himself to Metcalf's cliché of a shapely, blonde secretary, who dressed for the part replete with high heels, short skirt, and tight cardigan sweater unbuttoned to reveal cleavage that would make a Victoria's Secret model blush. She escorted Havenot into the superintendent's office, flouncing ahead of him and receiving a wide smile from the superintendent when she approached his desk and performed a quick curtsy for his benefit.

"Can I do anything else for you, sir?" she asked.

200

"Not right now but maybe some dictation later," Metcalf answered. They exchanged glances and smiles, then she sashayed out the door, pushing it closed behind her.

Metcalf rose and extended his hand across the desk. "She's fun to have around." He said, smirking. Metcalf extended his arm and they shook hands. "So, what's this about? You mentioned physical danger. I mean, I didn't lose any sleep over it but it's not something I usually hear. So, let's get right to it. I've got a lot on my plate." The staccato sentences belied his indicated calm.

"We didn't want to alarm you but thought you should be aware that Brad Wallace might pose a threat to you. We're just letting people he had run-ins with before know that he's back in Connecticut."

The superintendent's alcohol-reddened complexion paled at the mention of Brad Wallace. "But he's dead. What the hell are you talking about?"

"Actually, we think he's not dead and that he might be back here looking for a little revenge on people who treated him unfairly over the years." It was such a dramatic announcement that the incredulity that passed over Metcalf's face was instantly replaced by a far different expression.

"He was treated well here. He just didn't want to stay on our side and we gave him a way out. Our administration thrives on team work, Detective, and Brad Wallace was not a team player." His speech completed, he puffed up with indignation. "I assume you're looking for him with all the resources at your disposal and that you'd let me know when you find him."

Parker just glared at him. "Yeah, we are, but not just for your sake. I'll find my way out. Just pay attention to your environment and if, by any chance, you should hear anything from him or see him, give me a call." He tossed a business card on the desk and left a sputtering superintendent behind.

BRAD WALLACE WAS ON borrowed time in Connecticut and he knew it. With the proverbial reading between the lines, the information gleaned from Henry Bouchard's note could not be clearer.

Somehow, John Simms had betrayed them, probably in exchange for information that might help when his trial came up. Now it was up to him to, as Henry had not so subtly put it, take care of Simms and in an extremely tight time period.

He tilted his chair back and, with a minimal turn, was able to open the refrigerator and pull out a cold beer, almost in a single motion. "The joys of simple living," he mumbled.

Faced now with an immediate problem, the words of a single question came tumbling out in a hissed whisper.

"What the hell am I going to do about Simms?"

PARKER LEFT THE OFFICE of Superintendent George Metcalf in the most agitated mental state he had seen in a long time. He'd carried out his duty well, doing exactly what the situation required, but instead of gratitude, he received a bushel of attitude. It was almost three o'clock in the afternoon when he returned to his office, his anger diminished but nowhere near spent. As he barreled past Jim Corbett's office, the sheriff called out through his open door. Parker spun a neat one-eighty and returned. When he entered the office, his entire demeanor pantomimed the word tense. His thin-lipped mouth, flashing eyes, and rigid posture told the sheriff how his day was going.

"Have a seat, Detective," the sheriff said, his cordiality clashing with the formal salutation. "Want to tell me all about it?"

In spite of his emotional state, Parker smiled. "You sound just like a therapist I went to once. If I tell you all about it, you're probably going to ask me how it makes me feel." The brief bantering drained the stress almost immediately as Parker sat down.

"The 'Peter Principle' personified. That superintendent is an arrogant jerk. How the hell do people like that get into those positions? From what Josie tells me, this is one case where Brad Wallace was right." He paused for a breath, and Jim Corbett made him laugh again.

"Listen, Parker, I don't want you to sugar coat it. Tell me what you really think of him."

The rest of the conversation dealt with Parker's plans to see

Alison Regan and Robert Snyder later on in the day. Jim Corbett allowed that those visits would be less aggravating, if not more productive. Parker returned to his office and amused himself with reading through the file of Sam Olden's research again until it was time to leave for his appointment with the victim of one of those chips, so cleverly delivered by John Simms. It was then that he realized that perhaps the doctor should be on his list of people to warn about Brad Wallace.

ALISON EXUDED THE CONFIDENCE of a young woman in charge of her own destiny. After admitting to being a "little freaked out" by the flat tire incident, she told Parker that she wasn't worried about John Simms at all anymore. When he said that the purpose of his visit had nothing to do with Simms, she was genuinely surprised.

"It may sound really farfetched but there may be a much larger involvement of other people with this chip business and those folks may not be happy to see their secret exposed. All I can really tell you is that the guy who tried to keep you from your appointment with Dr. Capaldi was not John Simms, although Simms probably knew about it."

Alison reacted just as Parker thought she would.

"I guess John wasn't a very good choice, was he?" She smiled. "He treated me well, you know; well, that is, except for the drugging and stalking part." She continued to smile at him in a way that might make a man wonder if she preferred older men. "I promise I'll be careful, Detective, and I'll call if anything seems wrong."

"That all I can ask, Ms. Regan. Thanks for seeing me."

"I thought we were over the Ms. Regan thing, but that's OK. I really do appreciate your concern."

Parker left with a spring in his step. If only his call on Robert Snyder would go as well.

HE WAS A FULL half hour early for the appointment but decided to approach the house anyway. Robert Snyder opened the door but kept the screen door as a buffer. He pointed out that the appointment was scheduled for six o'clock. Parker would never have recognized Snyder. He calculated that he'd gained at least fifty pounds since he last seen him. As a younger man, he could be described as handsome in a rugged, Marlboro man way but that appearance had given way to a gentler, early-middle age maturity that remained attractive despite a rounded and clearly expanding pot belly.

The fumes drifting through the screen door reminded Parker of his early days in a patrol car in Philadelphia. If that same aroma wafted from a partially opened car window, Snyder would be outside the car trying to walk a straight line by now.

"Truly sorry to bother you, Mr. Snyder, but my first appointment didn't take as long as I thought. May I come in?"

With more than a hint of hesitation, Snyder relented and opened the screen door.

The inside of the home would have surprised anyone not familiar with it. Although the house was compact, the open floor plan made the kitchen, dining area, and living room seem almost spacious. Sheila, obviously caught in the middle of putting a meal on the table, was now reopening the oven and replacing the covered dishes.

Parker apologized again and made a decision. "I can come back later if this isn't convenient," he said. "I feel bad about ruining your dinner."

It was Sheila who answered over her shoulder. "That's not a problem. We'll just keep it warm." She smiled at him but he noticed that Robert was grimacing, as if he'd just been punched in his empty stomach.

"We can get this over with very quickly. It has to do with a fatal accident of yours years ago, Robert. You remember, right?" Snyder's grimace remained in place.

"Yeah, I do, but that's a long time ago and I've been clean ever since." His face said what his mouth did not. "So, what the fuck do you want with me?"

Parker picked up on it. "Their son caused you considerable

heartache back then, if you remember. The tire valve and all." The awkwardness of the conversation increased as the three of them continued to stand, as if waiting for a chance to escape. Neither Sheila nor Robert mentioned sitting down.

"Water under the dam or over the bridge or whatever. What's done is done and I ain't been in no trouble since."

Parker couldn't resist. "Hasn't stopped you from drinking, has it?" Snyder's reaction was swift and left no room for discussion.

"You've got no fucking right to come in here and say stuff like that. This is my home; I can do whatever I want to. I don't get behind the wheel anymore, Detective, and you are way out of line."

Shelia took two steps and put her arm around him, gently squeezing, then patted him on the back. "Let's find out what he wants then we can eat."

Parker, chagrined to have caused such an outburst, apologized for the third time in ten minutes. "You're right. I had no call to say that. Now, let's get to the purpose of my visit and I'll be out of your hair."

Parker started to explain about the potential dangers from the son of the couple killed in the accident. "Brad Wallace . . ." He hadn't finished the last syllable of Wallace before Sheila shrieked.

"He was here. Just the other day, he was here. I was going to tell you, Bobby, but we got . . .umm . . . busy that night when you came home and I forgot all about it." Her face looked like a ripened tomato, the table lamp across the room reflecting in her cheeks. She stuttered to a stop.

Parker looked at Snyder, whose alcohol-mottled face had added another layer of red.

"Yeah, I remember," he said as Sheila went to the kitchen and returned with a slip of paper in her hand.

She held out the paper. "Here, take it."

Parker looked down then back at Sheila. "You're sure about this?"

"Yep. I thought Bobby might want to know. He said he was an old friend."

Parker stuffed the note in his pocket. He gave the two of them no choice but to acknowledge a traditional greeting. He grabbed Sheila's hand first and pumped it then did the same with Robert as he walked to the door.

"I came here to warn you about Wallace. It's probably nothing but just pay attention."

"Thanks," Snyder mumbled.

Sheila was more effusive. "We really appreciate your coming, Detective! Don't we, Bobby?" He didn't answer.

Once in the car, he reached for the note and looked at it again.

Brad Wallace-Grey Escort
Mass plate WMB2578

"I'll be damned. Unbelievable!" he shouted as he sped off.

John Simms

BRAD WALLACE SPENT HIS entire working life as a professional educator. He believed in his ability to alter the path of his students but he also believed that sending a student in the right direction had to be accomplished subtly. The heavy-handed teachers whose interference in the lives of their students through the introduction of obstacles designed to make them fail instead of succeed were doomed to failure. A nudge here and nudge there could make all the difference. A push here and a shove there were usually met with resistance, sometimes even outright defiance, sending the student in the exact opposite direction. The same philosophy achieved his goals when he finally decided to assume an active role in correcting the injustices he saw around him. A gentle prodding was all that was needed. Inevitably, fate would then take over. He was not a violent man, although on occasion his nudges had brutal results.

As he sat at the table sipping his second beer and contemplating what to do about John Simms, he started doodling on the same pad where he had made his list. The doodles gradually turned into another list, a catalog of nudges he had supplied over the years after they had lost Brad, Jr. Each one provided a daydream, a succession of reveries that passed most of the afternoon away. Each one had at its center an emotional event capable of exacting a behavioral change in his quarry.

Now, he had one more to change before his exit from Connecticut and it had to happen today.

JOHN SIMMS LEFT HIS office at precisely five o'clock with a perfunctory "good night" to Clarisse Shearer, who then went to the window to watch him leave the building. She was wringing her hands so hard that she surely would need an ample supply of hand cream that evening. She hadn't even mentioned the crude phone call from Henry Bouchard. She knew him well enough to know that he didn't need to hear about that. In spite of his current travails, or perhaps because of them, normalcy and routine became paramount. His mind wandered from one morbid subject to the next.

He had treated just two patients the entire day, spending most of the time sitting in his office staring at the walls. A matter of days ago, he'd been looking forward to spending an evening with Alison. Now, he faced yet another evening alone in his condo. Just days ago, he had a burgeoning bank account and a degree of status from his work with TRAC and Henry Bouchard. Now he wondered how he would ever pay his bills. His stalking hearing was just two weeks away. Things were definitely not going John's way as he stepped off the curb into Highland Avenue. With his mind a jumble of negative thoughts, he didn't even realize that he was jaywalking.

Clarisse saw it coming from her window. The car was braking well before it struck him, but seemed to keep going just enough to knock him to the ground. The small grey sedan pulled to the curb and stopped. She ran to the phone, dialed O to report the accident, then ran out the door.

By the time she reached the street, a small group of onlookers surrounded Simms. One man was attending to him while a siren wailed in the distance. Clarisse pushed her way through and knelt by his side. He looked like he had just fallen asleep right on the spot. She stood up and looked over the heads of the crowd.

"Where's the car?" she screamed. "Didn't anybody see what

happened?" She looked from face to face, being met with a series of blank, uncomprehending stares.

BRAD WAITED UNTIL SEVERAL people gathered around the doctor. He slowly pulled ahead in the bus lane for a couple of car lengths then stopped again. In his rearview mirror, he could see that no one seemed to be paying any attention to him. He eased out into the first lane and continued down Highland Avenue. At the first service station, he pulled in and stopped at one of the self-service gas pumps. He got out and went to the front of the car as if to open the hood to check something. A small smudge on the bumper and a series of similar ones on the fender were the only evidence that he had hit Simms. His spontaneous plan to supply a meaningful emotional event to the doctor apparently worked.

He moved his car from the pump and parked next to a phone booth. Jangling his pocket full of change, he pulled out a handful of quarters, nickels, and dimes. He dialed the number and dropped in the exact change as requested.

Bouchard answered before the first ring stopped.

"Dr. Simms has had a lesson. It remains to be seen how hard that lesson was. I'll be in touch." Brad didn't wait for an answer.

Less than an hour later, he was on Interstate 84, heading for the used car lot in Massachusetts where he bought his Escort.

THE AMBULANCE AND POLICE arrived simultaneously. After the unconscious John Simms had been transported, the two officers circulated among the rapidly disappearing spectators, receiving negative nods from all of them until one turned his attention toward Clarisse Shearer.

"I saw what happened from my window up there. It was a hit-and-run." Her voice trembled as she struggled to maintain her composure. "He's my boss, he's a doctor, oh, God, he'll be all right, won't he?"

"You seem to be the only one who saw anything, Miss. Everybody else either didn't see the accident or just saw the aftermath.

If you can calm down a bit, maybe you can help us." The officer waited. The intimidation factor of a police interview often turned average people into bumbling idiots. Eliciting answers required patience.

"What exactly did you see from your window and, if I may ask, how'd you happen to be watching anyway?"

"I'm not sure; I just was stretching and looked out. It looked like he could have stopped but then he kept going, like he just wanted to nudge him with the car. It didn't seem to hit him that hard." She hesitated once more. "As I'm saying this, it sounds pretty silly. I mean, why would anyone want to do that?"

"Can you describe the car, ma'am? Anything at all might help." The officer held his notepad at the ready but dropped it to his side when she answered.

"A small car, maybe gray or black," she said. "He pulled over and stopped, I thought he was going to help but when I got down here, the car was gone."

The officer noticed that his partner had already made his way back to the cruiser. He handed her a card and asked her to call if she remembered anything else. All of the other potential witnesses had dispersed as he climbed into the shotgun position. Clarisse stared after the car as it pulled away then hurried to her own car to drive to the hospital.

Mass Plate WMB2578

PARKER CALLED DISPATCH RIGHT after leaving the Snyder household. First, he wanted them to call Josie informing her that he would be home later than he expected. The second thing was to have them run the plate number of the car that Brad Wallace was driving, assuming that Sheila was correct. As he was speaking with the officer on duty, it occurred to him that he had made a rookie mistake. He'd assumed that the Snyders were a married couple but that might be an inaccurate assumption. He gave the officer a third job: find out if Robert Snyder had a wife. When he arrived back at headquarters, he was sure to have the answer to the most pressing questions. Who was the owner of that Massachusetts plate and where was that owner living?

It was seven o'clock when he parked his car in the headquarters garage. He skipped the elevator, his adrenalin rush causing him to take the stairs two at a time. His rising excitement carried him down the hall at a record pace but when he arrived at his office, he was brought up short. Jim Corbett sat in one chair and Sam Olden was in another. Neither of them should have been on duty, and even if they had been called in, they would not be sitting in his office. Something was wrong. His first thought was that something had happened to Josie but he dismissed that out of hand. She'd be home from school for hours by now on a Friday afternoon.

211

"What's up, boys?" he asked, his attempt at nonchalance falling flat. Both men caught his concern but it was Jim who spoke first.

"Everything's fine, Parker. Relax and we'll fill you in."

His relief brought a broad smile to his face. "You've got a lot of explaining to do. You scared the bejesus out of me." He circled his desk and plopped down in his chair. "OK, let's hear it."

"John Simms was a victim of a hit-and-run this afternoon. Apparently, he just got bumped while he was crossing the street but his head struck the concrete real hard when he went down. He's unconscious and they're doing tests for brain damage. It's weird; not much else—a bruise or two but just minor stuff."

Parker sat in stunned silence, waiting for more information but none was forthcoming. Instead, the sheriff asked the question.

"How did your warnings go this afternoon?"

"As I told you, the superintendent was a pain in the ass; Alison Regan was fine with everything; Robert Snyder didn't seem happy at all to see me but his wife or girlfriend provided some startling information." He reached into his pocket, pulled out the scrap of paper, and handed it to Corbett. "This is the car that Wallace is driving. I called dispatch from the road and they should have tracked it down by now."

The sheriff passed it to Sam Olden with a telling expression, a mix of a raising of the eyebrows and pursing of his lips. The look did not escape Parker's notice.

"What's going on?" he asked, staring hard at Sam Olden. "And by the way, Sam, what are you doing here?" Sam looked to Jim Corbett for help.

"I called him in because he worked on the Regan and Simms case and he did all that stuff for you with those chip things."

"OK, I get that. Now what else?" Parker stood and started pacing back and forth, unable to contain his agitation.

Sam dropped his eyes to the paper. "Shit," he mumbled. He raised his head and met the detective's gaze straight on. "Simms was struck by a gray or black car, a small one, if our witness is correct."

"I guess I'm too late to warn him about Wallace." Parker picked up his phone and hit the button for dispatch. "This guy's getting more dangerous by the minute." He leaned against the edge of his desk and listened. About two minutes passed before he said "thanks a lot" and gently set the phone into its cradle. Olden and Corbett leaned forward.

"That plate isn't valid. It came from a car that was totaled and it should have been destroyed. They'll work on tracking it down tomorrow but technically, it shouldn't be on a car. If a small-time used car dealer used it, even temporarily, he'd be in big trouble."

Jim Corbett offered the obvious suggestion to broadcast a "be on the lookout" order to state and local authorities. It was now over two hours since the Simms accident and that plan didn't appear to have much chance of success, at least at night.

"He's long gone by now but there'd be no harm in trying it. At least we've got a place to start tomorrow."

A New Car

BRAD ROLLED INTO THE lot of Paul's Used Cars an hour and a half after packing up his meager belongings in Farmington. He parked in the shadow of a shack that passed for a closing office. The neon sign on the roof flashed intermittently with a message—*YES WE FINANCE.* The fluorescent lights in the building bounced off the bald head of Paul, who was watching a television mounted on a stand in the corner. Brad assumed that the owner, because of the nature of his business, was sure to be there and he wasn't disappointed.

He started to climb out of his Escort but with the instincts of a bloodhound posing as a used car salesman, Paul was at his door, panting from the exertion. When he saw Brad and recognized the car, he flinched as if a coiled rattlesnake faced him, ready to strike.

In the manner of so many of his colleagues in the business, he recovered his smooth demeanor in an instant, intent on the possibility of the next sale.

"How'd the car do for you?" he asked with a patronizing smile that almost made Brad gag.

"It's been fine but now I need a different one. As you know, I've got the cash." The word cash had an immediate effect and Paul shifted into his conspiratorial mode.

"I've got some great choices, new ones since you were here last. We could handle it just like the last time."

214

At first, Brad couldn't decide if this man really remembered him or was just faking it. As the conversation continued, it became clear that Paul was the epitome of the perfect salesman. He never forgot a face or a name, and certainly not the situation where that face or name originated.

"I think I'll need another plate with whatever I decide to get this time."

Paul, a seasoned veteran of the unethical used car wars, lowered his voice when he responded.

"I understand completely, Mr. Bradford," he said

After a short trip around the lot, Brad chose another bland car, a 1984 white Corolla four-door sedan.

"Want to take it for a test drive? It's really a good car but you should try it out."

"I'll take your word for it. I'm sure it'll be just fine."

When they returned to the office, Paul presented the asking price, ready to reduce it at any indication of resistance.

"I'll take it, under the same conditions as last time. You can have the Escort back but, as I told you, I need new plates."

Paul regarded him with the suspicion that said this guy was not someone to be trifled with. Greed erased the apprehension when Brad pulled the roll of bills from his pocket.

"It's important that I get going right away. My suggestion would be that you not use the plates you gave me again for a long time."

Paul excused himself and returned ten minutes later with an announcement.

"Your car awaits, sir, and the New Hampshire plates are good for another year. They don't stop anybody up there without good reason. It's the 'Live Free or Die' state, you know." His crooked smile unsettled Brad. "If anyone comes around asking, I've never heard of you."

An hour later, Brad and his Corolla crossed the border into South Nashua, New Hampshire. He stayed on Route 3 North-bound until the last exit before it became the Everett Turnpike. New Hampshire was not known for its large cities but the Manchester/Nashua combination was within easy driving distance of the 128 beltway around Boston with its expansion of high-tech companies and economic growth. The population of those two cities grew in proportion to the opportunities afforded and possessed the added attraction of affordable housing and low taxes. Extensive development of service industries accompanied that growth and motels and hotels peppered the neighborhoods surrounding the increasingly popular Manchester Airport.

The area was a perfect place for Brad to disappear as he mapped out his plans for a return to the Lakes Region.

Gone

PARKER BENT OVER AND kissed Josie goodbye as she lounged in bed, taking advantage of the Saturday morning opportunity.

"You're sure you have to go in this early?" she asked. "It is Saturday, you know."

He found her hand under the covers and squeezed it as he straightened up. With her other hand, she threw the light blanket and sheet off to the side.

"Maybe I could convince you to stay." Her short nightgown had ridden up to the top of her thighs. She stretched her arm out above her head and the gown crept up another inch.

"You're not playing fair," Parker said with a leer. "But I'll need you to hold that thought. I'll be home later this morning and I'll let you decide how we spend our lunch hour." He leaned over again and kissed her again, somewhat harder than the first.

"I'll let you know if we had any luck finding Brad overnight. I'm not holding out much hope," he said as he left the room.

ONCE AGAIN, JIM CORBETT was the bearer of news that could not have been much worse. Parker had just opened the container of a McDonald's artery-clogging breakfast platter of eggs, sausage, and English muffin slathered in butter on his desk when the sheriff knocked. He wasted no time in delivering the news.

John Simms suffered a brain aneurysm just after midnight, no doubt caused by the injury sustained in the hit-and-run accident. His prognosis was not good. The doctors were doing all they could and running all kinds of tests but he likely would not last the day.

"Shit," he exclaimed. "And Brad Wallace?" He looked at Jim, who had anticipated the question and was already shaking his head.

"Nothing," he said. "Absolutely nothing. That guy's like the invisible man."

Parker picked up the plastic fork and began to move things around the Styrofoam tray. He popped the lid off the large coffee to let it cool as the sheriff made his way to the door.

"I'll let you eat your breakfast in peace. By the way, I thought you and Josie always ate breakfast together. What's up with the McDonald's? Don't mean to pry or anything."

"Just gave her a break—Saturday morning and all." He stared down at the food, which had taken on the artificial appearance of its container. Suddenly, he slammed his fist down, causing the coffee to slosh over the sides. "Damn it, Simms was a jerk, but he didn't deserve this. Has anybody let that receptionist know? I've got a feeling that there's more than a professional relationship there."

"Not that I know of. Let me know what you're going to do." Then he was gone.

Clarisse Shearer greeted Parker with an apathy that broke his heart. He expected anger or grief or rage or some normal emotion that would suit the situation. When he called, her voice was flat, devoid of life, but he anticipated that in the time it took to travel to her home, she would recover. She hadn't. She was dressed in a bathrobe, although it was ten in the morning when he arrived and she knew he was coming. This was not normal behavior for any woman but then again, these were not normal circumstances. He was sure that she had not even brushed her teeth yet.

"What do you want, Detective? I've told the police everything I saw." They remained at an impasse, she halfway shielded by the door and he standing outside.

"I thought maybe something else might have occurred to you overnight, something that might help."

"Maybe when John wakes up, he'll remember something but the police didn't act as if my information was of any use whatsoever." She didn't miss the she-doesn't-know look flash in his eyes. "What is it? What's wrong?"

"Doctor Simms isn't doing well, Mrs. Shearer. If I could come in, I'll explain."

"No. No. You can't come in. Just leave me alone." She pushed the door closed. Just before the deadbolt snapped into place, he heard a male voice call out, asking if everything was all right.

"That went well," he murmured as he walked back to his car.

PARKER CALLED AN OLD friend who had served with him in the City of Philadelphia Police Department. Brian Borstad moved on to the Massachusetts State Police a month after Parker made the move to Covington County. They spoke to each other about once a year but continued to think of each other as close friends, the kind that can resume a conversation a year later as if no time had passed at all.

When informed that Patrolman Borstad had the day off, Parker went to his Rolodex file and pulled out his home phone number. The question he wanted to ask had a straightforward, uncomplicated answer so Brian wouldn't object to being called at home. After the initial bantering involving war stories from Philly and catching up on their current lives, Parker asked his question about the plates.

The process was a simple one. It only became complicated if someone deliberately decided to circumvent the regulations. When insurance adjusters determined that an automobile was a total loss, the car was towed to a salvage yard and soon was smashed into a two-foot-square block of metal. Most of the time, the plates were part of that block, unless the owner of the car wanted to keep them. Parker listened closely, then asked the follow-up question that was really at the heart of the conversation.

"So, how would a set of plates that were taken from circulation and supposedly destroyed wind up on another car?"

"Come on, Parker, you can't be that naïve. You were a cop in Philadelphia. Body shops can sell those plates for all kinds of illegal reasons. The most common one is to simply get a car from point A to point B without registering it. Less common but still popular is for someone to want transportation but they don't want their name in the system. Buy a car with cash, put phony plates on it, and you could drive forever without getting caught, as long as the plates are not out of date, and even then you might get by if you're careful. If a guy is obeying the traffic laws and has what appear to be valid plates, he'll never get stopped." Brian paused and waited for Parker to ask questions, which he knew he would.

"So, theoretically, if the person has a source, he could just change tags or even cars and tags and never wind up in the system."

"I always told people that you were smarter than you look," Borstad said, and both men broke into hearty laughter at Parker's expense.

The next few minutes of their conversation covered the details of Parker's case and Brian promised to assist him in any way he could when he returned to work on Monday.

"There is a trail. It sometimes takes a while to follow it but it's there. First step is find out where that totaled car went."

Toward the end of the conversation, Jim Corbett slipped into the office, motioned for Parker to ignore him, and leaned against the door jamb.

"Talk to you on Monday, Brian, and thanks a lot for the info." He hung up and invited Corbett to sit down. The offer was ignored.

"Simms is gone. He had another incident; guess that head injury was worse than they figured at first; there was nothing to be done. We've still got nothing but circumstantial evidence but we've got to find this Wallace character."

Parker bowed his head. "Poor Clarisse," he said to himself. "You're right. We do have to find him." He hadn't noticed that the sheriff was already gone.

The Trail: Part One

SATURDAY MORNING, OBLIVIOUS TO the drama unfolding in Covington County, Brad went in search of breakfast, finally settling on a nondescript IHOP that was filled with locals. His extensive summer experiences with New Hampshire had all come in the rural areas of the central part of the state where much of the population depended on tourism for a living. While the people went out of their way to be friendly to the flatlanders from southern New England, many of the natives' cars still carried the amusing but galling bumper stickers. *Welcome to New Hampshire, now go home* irritated those whose wallets the drivers of the cars were so eager to see opened.

The clientele of the IHOP in the heavily commercial section of downtown Nashua seemed more suited to Boston than the New Hampshire he knew. He found a seat at the counter, flanked by two men in suits. The briefcases held between their feet clearly indicated they were on their way to work, although both looked to him like nine-to-five, five-days-a-week businessmen. The waitress approached, wearing the obligatory smile etched on her face, and listened to his order of ham with two eggs over light and coffee. She turned and called it into the kitchen in a short order code, then returned with a pot of coffee that was still bubbling. She splashed the hot liquid into his cup while looking down the counter at another customer, somehow managing to stop before it overflowed.

The man on his right stared at the mound of pancakes on his

plate as if reading tea leaves in a cup so Brad decided to ask his question of the one to his left, who seemed more in touch with his surroundings.

"Excuse me, I hate to bother you, but I'm up here from Connecticut on business and wondered if there's a newsstand or maybe even a library where I could get a look at a paper from back home."

The man rotated on his stool to face him.

"There's a tobacco place right down the block and they've got a lot of papers there. Not sure if they have anything from Connecticut. Best bet probably is to go over to the library on Main and Cottage. You'll see a sign for it if you head south on Route 3 for two lights."

Brad thanked him and turned his attention to his breakfast, which had just been delivered. In typical city fashion, the three men ate as though each was in an isolation booth, exchanging not another word, keeping their eyes straight ahead and posture rigid like all of them wore neck or back braces.

Brad finished breakfast first, looked at the bill, and placed cash on the counter to cover it plus a generous tip.

"Thanks for the directions," he said, but only got a mumbled "sure" in return.

THE SOUTH NASHUA PUBLIC Library subscribed to virtually every New England newspaper and had them arranged by state on the quaint, old-fashioned long sticks which separated every section. Brad went directly to the rack with a fancy wooden sign announcing that it held papers from Connecticut. He was immediately disappointed to find that it was Friday's paper. He didn't expect that his incident with John Simms would make the front page but hit-and-run accidents usually found their way into the news, if only as a filler. The paper in his hand would have been printed well before Friday afternoon.

"When will you get Saturday's *Hartford Courant*, ma'am?" he asked the one staff person he could find, a dour older woman who sighed heavily, as if he had asked her to carry out extensive research for him. The name tag pinned to her ample bosom read Winifred Flowers.

"Connecticut papers are always a day behind. It's not like they're going to deliver way up here. We get most of them by next day mail." She turned away, engrossed in placing little stickers of some sort on each book of a teetering stack, one of the many small detail jobs that occupy so much time in a library.

He stared at her back, started to ask about Sunday hours, but changed his mind. On the way out, he checked the sign and found that the facility was open on Sunday from noon to five.

The Trail: Part Two

BRAD RETURNED TO THE library on Sunday, arriving just after noon. Winifred Flowers had the honor of loading the newspapers on the sticks. She had apparently started with Maine and was working her way southward since the Rhode Island and Connecticut papers remained in piles near their respective racks. Brad meandered over to the Connecticut pile. The *Hartford Courant* happened to be on the top and he picked it up. Winifred rushed over to him.

"You'll have to wait. Those need to be arranged before anyone can read them." She took the paper from his hand and placed it back on top of the pile. The memories of high school librarians he had known during his career came roaring back along with his timidity in the face of their authoritarianism.

"I only need to see one quick item then I'll be out of here, Winifred."

She glared at him as she handed the paper back. "Be quick about it." As he did the day before, he stared at her back as she returned to her duties.

He quickly found the article and, as he expected, it was a filler hidden in the midst of the local news pages. The short piece noted only that John Simms, a general practitioner in the area, had been struck while crossing the street. He was not in a crosswalk. His injuries were unknown but he was kept in the hospital for overnight observation. Police are looking for a small car, either black or gray, as the hit-and-run vehicle. The article closed with the usual plea for anyone with information to call the police.

Brad closed the paper, careful to fold it on the existing creases. The rattling of the paper brought his efforts to the attention of Winifred Flowers. He smiled at her and, with a flourish, placed it back on the pile of Connecticut papers and left the library.

As he returned to the motel, he passed the Crescent Tobacco Shop and Newsstand his breakfast companion had mentioned the day before. On a whim, he wheeled into the parking lot. A shop in Stoneham carried only the Sunday editions of some newspapers like *The New York Times* and perhaps the same held true for this store. His whim proved worthwhile. The shelves were lined with thick Sunday editions and about five copies of the Sunday *Hartford Courant* were stacked right in the middle of them.

Back in his motel room, he reclined on the bed and pulled out the section containing local news, not expecting to find anything further about his incident with Simms. Instead, a headline just below the fold stunned him.

DOCTOR IN HIT-RUN DIES

He skimmed the story, which recounted the requisite how, when, and where of newspaper articles but naturally couldn't address the why. Once again, fate had taken an active role in one of Brad Wallace's attempts to see that justice was served.

Brad rose from the bed, went into the bathroom, and gazed at his reflection in the mirror.

"Poor bastard," he said aloud. "I never intended . . ." The finish of the sentence just hung in the air. His watering eyes caught him completely by surprise.

He threw his suitcase on the bed and began to round up the few things he had unpacked, mostly toiletries, all the time muttering to himself.

"That faux gravesite up on the lake will have to do. I need to talk to Brad, Jr. and I sure as hell can't go back to Mountain View Cemetery."

MONDAY MORNING, BRIAN BORSTAD met with his supervisor, explained the situation to him, and asked if he could take just an hour away from normal duties to do some research. An officer with Brian's stellar reputation did not have to ask more than once. The commander knew what he had and granted his request immediately.

In a single call to the Division of Motor Vehicles, he had the information he needed and minutes later was on the phone with Parker Havenot.

"I've got the name of the company that took care of the totaled car. I remember how you feel about coincidences but amazingly enough, they're actually in our neighborhood up here. I'll just drop by on my rounds later this morning and see what I can find out."

Parker expressed his profound appreciation and they agreed to talk again if Brian had any information for him. "I've got a meeting with the Feds this morning but it should only take an hour or so then I'll be hanging on the edge of my seat waiting for your call."

Brian was startled by the announcement.

"The Feds! What'd you do to deserve that?"

"It's a long story but it's actually related to this case in an obscure sort of way. I'll fill you in when we can get together in person which may be sooner rather than later. Thanks a lot, Brian; I really appreciate your doing this."

JIM CORBETT CALLED A moment after Parker ended his conversation. "They're here," was all he said. Parker walked briskly to the conference room, his stomach fluttering.

Introductions, as expected in the situation, were formal. The sheriff introduced them as Special Agent Aaron Thomas and Special Agent Harold Smythe of the FBI. "This is Detective Parker

Havenot," he said, and the four men sat at the table, Corbett and Parker on one side and the two agents opposite them.

"So, Sheriff, we go back a long way and we're all friends here so why don't you just cut to the chase, as they say, and tell us what we're doing here."

"Actually, I'd prefer to turn it over to the detective, if that's all right with you. He's the one that ferretted this whole thing out." The two agents looked at each other and shrugged their shoulders in unison.

"Go ahead, Parker. You've got the floor."

The sheriff had informed him of the meeting late Friday but with the drama of the Simms accident and the subsequent contact with Jim O'Brien, he had only thought about it again on Sunday. He'd experienced interviews with FBI personnel on many occasions but he still was nervous about it, especially in this case where he had little concrete information to give them. He was prepared for it but hoped he didn't get laughed out of the room.

For almost twenty minutes, he spoke without interruption, explaining the Alison Regan case first then segueing into the connection of John Simms with Henry Bouchard and Univac Redux. He never mentioned Brad Wallace. He finished with an apologetic gesture, opening his palms and spreading his arms apart. "That's about it. We just thought that this experiment they're conducting might be against some federal law."

Agent Thomas reacted first. "Off the top of my head, only the part that Simms played seems illegal and that's purely local jurisdiction. It appears that's moot now anyway. There are dozens, if not hundreds of companies, especially in the Northeast, that are doing research that is borderline but this is the first of this kind I've heard about." He turned to Smythe. "What about you? You aware of anything like this?"

Smythe's answer put a period on the whole conversation. "I've heard of the medical research into chips and some of the stuff they're doing with tracking but we can't possibly step in if it's legitimate. Apparently, all the subjects in this case except for that woman are willing and know what they're doing. It just sounds like good old American ingenuity and corporate competition to me. You folks can handle the Simms type of characters. There are always some of those, especially when good-looking women are involved. We do appreciate your letting us know about this and we'll keep our notes on file in case something comes up later."

The agents, who appeared to do everything in tandem, rose from the table together, a clear signal that this meeting was over.

After the usual handshakes, the agents left the room.

Parker shook his head. "Notes? Did you see them take any notes?"

Jim Corbett smiled. "I'm sure they'll write them up when they get back to the office."

"RUDY'S SCRAP AND SALVAGE Company in Brockton is the name of the outfit. They've got about ten guys who would have access to totaled automobiles before they are loaded into the masher. I guess they try to remove anything of value if it's not too much of a problem," Brian explained.

"Yeah, like license plates." Even though it wasn't even close to his jurisdiction, Parker thought he would ask anyway. "What would be the chances I could talk to those guys, unofficially, of course?"

"I'd say pretty good, but only if I get to go along and watch the master detective in action."

"Agreed. I'll get back to you with some options. It'll have to be later in the week, though. I'm booked until then. And again, I can't thank you enough, my friend. I'll try to live up to my reputation." Parker chuckled as he hung up.

THE MEMORIAL OBSERVANCE FOR John Simms was a simple affair, conducted at the Manlove Funeral Home in West Hartford on Tuesday. Parker rushed to clean off his desk of immediate attention types of things and arrived with ten minutes to spare. The few cars sprinkled throughout the huge parking lot spoke volumes for the personal and professional regard of the doctor.

As he anticipated, Clarisse Shearer's name was the first in the remembrance book, followed closely by Alison Regan. Toward the bottom of the first page, Havenot noticed the dramatic signature of Henry Bouchard. He didn't recognize any of the other names and, after some consideration, squiggled his halfway down the second page. A small sign beneath the book signaled that visitors should follow the hallway with the beige carpet to the Peaceful Room on the left.

The room lived up to its name. Nothing but profound silence greeted him when he entered. He stood facing the backs of the other attendees, all of whom were seated and not moving. It was as if he had been dropped into a movie set where he was the only live character surrounded by cardboard cutouts. Henry Bouchard sat by himself in the last row, even though five rows in front of him were empty. An altar framed by several baskets of fresh-cut flowers and topped by an ornate urn centered the front of the room. Parker scanned the assembly, searching for Alison Regan and found her in the second row. There was a seat next to her and he walked down the center aisle, his squeaking shoes echoing off the walls. He silently excused himself as he bumped into several pairs of knees to get to the seat.

Alison turned, acknowledged him with a nod, then leaned toward him and whispered in his ear.

"I need to talk to you afterward." She then assumed her cutout position with the rest of the gathering.

The service was the shortest one he had ever attended. A minister, who glanced around the room as though hoping for an interruption, opened with the Lord's Prayer, which was unintelligibly mumbled by the group. He then launched into a five-minute cookie cutter eulogy that demonstrated his complete lack of knowledge about the deceased. There was no attempt to sing a hymn. The pastor's request for anyone to stand and say anything they would like about John Simms was met with blank stares with one exception. A young man seated next to Clarisse slowly rose to his feet.

"He was my dad; I didn't know him too well but I remember

him being nice to me when I was little." With that, he sat down. A few sniffles like those heard at the end of a sad movie drifted through the room. After that, no one else opted to make any kind of a speech, although the minister stretched the silence as long as he possible could.

The requisite Psalm 23 was read, as always causing a few to wipe away a tear with its poignant and elegant statement of hope in the face of the finality of death. The group was dismissed with the traditional Christian benediction but everyone waited for Clarisse and John Simms's son to exit first. They formed a receiving line of two at the rear of the room, accepting the condolence clichés with grace as people moved by. Henry Bouchard was first in line thanks to his seat in the last row and was nowhere in sight when Alison and Parker came out to the parking lot.

They walked to Alison's car in the silence that feels mandatory after leaving a funeral service. "What was it you wanted to talk to me about?" Parker asked as she unlocked the door.

When she turned to face him, her eyes were filled but not quite overflowing. "It's my fault, isn't it?"

"What do you mean? He was just in the wrong place at the wrong time. I'm not sure how you can say it was your fault. A few seconds here or there, he wouldn't have been crossing right then. I guess I'm pretty much a fatalist. You do what you can but there's not much you can do when it comes to fate stepping in. You know the old saying; man plans and God laughs."

Now the tears bubbled over. Parker shuffled his feet and waited. "That was a great speech, Detective," Alison said after she recovered her composure. "The truth is that John was not the same after that whole chip thing. I almost feel like he could have stepped in front of the car on purpose." She got into the car and wound the window down.

"The investigation is ongoing but I'll tell you this. Dr. Simms's death was not his doing."

Alison stared straight ahead, giving up on stemming the tears rolling down her cheeks. "I didn't even know he had a son, for God's sake. And one more thing, Detective. As his son said, I remember him being nice to me." She clicked the car into gear and drove off, leaving Parker standing alone in the lot.

THE PLACE LOOKED THE same. Brad entered the long winding driveway and stopped the car. A momentary euphoria gripped him. It was here that destiny had led him. The August rendezvous with the *Belle* hadn't turned out as he expected but he had developed a sense of purpose. That purpose would be fulfilled here. It was here where he would either live free or die.

Nature had begun its reclamation project on his property. The five acres would soon look like so many other abandoned parcels of land sprinkled around the Lakes Region of New Hampshire. As he drove toward the cabin, tendrils from overgrown bushes scraped along the side of the car. As the building came into sight, the lack of care became more evident. Where there had been patches of grass, tall weeds waved back and forth. The towering oak trees had tightened their canopy over the small cleared area circling the cabin, which itself had adopted the forlorn look of disrepair so common with old, deserted farmhouses.

Without proof of his death, the property was doomed to languish for a long time. The deed was solely in his name; eventually the courts would have to decide what to do with it. His most immediate concern was to check on the duplicate gravestone he had set in the ground for Brad, Jr. His second concern was how to hide the fact that he was back. Havenot was sure to investigate the possibility that he had returned to New Hampshire. In some ways, he relished the prospect of his meeting with Parker Havenot on his own turf. He just had to be adequately prepared for it.

The Trail: Part Three

PARKER AND BRIAN BORSTAD met for lunch in Watertown on Thursday. Much of their discussion over the meal focused on which of their vehicles they should drive to Brockton. Brian thought that an official Massachusetts State Police cruiser would send a more intimidating message and might make the folks at Rudy's Scrap and Salvage Company more inclined to cooperate. Parker preferred the low-key approach, using his black, unmarked Covington Sheriff's Department car.

"I guess we'll go with your car. After all, you outrank me. You're a real detective and I'm just a sergeant," Brian conceded.

"Ah, but we're in your jurisdiction, so we should go with your recommendation."

"I feel like we're back in Philly. Remember how we used to argue back then?" Brian smiled. "And you always won."

"Tell you what. We'll just take a bus." They grinned at each other.

When they finished lunch, Parker followed the cruiser back to Troop E headquarters where Brian parked it.

"CAN YOU IMAGINE THE hearing loss rate for workers here?" Brian shouted as Rudy Cappola escorted the two policemen into his private office. The noise level outside prevented any chance at a conversation. The office, despite obvious soundproofing on the walls and ceiling, wasn't much better. The entire building shook and vibrated as though a freight train was rumbling by on a regular basis.

"What can I do for you? We don't get visits from the police very often, and certainly not two at a time," Rudy, the owner, asked over the din. From the reaction of his employees as he walked by, he also was clearly the man in charge. About fifty, he retained his youthful and rugged good looks. Dressed in a uniform identical to his workers, he looked like the kind of boss who's not afraid to get his hands dirty. The image he presented was much different than Parker expected.

The two friends had agreed at lunch that since this was a Connecticut inquiry, Parker should take the lead. The subject of the interview was somewhat new territory for him but Rudy's friendly handshake set him at ease as did the owner's insistence that they take the two comfortable chairs while he unfolded a metal card table chair and sat down facing them.

"We're really sorry to bother you with this. You obviously are a very busy guy." Parker realized that he was shouting, a conscious reaction to the racket. Rudy either was deaf already or was so used to it that he showed no signs of even noticing it.

"We've come across a set of Massachusetts plates being used illegally," Parker continued, toning down his voice slightly. He noticed Randy squinting and wrinkling up his nose, as if to say, "So?" He plowed on. "The car those plates came from was totaled and your company is the one that destroyed it." Randy's squint dried up as he caught on.

"Ah-ha! Now, I know what you're doing here." He got up and went behind his desk to a file cabinet. He pulled open the third drawer and removed a file from about the middle of it.

"This is our SOP manual for dealing with automobiles that are to be scrapped. Every one of my employees is familiar with it, or at least they'd better be." He opened the file and selected a page but did not share it. Instead, he told them what it said.

"Nobody takes anything home from here. We salvage any usable parts first, then, as you can hear, we do an awful lot of smashing and mashing. If the owner of the car has not removed the plates, they get smashed right along with everything else." Randy replaced the paper in the file, and then the file in the cabinet. He closed the drawer with authority, as if to place an exclamation point on what he had just told them.

Brian, with some hesitation but with a nod of approval from Parker, joined in.

"So, how did the plates get on another car if they were destroyed?

Rudy's demeanor changed as the question seemed to challenge everything he had told them. He stood and looked out the window at the facility. "I've got good guys working here. If you're saying that one of them is doing something illegal, I just don't buy it. Why don't you talk to them yourself and you'll see what I mean? I can call them in one at a time or you can go out there, whichever way you want."

Parker also stood. "We've bothered you enough. Why don't we just go out there and chat with the guys in their element? It usually is more comfortable that way."

"Suit yourself," Randy said, extending his hand. "Oh, and by the way, Officer Borstad, the answer to your question? Maybe the plates weren't on the car when it came in."

THE CHALLENGE OF INTERVIEWING Randy's workers in their environment proved daunting. The noise was deafening; no one seemed to appreciate the interruptions, especially by two police officers; the integrity of each employee was being called into question or at least that was how they saw it. The entire process led only to frustration. As Rudy had said, this group of employees seemed above reproach. After the final conversation, Brian and Parker discussed returning to the office and thanking Rudy for his time and for allowing them to talk with his workers. Their consensus was that they didn't want to bother him again. They headed for the car, their strides lacking the resolute determination which they had on the way in.

"What did you think about Rudy's comment, that maybe the

car didn't have the plates when it got here?" Brian asked. Before Parker could answer, he heard footsteps behind him and turned to find one of the men they had interviewed hurrying to catch up with them.

"I think one of you might have dropped this back there." He handed Brian a smudged sheet of white lined paper that looked as if it had been torn from a spiral notebook. "Hope you find what you're looking for." He started back, then stopped suddenly. "Please don't come back here to ask me any questions; I'm taking a chance as it is," he said over his shoulder, his darting eyes pleading. Then he hustled back toward the plant.

Both men had done enough police work to recognize the signs of a nervous informant. Brian casually slipped the note into his pocket. It was back out before he snapped his seat belt together. He scanned it first, then as they left the facility, read it to Parker. The hastily written squiggles left a clear message.

Paul's Used Cars-Framingham-always looking for used plates

"I know exactly where that place is," Brian said. "It's in the direction we are headed, maybe a little further. It's still early. How about if we give it a try?"

"Why not?" Parker answered.

The Trail Ends

WITH HEAVIER THAN NORMAL traffic, the trip to Framingham stretched well beyond its expected half hour, allowing Brian and Parker to swap old stories about the time they served together on the Philadelphia Police Department. As they approached Route 9, with just a few minutes to go, the talk turned to the case at hand. Brian listened, fascinated by the twists and turns the story of Brad Wallace had taken over the years. When Parker filled in the details of the last two years and Brad's double life as a hermit and a supposed avenger, his friend was shaking his head in disbelief. The tale was so engrossing to both driver and passenger that the Route 9 intersection caught them by surprise.

"Take the left and head west. The lot we're looking for is on our right."

The neon sign shone through the overcast and chilly afternoon. It was the kind of a sign that likely stayed on twenty-four hours a day. Parker was observing the number of cars in the lot and didn't make the first driveway.

"I expected a small operation; this guy must have forty or fifty cars here," Parker remarked.

"Pretty typical for a dealership that does its own financing. He probably sells some of these cars three or four times before they're gone for good. He uses a professional for the repossessions so he doesn't get dirty but I'm sure he's got his share of enemies."

They rolled to a stop directly in front of the entrance to the office but before they could exit the car, Paul was out the door and waving at them through the closed windows.

His enthusiasm vanished as he realized he was looking at an unmarked police car, not a potential customer. His wave diminished to an awkward dropping of his hand to his side.

Brian was first out of the car. Paul, ever the salesman, pumped his hand as if greeting an old friend. Parker joined the two and was treated to a similar bone-rattling handshake.

"How can I help you fellows today?" Paul asked, the smallest hesitation in his voice.

As he had done at the salvage plant, Parker assumed the lead. "We've just got a few routine questions for you, if you have the time."

"Do you mind if I, uh, you know . . ."

Brian stepped in with an apology, "Sorry about that, sir," he said as he opened the wallet with his credentials. Parker started to reach for his but Paul stopped him. "No need for that, officer. Let's go into the office and get out of the weather." Paul's nervousness increased with every word.

The policemen looked at each other with a mutual expression that asked "what weather?" as they glanced up at the partly cloudy skies overhead.

The office of Paul Braun defined what an automobile dealer's sales office should be. The chairs for the customers were well-padded for comfort. The wall behind the desk had the requisite certificates of attendance at a variety of sales seminars and conventions with two awards for community service framing them. The room projected an air of professionalism which contrasted with the demeanor of the owner.

"I don't get many visits from the Massachusetts State Police," he said, addressing Brian Borstad. "When I do, it's usually just one of my friends dropping by for a cup of coffee and a doughnut. By the way, can I get you boys anything—coffee, soda, something stronger?" He grinned. "Sorry, you must be on duty, right?" The conspiratorial smirk disappeared when neither man reacted.

"We don't want to take up too much of your time here," Parker said, then explained their reason for being there, watching closely as Braun's face crumbled slightly with each sentence.

"I'll admit I do collect license plates but I don't think there's a law against that, is there?" He had adopted the posture of the wrongly accused citizen, sitting straighter in his chair.

Brian Borstad entered the conversation. "No, you're right. There is no law against collecting them. There is one against using them again for illegally transporting vehicles."

Paul Braun folded his hands on the desk, squeezing his fingers tightly enough to turn his knuckles white. His wrongly accused citizen posture was replaced by a visible tension. "I'm not sure what you mean, officer. Sometimes, I'll help a customer get a car somewhere but I don't see . . ." He stopped talking when Parker abruptly stood up.

"Look, Mr. uh . . .I didn't catch your last name."

"Braun," he sighed.

"Officer Borstad may want to know all about your use of the plates. I could care less. I'm looking for a guy who might have bought one of your cars, would have paid cash, would've been pretty secretive about it, and might have needed your help with getting the car to look legal. This would have been a while back, a few weeks maybe. How much trouble would it be to check your records . . .?"

"Don't need to. I remember him—not like guys like that come through here every day. He bought an Escort and said he wanted to get to Connecticut and would do the paperwork there. I put Mass plates on it for him temporarily." Braun's eyes were now trained on a spot on the floor. "Was just back here recently," he mumbled.

Parker shouted his response. "What the hell did you just say? He was back here?"

Braun surrendered all pretense of being in charge of this situation. With sagging shoulders, he told his story. "He showed up with the Escort; wanted another car and he had the cash. Do you know how tough this business is? I mean, a guy comes in with cash, what am I supposed to do? I help him out."

"I really don't need the sob story. Help him out how, exactly?" Parker hissed. Brian stood back, admiring his detective friend in action.

"I asked, Mr. Braun, how exactly did you help him out this time?"

"He wanted to trade cars, said he needed new tags, so I set him up. Gave him New Hampshire tags this time. They're not very good at checking stuff like that up there."

Parker spoke through gritted teeth. "What kind of car and what's the plate number? We'll need that right now."

"It was a white Corolla but I have no idea about the tags. I can't even remember where I got them."

"But they were valid, right? So, you must have gotten them recently. But you don't remember . . .Jesus!" Parker was pacing back and forth. Braun took this as a bad sign.

"I could get the VIN for you. Would that help?" he asked in his most ingratiating salesman's tone.

Parker didn't answer but just stared at him. Wilting under the glare, Braun backed toward a filing cabinet behind his desk. He reached backward and when he made contact with it, he turned around. The back of his sport coat was spotted with a sizable round stain of sweat. A minute later, he walked over with a single sheet of paper.

"Here the car's description and information. Sorry I can't help you with the tag numbers," he said, as if their business was finished.

"I'm sure that someone from either the Massachusetts State Police or Division of Motor Vehicles will be in touch. Wouldn't you think so, Officer Borstad?" Parker smiled for the first time when Brian grinned and nodded back at him. Almost as an afterthought he asked Braun a final question. "By the way, you wouldn't still have the Escort, would you?"

"First row, last car down. It's gray with a gray interior." He said it like a prayer that it was the last question they would have.

They left without saying another word, leaving Paul Braun to contemplate his future as a used car dealer.

Once outside, they walked down the row of cars, every one of them having a "Special Sale" sign taped on the windshield. When they arrived as the Escort, Parker knelt by the right front fender and ran his hand over the finish.

"Obviously been compounded and waxed," he said. "At least the trail you mentioned has come to an end. Now I've got to follow the next one."

Gordon Tibideau

"HOW WOULD YOU LIKE to spend the weekend up at the cabin, Jos?" Parker opened the conversation as they sipped their glasses of Merlot before dinner.

"I always love to go up there but this is kind of sudden. I had planned to do a lot of catching up on things around here this weekend and it's already Thursday. What's going on?'

"Maybe we haven't been married long enough for the 'how was your day' ritual but I think if I tell you about it, you'll understand."

"Do you really think he's gone back to New Hampshire?" she asked, after Parker related the details of his entire day spent tracking down the car.

"I honestly think he might have. He's got a car with the right plates on it. I can't believe that he would go back to his old cabin but you never know. I'm going to make some calls tomorrow morning and then I thought it might be kind of fun to take a look at his old place. I'm not on call this weekend and you're a typical teacher who has every weekend off with nothing to do; so, what do you think?" He ducked and grabbed his wine glass as a pillow from Josie's chair came flying across the room.

"I'm in but only if you take me with you to see his place. You wouldn't let me go with you when he died. And I earn my money, by the way!" She laughed as she said it.

"I appreciate it, Josie, except if I think there's any danger involved, you're not going to his house. And, by the way, we need to start talking about Brad in the present tense again. He's definitely not at the bottom of Lake Winnipesaukee."

Josie crossed the room and sat on Parker's lap, snuggling as close as possible. "This is like a plot in a bad novel. You know, crazy ex-husband fakes his own death then returns to wreak havoc on his wife and her new husband." She stayed on his lap but sat up straighter and looked into his eyes. "I'm a little afraid, Parker. Brad never liked you, although he always told me that he admired you. I'm sure he's more than a little upset that we wound up together."

Parker pulled her back in her snuggling position and lightly ran his fingers through her hair as she relaxed against him. "I'll confess to feeling a little sorry for him. You never know what pushes some people over the edge but he obviously figures he's just following his conscience. It's like his ability to think rationally veered off the tracks when you lost your son. Ever since then, he's thinks he's been trying to make things right but in some awfully weird ways."

Without changing positions, she whispered, the words drifting up to him soft in tone but harsh in content. "Now it's my turn to confess something and it's not easy. I'm not just a little afraid, to tell you the truth. I am more like a lot afraid. I think he's capable of almost anything. That's why I'm going with you tomorrow."

FRIDAY MORNING, JUST LIKE most of the days of this particular week, Parker was in his office earlier than usual. He fanned through the Rolodex and found Gordon Tibideau's home phone number. He dialed the number, sure that his young friend would be up and about on a Friday morning preparing for what promised to be a gorgeous early fall weekend on the big lake.

When Gordon answered, Parker knew he had made a mistake. His voice had the telltale huskiness of just being awakened.

"Sorry, Gordon, did I wake you?"

"No, no, I'm just a little slow getting started this morning," he said.

"I've never yet had anyone admit that I had awakened them but that's OK," Parker said. He was about to continue with his reason for the call when he heard a faint female voice in the background saying something unintelligible.

"Oh, shit, now I'm really sorry. Listen, just call me back when you get a chance. I'll be in all morning." He hung up before Gordon had a chance to protest.

One of the few photographs on Parker's desk pictured Gordon in the cockpit of his lake patrol boat that Brad Wallace had sunk just before his supposed suicide. The instant rapport with the young law enforcement officer began with a phone call, one that added to the suspicion that Brad Wallace was in a spiraling and unhealthy mental descent.

The memory of that phone call had Parker reaching into the bottom drawer of his desk, a drawer reserved for purely personal items. His organization of the drawer left much to be desired but he visited it on a regular basis and he was able to put his hand on the doodles he had made when discussing Rich Lane's waterskiing accident with Gordon Tibideau. The notes indicated the possibility that Rich's devastating accident may not have been an accident at all. When he had asked if a skilled operator could cause a spill like the one that Rich had taken, Gordon's answer was simple and to the point.

"I'm not sure why you'd want to but it's easy to do. That's why it's so common," Tibideau said, and Parker wrote down his exact words.

That was his first contact with the young lake patrolman and his respect and admiration for him had grown dramatically over the years as they became close friends. Now he was seeking his help once more.

THE MORNING DISAPPEARED UNDER a flurry of paperwork. The intercom buzzed at about ten thirty. "Call on line two, Detective," the dispatcher said. Parker pushed the flashing button.

"This is Havenot. Can I help you?"

"I'm embarrassed," Gordon said without any greeting. "And

I'm really sorry I didn't get to talk to you earlier. Wouldn't you know the one time I decide to take the later shift, you would call?"

"Sounds as if the morning held out some promise for you and I should be the one who's sorry for interrupting." He had known Gordon long enough that he was certain that the younger man was blushing furiously. He half expected to hear an "aw, shucks" come from the other end of the line.

"I was a little busy; you know how that is, right?"

Parker knew his good friend's face was still flushed. "Actually, I don't, but maybe when we get together, you can tell me all about it." He laughed out loud, enjoying his position on the giving end of the teasing.

"So, what can I do for you? You obviously didn't call just to give me all this grief." Gordon was laughing right along with him now.

Parker provided a summary of the tracking of Brad Wallace, including at its conclusion that there was no longer any doubt that Brad was alive.

"Josie's afraid that he's become more dangerous than ever. I feel like I've got to find him to set her mind at ease. Plus the fact that I tend to agree with her."

"You know I'll do anything to help. What do you have in mind?" Gordon's interest in the case carried a personal grudge along with a professional law enforcement connection. Brad might have killed him the day he planned to attack the *Winnipesaukee Belle*. Josie's concern, in his opinion, was justified.

"The car he's driving is a white Corolla with New Hampshire tags. I'm going to talk to the state police up there and see if they are willing to do anything to help; in the meantime, what would you think about just doing a drive-by of his house—see if anything looks different. I can't believe he'd come back there but I'm not sure he's thinking too rationally right now."

Gordon's joyous exclamation stopped him. "That would be great! I'd love to do that!" He hesitated for moment then asked the obvious question. "What about George Grover? Why not ask him?"

While Parker didn't harbor any particular ill feelings toward the local police chief, he wasn't exactly overwhelmed with confidence in his abilities. "Grover's never been on board with us in this. If you remember, he gave us that live free or die speech more than once when we wanted him to check out Wallace's house up there. 'Man can do whatever he wants on his property' or something like that, he said. I'd prefer you to just do a low-key, and I stress that, Gordon, LOW-KEY, undramatic, casing of the place for any signs of activity. We'll be up there late evening tonight and I'll call you tomorrow."

Gordon's palpable excitement radiated through the phone lines. "You can count on me, don't you worry about that," he said, sounding so much like Barney Fife making a promise to Sheriff Taylor in Mayberry that Parker laughed out loud once again.

"Just be careful and I'll see you tomorrow," he said, still chuckling.

Immediately after disconnecting his conversation with Gordon, he instructed his dispatcher to contact Colonel Quint Jacobs, the director of the New Hampshire State Police. A minute later, he had Jacobs on the line.

After summarizing the Wallace case in broad strokes, he made his appeal, a request that to Parker Havenot was an easy one to grant. "I'll fax you a copy of the description and VIN of the car along with a description of Brad Wallace. If you could have your folks looking out for the car and let us know if you find it, we'd appreciate it."

Jacob's response to the request was totally unexpected.

"Do you have any idea how many white Corollas there are in this state, Detective? If we start pulling over people for no reason just to see if it's the one you're looking for, we're going to have a lot of upset natives up here. Have you never heard of just cause? We'd love to help you out but from what I'm hearing, you're not even sure that the car is in New Hampshire. Maybe your guy headed south or west. I'll let our guys know but I can't promise they'll be pulling anyone over without some reason. Send me the stuff and I'll let you know if anything happens." The colonel hung up.

Parker sat there, stunned, then called Jim Corbett and asked him to come to his office. When he arrived, Parker motioned for him to have a seat then related the details of the phone call debacle with Quint Jacobs. He finished with what the sheriff found to be a comical aside.

"If I may speak candidly . . ." he began.

Corbett giggled. "No, you may not! What is this, Parker, some kind of joke?"

"No joke. I just want to say that I'm just getting pretty weary of listening to live free or die lectures."

GORDON DROVE PAST THE entrance to Brad's house on the south side of the big lake twice. On the second pass, he slowed down just enough to glance down the driveway, which appeared unused. He saw no sign of life; he made a quick U-turn, pulled off the road, and parked. He sat thinking about his best course of action. His two choices were plain—either he could drive right in, which would automatically alert anyone in the cabin, or he could walk in, using the edge of the forest as cover, and surprise whoever might be there. Parker's warning had unnerved him enough that he decided to move the car down the road to a less conspicuous place and walk back. If Brad Wallace had returned to New Hampshire, he very possibly could have returned to this property, as isolated as it was.

About a quarter of a mile down the road, Gordon turned into an old logging road, now just two ruts with knee-high weeds between them. It looked solid enough and he crept the car forward far enough that it couldn't be seen. He walked back to the road and turned toward Brad Wallace's cabin. Twice, he heard cars approaching and ducked off into the woods as they passed. About fifty yards from the entrance, he turned into the forest at an angle that would intersect with the driveway about the same distance from the road. As a seasoned hunter, he knew how to navigate thick brush and woodlands with stealth and wiliness and soon found himself standing next to the driveway. The breezes of the last few days had brought down a fresh layer of poplar and maple leaves, eliminating any possibility of finding car tracks at the juncture where he stood. The cabin barely peeked through the growth of sizable trees that lined the long curved path. There was no sign of any vehicles parked at the house but Gordon decided he needed to get a closer look. He moved a few feet into the woods and picked his way toward the house.

Less than an acre of the five on the property was cleared. The thick forests around Lake Winnipesaukee tended to reclaim their space quickly and in the short while since Gordon had been there last, nature had been hard at work, if only in his imagination. The canopy created by the overhanging branches darkened the open space, as if it were two hours later than it really was. He hung on the edge of the woods, staring at the cabin for any indications of movement within. Satisfied that no one was around, he left his cover and started across the yard. The place was exactly as he remembered it on his last visit there with Parker when they discovered the newspaper. The partial boat hulls lay scattered about, the experimental holes put there by Brad still obvious.

"That was one sick soul," he said aloud. He ventured toward the stone bench and the mock gravesite Brad had constructed. As he approached it, he happened to look down to avoid tripping over some of the dead branches brought down by the winds. He stood in the middle of a fresh set of tire tracks, clearly evident in the dirt. With the hair on the nape of his neck standing straight out, he literally spun around in a three-hundred-and-sixty-degree circle. No car or person made an appearance. He followed the path of the tracks with his eyes. They led between the cabin and the storage shed where he and Parker had found Wallace's scuba gear and weaponry. He walked slowly toward the shed, staying in the center of the tracks with eyes scanning in both directions.

When he reached the shed, he couldn't resist the temptation to peer through the window. At first, everything appeared to be just as they had seen it on the previous trip. Glancing around a second time, his attention came to rest on the corner where one of Brad's spear guns had been. He moved around to the door and pushed it open. A loud creak startled him and he recoiled but recovered quickly. The thudding of his heart in his chest told him that his adrenal gland was functioning properly. He entered the shed and walked directly to the corner where the weapon had been, certain that his memory had not failed him. The gun was not there. He knelt down to look under the bottom rows of shelves that lay close to the floor. The intuition of a law enforcement official kicked in but too late. In the instant that the synapses sent the message that he was in danger, Brad Wallace slammed the two by four into the side of his head, first sending blinding sparkles of light flitting around in his brain, then the blackness enveloped him.

A CURSORY SEARCH OF Gordon's pockets produced the keys to his car. Brad looked down at the crumpled Tibideau and decided that it was safe to leave him. He left the shed and hurried down his driveway to the road. Tibideau must have parked reasonably close by. He started off in one direction but then remembered the tote road to the north. Five minutes later, Gordon's car was parked beside his Corolla, both hidden behind the cabin and somewhat obscured by the thick underbrush.

He returned to the shed.

"I'm guessing someone's going to come looking for you, Gordo," he said to his victim, who lay perfectly still in the same position where he had left him.

The Havenots in New Hampshire

JOSIE LEFT SCHOOL ON Friday afternoon as soon as the secretary placed the "Staff Availability Chart" on the counter. The chart supposedly was designed to let the administration know if any classrooms had to be covered in the morning should a teacher be late for some reason but everyone knew that it served a dual purpose. When the secretary whisked it away at exactly seven o'clock every morning, she marked a red X next to the name of anyone who was late. Two of those X's earned a meeting with the principal and a third led to a written reprimand in the teacher's personnel file. Josie knew that some of those in line to sign out exactly at 3:30 had a fair share of red X's from the mornings. Since it was Friday, the line to sign out for the weekend was longer than usual. It was a rare occasion for her to be leaving the school before four thirty or five in the afternoon and she kept her eyes averted as if ashamed to be in the company of this particular group.

Parker had been uncharacteristically adamant about going to New Hampshire for the weekend and she felt that she should honor his request. An early escape from school would give her time to pack some last-minute items for the trip and have everything ready when he came home from work.

PARKER LEFT HIS OFFICE a full hour ahead of his usual schedule, determined to get a relatively early start on the three-and-a-half hour trip to the cottage on the lake. As he passed Jim Corbett's office, he gave a goodbye salute and was chagrined to see the sheriff jump out of his chair and motion to him. He stopped but stayed in the hall just outside the door. To enter the office would mean sitting down and sitting down conversations always lasted longer than standing in the hall chats.

"What are you up to for the weekend?" Jim asked. "Anything fun?"

"We're going up to the cottage, do some old-fashioned leaf-peeping, enjoy the fall weather, you know, that sort of thing."

"Why do I have the feeling you're holding back on me, Parker? You wouldn't be including a little Brad Wallace hunting while you're there, would you?" Corbett smiled. "I know you pretty well by now."

"My friend Gordon's checking out his house today, and I'll see him tomorrow for a report. Like the colonel said, Wallace is probably headed in the exact opposite direction by now. I think Josie and I will be having a goodly amount of quality time and I'm really looking forward to that!" Parker's body language had him leaning toward the exit.

"See you Monday and have a great weekend. Drive safe and be careful, will you?"

"Always," Parker said with a grin.

GORDON TIBIDEAU EXHIBITED THE signs that Brad had learned during his coaching days were symptomatic of possible brain injury. As he lay on the floor of the shed, his body gradually shifted involuntarily until it looked as if he had worked his way into a comfortable position and simply fallen asleep. Obviously, Gordon was comatose; he could wake up momentarily and he may never wake up. Brad's rudimentary medical knowledge told him that the large swelling on the side of his head was a good thing since internal swelling would place potentially life-threatening pressure on the brain. He gazed down at the younger man, then reached over and picked up the four-foot section of two by four he had used in the brief attack. As if awaiting his turn at bat in a World

Series game, he twisted it in his hands, picking up several splinters in the process. The pain from the slivers of wood finally penetrated his consciousness and he ceased grinding.

"What the fuck is wrong with me?" he hissed. "This guy never did anything to me!"

He propped the shed door open, using the two by four, then returned to Gordon. He pulled him into a sitting position and circled around behind him. Without losing contact, he slipped his own arms under Gordon's armpits. With a hard tug, he was able to gain some momentum, and in a short time, managed to drag the stricken man all the way into his cabin. He flopped him onto the futon in his small living room, gently raised his head and slid a small pillow under it. Gordon showed no sign of being aware of anything in his environment, another symptom of a deep coma, one so deep that the man could not feel anything, even intense pain. Brad lifted his legs and they fell into place on the futon. The swelling just above Gordon's right ear appeared to be worse but he lay there as though enjoying an afternoon nap.

It was time to have a chat with Brad, Jr. or at least, his proxy.

THE HAVENOTS DID NOT arrive at the cottage until well after ten o'clock that night. The fall weekend traffic mimicked what it was like in the summer, turning the trip into an interminable four and half hours.

The only positive side of the prolonged journey was the opportunity for Parker to share all of the details of the past week instead of the condensed version. Josie listened with keen interest but with minimal commentary, mesmerized by the apparent exploits of her ex-husband. In the retelling of the story, Parker became more and more convinced that Brad Wallace would never return to the scene of his last crime in New Hampshire. As Josie gently reminded him, Brad was ready to sink a boat with dozens of innocent people aboard just so he could avenge what he perceived as injustices toward him personally. It had nothing to do with his furious reaction to major issues like the Vietnam War or racial hatred and inequality. His attack on the *Winnipesaukee Belle* was to be a settling of personal grievances against the educational establishment and people in leadership positions like George Metcalf. Had his plan not been foiled, the collateral damage from the attack would have been devastating. In the end, she agreed. Brad Wallace surely would be pulling another of his disappearing acts once again.

"If we had gotten in here earlier, I might have called Gordon. I'm really curious what he found at that cabin," Parker said as they brought the last of their supplies in.

"From what you told me about this morning's call, I think maybe you shouldn't bother him until much later in the morning tomorrow." She batted her eyelashes and grinned. "Hearing about Gordon made me a little jealous. Maybe we could sleep in for a while tomorrow morning as well." She sidled over to him. "If you know what I mean," she purred.

"Sounds good to me, just so we don't use up too much of our strength in case we want to take a nice afternoon nap; that is, if you know what I mean." They giggled like a teenaged couple hiding in a dark closet.

Saturday Morning

DESPITE THEIR LATE ARRIVAL and the promise to sleep as long as they could, Josie and Parker found themselves having coffee on the deck as the spectacular sunrise behind them cast a myriad of colors and cloud reflections across the lake spread out before them.

"This has got to be a good day with a start like this," Josie offered.

Parker seemed not to hear her as he absorbed the humbling display of nature around him. When he realized what she had said, he apologized.

"Sorry, Jos; I was just kind of caught up in the moment. Yep, you're right. It's got to be a good day."

"So, why don't we start it off on a positive note?" she said, setting her coffee cup down. She took his hand and led him back into the house.

"YOU ARE ABSOLUTELY AMAZING!" Parker said an hour later as they enjoyed their second cup of coffee on the deck.

"On a more mundane note, when do you think I could call Gordon, you know, without interrupting the same kind of activity we . . . umm . . ." Parker, a fifty-plus-year-old and a seasoned veteran of police affairs, stammered, blushing like a teenager.

"You are so cute, you know that!" Josie chuckled but kept her

253

composure. "He's a lot younger than we are so give him another hour or so. I'm sure he can't wait to hear from you but everything in its time."

At ten o'clock, Parker could wait no longer.

"I'm calling him. I don't care what I interrupt at this hour." Parker dialed his number and waited.

"You've reached Lake Patrolman Gordon Tibideau. Please leave your name and number and I'll get back to you as soon as possible." The generic answering machine message made Parker sit up straighter in his chair.

"I'm trying him at headquarters," he said to Josie, whose feet stretched out before her on the hassock. She looked ready to take a mid-morning nap.

Parker took the phone and went into the bedroom. When he came out, his complexion had turned from healthy tan to ghostly white.

"They haven't heard from him this morning. He called in yesterday, probably right after I talked to him; told them he'd like someone to cover his shift because something came up. He was supposed to be on the eight to four shift today but hasn't shown up yet. Something's wrong, Jos. I'm going over to his house."

"I'm going with you," Josie said.

BRAD SLEPT BUT NOT well. At least once an hour, he came out of the bedroom to check on Gordon, each time finding him in the same position on the futon. His respiration rate seemed normal and his pulse was regular, but when Brad shook his shoulder, there was no reaction. It was as though he had been given an anesthetic in preparation for a medical procedure. He had been out for close to eighteen hours.

The September sun finally succeeded in forcing the chill from the morning air. Brad peeked through the front window at the splashes of dazzling light spreading across the yard. The brightest reflection ricocheted off the marker he had planted almost two years before. The effect was mesmerizing, like someone was signaling him with a mirror. A second sunbeam illuminated the stone bench where he had sat for so many hours during his refreshing black periods. As though in a trance, he opened the front door, walked straight to the bench, sat down, and began to speak.

Fifteen minutes later, he knew what he had to do. He stood up, stretched, drew in a deep breath, and headed back toward the house. After one more quick examination of Gordon, he went into the bedroom, found his briefcase, and returned to his favorite chair in the living room. As he pulled the aging yellow legal pad out, the slip of paper with the list of names came with it. He glanced at it then shoved it back into the briefcase.

The note he wrote was brief, to the point, yet enigmatic.

It will end where it should have ended before.
I'm sorry to have caused so much grief.

He ripped the sheet off, leaving jagged edges behind, and dropped the pad on the floor. He got up and approached Gordon one last time. He lifted his limp arm, slid the note under it, and set it back down across his chest. "Hope everything will be OK with you," he said, speaking in a conversational tone.

After one long look around the cabin, he grabbed the car keys from the hook by the door and left. As he drove across the yard, he stopped the car, rolled the window down, and waved in the direction of the simulated gravesite.

"We really would've had a good time, my boy," he called out. Then he drove off without looking back.

GORDON'S HOUSE WAS LOCKED up tight. After peering through all the windows, Parker and Josie came to the logical conclusion that he hadn't come home. There were no dishes, no coffee pot, the bed was made, and there was no sign that he had occupied the house overnight. He always kept his car garaged but a quick glimpse through the side window showed just an empty space where his car should have been.

"We've got to check out Brad's cabin. We can be over there in forty minutes." Parker voice shook. "If something's happened to him . . . Dammit, why did I ask him to check things out!"

"Shouldn't we call the police or something?" Josie asked. Parker stared at her. Even in the seriousness of the moment, they both laughed. "Sorry about that! Let's get going."

BRAD DROVE INTO MEREDITH and stopped at the first marina he saw that had a boat rental sign. Although the season was coming to a close, the town docks were crowded with tourists, even at nine in the morning, and Avery's Marina had more than its usual share of customers. By the time Brad had completed the rental transaction, it was 10:15. A brief impasse ensued regarding his lack of identification, but the upfront cash payment turned that into a nonissue. He told the owner he'd be back later to pick up the boat. As he left the shop, he noticed a pay phone across the street. "Oh, hell," he said to himself. He went back in and asked for change.

The phone booth was decorated with the usual scratched initials and graffiti. The phone book hung by a chain but the inside had been decimated, probably by the same vandals. Somehow, the first few pages for town offices and services had escaped unscathed. He found the number for emergencies in the Gilford area and dialed it. As soon as the connection was made, he dropped in two quarters.

"Please send an ambulance right away. A guy in the front room of the cabin needs help." He supplied brief directions then hung up to the sound of the operator asking for his name and his connection to the request.

PARKER AND JOSIE ARRIVED at the cabin in a cloud of dust as he brought the car to a skidding stop in the yard. They were out of the car in seconds, glancing around in search of any sign of Brad. All pretense of being careful was cast aside. Josie came around the front of the car, which had stopped well past the front entrance. She noticed the glint of sunlight reflecting off a metal surface at the rear of the house.

"Parker, a car!" she called out. He hurried to her side and

together they walked toward the reflection. After just a few steps. Parker froze.

In the distance, they heard the wail of a siren but ignored it. "That's Gordon's car. He's got that Lake Patrol sticker in the window. Shit! He's here." The siren was louder and clearly was getting closer.

Parker didn't hesitate. "You stay right here and don't move. I'm going to the front door." Josie did as she was told and watched as Parker disappeared around the corner. She heard him rap loudly on the door, calling out at the same time.

"Police! Open up!" There was no response. He tried the door, which was not locked. He gave it a gentle push and it swung open, revealing Gordon, apparently sleeping on the couch. He called for Josie just as the ambulance, siren still blaring, swung into the driveway.

"What the hell is going on?" He crossed the small room to his friend and felt for a pulse. As he lifted his wrist, the yellow paper first stuck to Gordon's arm then fluttered to the floor. Josie bent to pick it up just as the first emergency technician came through the door. She rammed it into her pocket, all of her attention riveted on their friend lying on the futon.

"Pulse is strong," Parker said. "We'd better get out of the way so they can do their job." It was then that he noticed the bluish tinge and swelling on the right side of Gordon's head.

"What in God's name happened here?" he asked, framing the question for himself as much as for anyone else.

While Gordon was being prepared for transport, Josie and Parker walked around the property. Josie gasped when he showed her the marker with Brad, Jr.'s name inscribed on it. Even though Parker had told her about it from his previous visits, the shock of actually seeing it showed in her disturbed frown as if she had just witnessed the abuse of a child.

The shed door remained propped open by the two by four. After a cursory examination, Parker could see what likely happened. Although weeds prevented the path of the drag marks showing in some places, enough dirt remained to clearly outline the trail from the shed to the front door of the house. The weapon used for the attack stood in plain sight.

A quiet conversation caught their attention and they turned to see the technicians carrying the stretcher bearing Gordon, still appearing to be in a deep sleep.

"Any prognosis?" Parker asked. Their negative head shakes answered the question.

"I understand. What hospital?"

"Lakes Region General. It's the closest. Will you be heading over there? I'm sure the police will be getting involved in this somehow or other and they'll want to talk to you."

"We'll be right behind you. How'd you hear about this anyway? We just happened to be checking on a friend. "

"Anonymous caller. If you wanted to, our dispatch guy probably has figured out where it came from by now. Give him a call down at our headquarters if you're really interested. We gotta get going."

Parker reached out and touched the stretcher just before they slid it into the vehicle. He turned sharply away and didn't turn back until the ambulance left. Then he grabbed Josie, hugged her, and put his head on her shoulder. "My damn fault," he said.

His sobs shook them both. It was several minutes before he was composed enough to drive.

As they pulled into the hospital parking lot, Josie snapped her fingers. She unsnapped the seat belt, reached into her pocket, and pulled out the yellow sheet of paper.

"This is now contaminated evidence, I guess. I forgot about it with all that was going on."

"Wouldn't worry about that for now. What's it say, anyway?"

She smoothed it out and read it to him.

It'll end where it should have ended before.
I'm sorry to have caused so much grief.

"What do you think it means, Parker? Any ideas?"

Saturday Afternoon

THE FALL SUNSET CRUISES of the *Winnipesaukee Belle* started earlier than they did in the summer. They still had the reputation of being booze cruises with the only differences being that the drinking started earlier and more natives took advantage of them with fewer tourists around.

Brad picked up a fall schedule and figured he should have his boat in place by late afternoon if the timing was going to be right. His preparations would not take long but this was to be his signature moment as an agent for justice and failure wasn't an option this time.

THE RELIEF WAS SO intense that Josie and Parker could only cling to each other. They could only pray that the head trauma specialist who examined Gordon was correct but there seemed no reason to doubt him. The three hours of waiting had drained their optimism but the doctor's announcement refilled their half-empty glass to overflowing.

"Once we get that swelling down, I'm certain Mr. Tibideau will come around. He actually showed some good signs while we were testing. I see no evidence of permanent brain damage and the injury looks a lot worse that it really is. I've seen more of these than you would think, especially from motorcycle accidents where the boneheads . . .umm . . .sorry, that's unkind . . . the guys aren't

259

wearing helmets. Anyway, I think in a day or so, we'll see marked improvement." Parker grabbed the doctor's hand and squeezed it so hard that he let out a small yelp.

When they left the hospital, they practically ran to the car. Their joy lasted only long enough for Josie to pick up Brad's note. "What are we going to do about this?" she asked.

"We're going to visit the marina near where that phone booth is. When I called that dispatcher, he said the number's assigned to a pay phone with the nearest building a place called Avery's Marina. We'll just see if they happened to see him. I guess I'm not sure what happens after that. I'm just a little out of my jurisdiction up here."

They drove in silence for a few minutes before Parker spoke up.

"What do you think he means in that note, Jos? You were married to the guy for almost twenty-five years. Any hints whatsoever?"

"This is a different Brad Wallace than the person I married. He was a gifted teacher; he cared about his kids and people in general; he was a good, kind man; and now he's mentally screwed up. The guy I knew would never have cracked someone over the head. It's not about his disenchantment anymore. He barely knew Gordon. It's like he's lost touch or doesn't care or something."

"Hmmm . . ." was Parker's only reply.

The parking lot at Avery's was full so Parker pulled into a fire lane directly in front of the entrance. "I'll be right back. This shouldn't take long. Move the car if anyone hassles you."

Josie kept glancing around, ready to drive around the block rather than be sitting in a car in a no-parking zone. Parker hadn't even put his official police sign in the front window. Ten minutes later, which seemed like hours to Josie, Parker emerged from the marina. He literally started the car before he was fully seated. He accelerated out of the lot, spraying accumulated sand and gravel across the blacktop.

"Tell me again what you said there at the end," he said as they sped onto Route 3 heading north and east toward Stoneham and Wolfeboro.

"What is it? What's going on?" Parker attention focused on the road but Josie's shaking voice forced him to answer.

"He rented a boat, a powerful outboard, and he made the damn phone call. The guy remembered that he asked for change. Now, you said something that made me think back there when you were talking about him."

"What? Like he doesn't seem to care?"

"I think I know what he means by that note. He just doesn't care what happens anymore."

BRAD PICKED UP HIS boat just after two o'clock. He promised the owner of the marina that he would be finished with it by six then engaged in a semantic discussion over whether he meant he would return it by six or be finished using it by six. That exchange ended with no conclusion. The *Belle's* cruise would start at three. He would have some time to drift then set the anchor in about the same place as he was during his last encounter with the *Belle*. By the time it maneuvered into position for the best possible sunset viewing, many of its patrons wouldn't be sure which direction was east and which was west and would not be paying any attention to a boat anchored nearby.

His extensive knowledge of the big lake allowed him to use little-known shortcuts from Meredith to cross the broads to the north side and he was in exactly the right place in less than forty-five minutes. He changed his mind about drifting as the boat traffic was sufficient to cause a light to moderate chop, a surprising development considering the time of year. Normally, most boaters had their crafts pulled from the water by now, a couple of weeks into the fall season. Rather than constantly adjusting for the drift to make sure he remained in position, he anchored and began preparations for the upcoming event.

THE HAVENOTS PULLED INTO the Stoneham Police Department lot at 4:10 in the afternoon and hurried into the station. In the summer, a full staff of patrolmen would be on duty, ready to respond to the needs of a community whose population quintupled during the high season. Instead, even with the Chamber of Commerce weather for the fall weekend, they found just the officer on duty at the desk.

"I need to speak to George Grover," Parker said. "It's very important."

The young sergeant yawned without excusing himself. "The Chief's not on duty. I can't contact him unless it's an emergency."

"And who determines that?" Parker asked, his patience evaporating.

"I guess I do so you'll need to tell me what it is that you want." He stifled another yawn.

"Look, I'm a detective with the Covington County Sheriff's Department in Connecticut." He yanked his wallet out of his pocket and flashed his badge. "We need to get a lake patrol boat out to the *Winnipesaukee Belle.* There could be a dangerous situation out there."

Without answering, the policeman opened a gate and came around from behind the counter. He went directly to the window and peered out. The building had a clear view over the stores on the other side of the street to the town docks. "You're in luck, Detective. There's a lake patrol boat docked right down there. Lake's not our jurisdiction anyway so I don't know what Chief Grover could do for you."

"Shit!" Parker exclaimed. He grabbed Josie's hand, led her out the door and down the flight of stairs leading to the street. They found the nearest crosswalk and started across toward the docks only to be greeted by a blast from a horn and a squealing of tires.

"Goddamned idiots," he swore. "These yield to pedestrians in crosswalk signs are worthless," he mumbled as he dragged Josie behind him, ignoring the motorists' bellowing.

The squeal of the tires on the street above captured everyone's attention down by the docks, including the lake patrolman, who was watching curiously as the couple ran straight at him.

Parker raised his hand as if to ask for a time out, caught his breath, and launched into his story. The patrolman interrupted before he had uttered two sentences.

"I know who you are, sir. I was in the other patrol boat, the one that brought you on board after Gordon's exploded. You're a good friend of his, right?" The calmness in his voice relaxed the Havenots but the obvious urgency in their demeanor had its desired effect.

In typical law enforcement verbal shorthand, Parker related what they thought might be happening.

"I'm going to call for backup just in case, and I really hate to ask you this, Mrs. Havenot, but I think it might be best for you to come along in case we have a situation with your husband that you can help us to handle."

"It's ex-husband, and there would be no way you'd have left me standing here."

A minute later, the patrol boat roared away from the dock, nearly washing away the "NO WAKE" sign.

BRAD ESTIMATED THAT THE Evinrude engine weighed about one hundred and fifty pounds. If all of the attachment hardware, including the motor mounts, were loosened, a solid push would send it overboard. He unzipped the equipment bag he had grabbed as he left his house and felt around for his small toolbox that should contain everything he would need. After spreading the tools out on the rear seat, he went to work. The years of experience working on his father's boat made the job relatively easy, with the only hesitation coming when an unwelcome yet wonderful memory of working alongside his dad caused him to pause as he wiped his eyes.

Fifteen minutes later, all but one of the connections had been removed. He picked up his shears from the seat and went to the storage bin in the bow where a coil of waterskiing tow rope was stored. About twenty feet would be sufficient. Making an approximation, he cut the coil, unrolled a section of the rope, and returned to the stern where he wrapped several loops tightly around the

motor and secured it with his best bowline knot. He checked the
two cleats used for attaching the skiing tow rope. Satisfied that
they were both secure, he selected a spot about in the middle of
the rope that remained and wound it around each of the cleats
twice, leaving a coil of about six feet loose on the floor near the
stern.

After removing the last of the bolts on the motor mounts, he
gently rocked the teetering engine back and forth. With a final
push, it came loose and toppled into the water, pausing briefly
on the surface then sinking. Brad was sweating despite the cool
temperatures of both air and water as he watched the engine pull
the rope taut as it sank. The loops on the cleats held; the motor
was submerged out of sight, about ten feet down. He went back
to the bow and sat on the bench seat; the *Belle* would not make an
appearance for another hour so he had time to regroup for what
was sure to be the most difficult part of his plan for this final act
in the drama. He let his chin drop toward his chest and closed his
eyes to wait.

THE WINNIPESAUKEE BELLE ROUNDED the peninsula, coming
into sight right on schedule. The music drifted across the water
toward Brad, who had spent the hour in solitude, not allowing
any passing boats or other distractions to interfere with his mental
preparation. As soon as he saw the *Belle*, he stood and went to the
back of the boat. He picked up the end of the rope in the remaining coil and began to thread it through his belt loops when he
heard the sirens. He looked to the north and saw a lake patrol boat,
red and blue lights flashing, heading directly at him and closing
fast. A second siren came from the south. It was also a patrol boat
but was much further away.

"What the hell . . .?" he shouted as he pushed the rope through
the final few loops, his hands shaking violently.

After pulling the rope snugly around his waist, he tied another
bowline knot, checking it twice to make sure it would do the job.
He climbed onto the back of the boat and slid down onto one of
the steps just above the surface and unwrapped the rope from the

cleat nearest the submerged engine, which dropped an additional two feet then stopped as the last cleat held. He lowered himself into the water, holding on to the step with one hand and reaching for the final cleat with the other. Two loops held the motor. He could unwind them in seconds.

The patrolman manning the police boat had begun hailing him through his megaphone as it circled around to the stern. When he saw Brad in the water, he shouted to him.

"Get back in the boat and wait until we come along side. Now!"

Brad looked over his shoulder and saw Josie and Parker leaning over the side. The patrol crept closer and then it was Josie hollering to him.

"Do what he says, Brad. Please! We'll help you. We'll do whatever you want." Her voice cracked with desperation.

Parker called to him. "She's right, Brad. It's all over but we can help you if you'll let us. Just get back in the boat." Then he noticed Brad gripping the rope and the missing engine. Everything became clear.

"DON'T DO IT! BRAD, PLEASE!" Parker shouted.

"It's all too late," Brad shouted to them. "I'm the one who deserves an agent for justice. It's live free or die, right? And I'm never going to live free."

He already had one loop undone and he hadn't even finished with the second before the weight of the motor caused it to pull loose.

Brad let go of his hold on the step.

"Goodbye, Josie," he said as the rope tightened around his waist. The motor tumbled toward the bottom of the lake, pulling him down with barely a ripple.

For the second time in less than two months, Josie watched as he disappeared beneath the surface.

Preview of *Cracks in the Wall*,
the next Parker Havenot novel

Monday, May 10, 1993

"I FUCKING HATE YOU!" The message ended with the resounding crash of a phone being slammed back into its cradle.

Detective Parker Havenot, Sheriff Jim Corbett, and Sergeant Sam Olden huddled around the desk, staring at the telephone answering machine. They listened to the message for the fifth time, as if hearing the four words repeated over and over again might provide additional insight.

"This has got to be our guy," the sheriff said. Sam nodded in agreement but Parker brought him up short.

"Sometimes it seems like you've got a slam-dunk proposition, but you folks know that things aren't always as they seem." His pronouncement deflated them as surely as air escapes from a pin-pricked balloon, but Jim Corbett recovered quickly.

"This guy's been stalking Linda Phillips for months now, and especially over the last two weeks. All of her friends are in agreement about that. I say we bring him in and have a chat."

"OK. I'll go along with it but I want it to be voluntary, make it seem like he's doing us a favor, at least to get him in here without issuing any paperwork."

"What about the state police?" Sam asked. "Aren't we going to get into some kind of jurisdictional hassle? They're the ones processing the crime scene."

"Hampton Village is right smack in the middle of our county

and I've already spoken with them. We'll be taking the lead with their role just being support. With his Philly experience, Parker's got more skills in homicide than most of their guys anyway. That won't be a problem but thanks for the concern, Sam." The sheriff turned his attention to Parker. "You're OK with taking this on, right?"

Parker's answer was just to flash a wide grin at him.

"I'll get in touch with Tommy Iverson and have him in here this afternoon," he said. "You guys can watch the interview through the window."

"We'll be recording this. That's not a problem for you, is it?" Parker asked, his question sounding more like a statement of accepted fact.

Tommy nodded, staring at the two machines on the narrow table separating the two men. Their knees were almost touching. "I've got nothing to hide. Why do you have two?"

"Just standard procedure; you know, backups for each other. I know I asked you this on the phone but I'll ask it once more." Parker pushed the record button and the sound of the whirring tape seemed to hypnotize Tommy momentarily.

"This is May 10, 1993. The time is 3:20 in the afternoon. Mr. Iverson, will you just repeat that it is all right with you that we are recording this interview and that I've offered to postpone it if you wanted to have a lawyer present?"

Iverson scanned the room, his glance stopping at the window exactly opposite him. The stark reflection of the back of Havenot's head and his face told him what it was. "Who else is watching this?" he asked.

"Again, just standard procedure; nothing to worry about. More for your protection than anything. I've got the sheriff in there. Now, if you could answer the question and we'll get this over with as fast as we can."

"Yeah, I'm good with the recording and I sure as hell don't need a lawyer."

"OK. We'll get started." Unlike most interrogators, Parker

always sat while conducting his interviews. He could be equally intimidating with his words and tone of voice as with his body language from a superior standing position.

"So, how long ago did Linda dump you, anyway?" Parker asked the question with one of his confident smiles, the "we've got you nailed" look sparkling in his eyes.

"She didn't dump me. We were just working some stuff out." Tommy Iverson's sweat-drenched shirt belied the fact that the interview was just beginning.

"Come on, Tommy. We've spent most of yesterday and half of today talking with the friends. Everybody in town knows you two were finished. She even told one of her friends that you used to be a friend with benefits but she shut off the benefits."

"She really said that? I can't believe she'd ever say that."

Parker reached for the answering machine. He pushed the play button, leaned back in his chair, and watched for Iverson's reaction. It was predictable.

"Is that you on that phone call?" he asked, almost whispering.

Tommy Iverson reached into his back pocket and pulled out a crisp, clean handkerchief that looked as if it had just been ironed. Without unfolding it, he wiped his mouth, gathering the droplets of sweat that had formed across his upper lip. Parker kept watching him as he gazed at the now-silent machine. Without saying another word, Parker again hit the play button and the message repeated, echoing off the bare walls. It hadn't finished when Tommy bounced out of his chair.

"Shit," he shouted. "That was the other day. Must've been Friday night." He paced around the room while Parker remained in his chair, waiting for the inevitable letdown. A minute later, Tommy sat down in stunned silence.

"She left it on the machine. Didn't even erase it. Guess she loved hearing your voice over and over again."

"I can't believe this is happening. I can explain that. I was just pissed off, that's all. Wouldn't you be if you saw your girlfriend making it with another guy?" The words ran together as Tommy's voice trembled.

"And just how did you see them making it?" Havenot spoke softly, the relaxed cadence disarming.

"It was Friday night; I stopped by and saw them through the window. I even talked to them."

"So, you just happened to stop at your old girlfriend's house and peek in the window. Let's run through this again. Linda dumps you two weeks ago. You don't want to admit it so you keep hanging around, even peeking in her windows late at night. Then, you call to tell her that you hate her. Then, she shows up murdered. You live two blocks away and never left your house that night but no one can corroborate that. You're a hunter and have a hunting guide business with access to who knows how many different kinds of knives and are likely very good with them. You practically lived at her house for several months while you two were going together so you know your way around. Seems like a pretty good combination of motive, means, and opportunity to me."

"You know damn well that it was Shane. He's the fucking ex-husband, for God's sake, and he was thoroughly nuts about the divorce settlement. A sixty/forty split of all assets? Plus, in two days, actually it would have been this morning, there was going be that final hearing. After that, he was toast!"

The volume of Tommy's voice increased with the realization that the detective was staring at him.

"Shane was fighting that down to the wire and you know it! What about him? He was always threatening her."

"I don't have to tell you this," Parker said, "but I will. He's in the clear. Two of his friends swear they were together at an overnight camping expedition, scouting out some hot spots for deer on the night Linda was killed."

"Then you've got three goddamned liars. That's how I met Shane. I did all his scouting for him. He's clueless in the woods without help."

"Yep, and all you've got is one liar. Right now, we've got probable cause and I'm guessing about a 95 percent chance of conviction, even with just the circumstantial stuff. And, by the way, where'd you get those scratches on your hand and face, again?"

"I told you I was doing yard work on Saturday; got into a damned rose bush and Linda helped me later with some splinters I got picking up brush." The color drained from Tommy Iverson's face as the detective waved at the window.

Sheriff Jim Corbett entered the room and greeted him.

"Hello, Tommy," he said. "Been a while since I've seen you." As he removed a small card from his vest pocket, Iverson reacted.

"You've got the wrong fucking guy. I'd never do anything to hurt Linda. I'm telling you, this is all wrong."

The sheriff began to read from the card. "You have the right to remain silent…"

Friday, May 7, 1993

COVINGTON COUNTY, A SPRAWLING rural area west of Hartford, Connecticut, had not seen a murder since early in 1991 but the county was gradually falling victim to the encroachment of an imaginary boundary line, one which separated the city from the bucolic horse farms and forests to the west. While the city limits signs stayed in place, the appearance of bargain-priced housing developments, shopping malls, and automobile traffic threatened to destroy the quiet neighborhoods that served as an escape from the rat race that was the city. With the growth came the inevitable increase in crime, but thus far, the populace had been subjected to nuisance offenses such as graffiti sprayed on bridges or minor intrusions like the occasional sliced tire or property vandalism. The possibility of violent crime remained just a niggling itch, the kind of worry which was easily scratched.

LINDA PHILLIPS HAD LESS than thirty-six hours to live. She would not see the dawn of Mother's Day on May 9, 1993. That festive weekend of celebration with special family gatherings would be a bittersweet one for her. As the residents of Hampton Village relished the thank-God-it's-Friday moments and anticipated a relaxing few days of gardening and puttering around the house, Linda could only look forward a Mother's Day weekend without her three young children. As only he could, Shane Phillips cajoled, pleaded, and begged with Linda to allow him to have them for the weekend. When all else failed, he resorted to his usual intimidation and threats. With their final divorce settlement hearing just days away, Linda would soon be rid of him and his influence permanently so she finally relented. She would use the weekend to sort out the myriad personal problems that were bedeviling her in the nine months since she separated from Shane.

SHANE, JR. CAME BOUNDING through the door to the real estate office of Chambers and Stone first, followed in rapid succession by Tonie and Jackie. All three ran directly to their mother sitting behind the receptionist's desk. She smiled as they jockeyed for position to give her the usual hug. At nine years old, Shane won the battle over his younger twin sisters and squeezed Linda hard around the waist.

"Do we have to go with Dad this weekend?" he asked as he allowed the girls enough space to make the gathering into a group hug. "I don't want to."

"Your father has some fun things planned for the weekend. You'll have a good time with him." The hug broke apart and she looked at Shane. "He's looking forward to it and you don't get to see him that much."

"He's not always fun, Mom. Sometimes it's like he doesn't even like us." Linda noticed the seven-year-old twins nodding in agreement.

"It's all arranged and he'll be at the house in a little while so we better get going."

Steve Chambers appeared at the door of his office and greeted the children with a warm smile. "You take good care of your mom this weekend, and behave yourselves, especially on Sunday. It's Mother's Day, you know!"

"Shane's taking them for the weekend. He's picking them up this afternoon. I'll be back to close up after he leaves."

Steve's surprise was evident. "Really? On Mother's Day weekend? Wow!" He hesitated as the words caused Linda to frown. "Listen, don't bother coming back. I'll take care of things here. You just enjoy your weekend."

"I don't want to go, Mr. Chambers," Shane, Jr. whined.

"Me neither," Jackie added.

Linda blushed and shrugged. "We've got to go, kids. Thanks, Steve, and I'll see you tomorrow morning. It's my Saturday to work." She hustled the three children out the door.

SHANE PHILLIPS, AS USUAL, was more than an hour late. Linda had the children ready to go on time and the four of them sat on the veranda waiting. When Shane roared up the driveway, spraying gravel and dirt behind, Jackie began to cry. She moved against her mother, clinging to her blouse while Shane, Jr. dragged his small suitcase toward the car, thumping on each of the five wooden steps. Tonie followed him and they both climbed into the car without a word.

"Jackie, get in the car," Shane shouted through the open window on the passenger side. When all three children were in the back seat with their faces pressed against the window, he began to back down the driveway. After returning their tentative waves, Linda watched as they struggled with their seat belts. Shane had not said a single word to her.

The children would not see their mother alive again.

About the Author

DUKE SOUTHARD IS A retired educator. He has published professional articles in *Media and Methods* and served as president of the New Hampshire Educational Media Association. In 1997, he was awarded an "EDie," the New Hampshire Excellence in Education Award, for his contribution to the school library/media profession in the state. His  educational credentials include a BS from Villanova University, a MA in English education from Glassboro State University, and a CAGS in library/media technology from Boston University. He is married, the father of three. He lived in New Hampshire before moving to Green Valley, Arizona.

The original version of *A Favor Returned* was published by Peter Randall and distributed by University Press of New England. Southard's second novel, *Agent for Justice*, was published in 2003 by Hot House Press. He is also the author of two non-fiction books. A memoir, *The Week from Heaven and Hell*, describes the family's struggles while dealing with the sudden and tragic loss of a young adult son, and *The Nick: A Vision Realized* is a commissioned history of a large recreational facility in New Hampshire.

In 2010, Southard won awards in both the short story and memoir divisions of the Society of Southwestern Authors writing contest. His novel, *A Favor Returned*, was a 2013 finalist in the New Mexico/Arizona Book Awards. The second edition of *Agent for Justice* was a finalist in the 2014 New Mexico/Arizona Book Awards.

Visit the author's website for more information on his work, works in progress, and free programs for schools, libraries, and community groups:

www.DukeSouthard.com

CPSIA information can be obtained at www.ICGtesting.com
Printed in the USA
BVOW03s1254120215

387259BV00002B/72/P